SILENT
ANGEL

BOOKS BY HELEN PHIFER

DETECTIVE MORGAN BROOKES SERIES

One Left Alive

The Killer's Girl

The Hiding Place

First Girl to Die

Find the Girl

Sleeping Dolls

BETH ADAMS SERIES

The Girl in the Grave

The Girls in the Lake

DETECTIVE LUCY HARWIN SERIES

Last Light

Dark House

Dying Breath

Lakeview House

SILENT ANGEL

HELEN PHIFER

Bookouture

Published by Bookouture in 2022

An imprint of Storyfire Ltd.
Carmelite House
50 Victoria Embankment
London EC4Y 0DZ

www.bookouture.com

ISBN: 978-1-80314-403-0
eBook ISBN: 978-1-80314-402-3

For all the wonderful, supportive book bloggers. You are amazing and so very much appreciated. Love Helen Xx

PROLOGUE

Bundled up against the cold he sat in the cab of his converted ambulance, watching the group of rowdy teenagers pushing and shoving each other around. They were friends, he could tell by the loud screeches and giggles, but even if they weren't he wouldn't intervene unless it suited him. He didn't care if anyone got hurt, in fact he would enjoy it. He was hanging around McDonald's waiting for the perfect opportunity. He knew he was less conspicuous parked in the faded yellow private ambulance he'd bought off eBay last year than he would be in a car, and had spent hours lovingly converting it to suit his needs. Men hanging around in cars were noticed more than even stranger men hanging around in the cabs of emergency vehicles. People assumed you were on a break, had been working for hours and were now catching a nap. It really was the perfect vehicle for what he wanted to do. He glanced behind him at the small sleeping and living area. Once he pulled those curtains across the pane of glass in the panel no one would have a clue how many people were in the van, what they were doing behind there or who he had with him. He didn't know why more killers didn't use this method of transport; it was far easier to slip through unseen.

And he'd picked his parking space deliberately. Although he wasn't from Blackpool, he knew the area well. He'd been visiting since he was a kid, and he was aware of all the main spots that the teenagers frequented. The McDonald's in the town centre and the one in the retail park, the cinemas, the bargain shops that stayed open late selling energy drinks to fuel their idiotic behaviour, KFC, all of them were in places he could have chosen. No one had a clue what he did or where he came from. He liked the anonymity it gave him and the complete freedom to do what needed to be done. He had stalked potential victims and his pretty young copper without anyone paying him the least bit of attention. Wear a high-vis jacket and you could turn yourself into the invisible man. Ironic that.

The group were dispersing, a boy and girl lingered behind and he could tell by their body language that they were arguing. She had her phone in her hand and was pointing at the boy's chest. He shrugged, turned away from her and ran to catch up with his friends, leaving her alone. *No, boy, you don't want to be leaving her all alone there like that. How are you going to live with yourself the rest of your life when you find out she's gone, taken because you left her over a stupid disagreement?* Shaking his head, he glanced at the clock on the dash. It was almost ten thirty, time for most teenagers to go home. His hungry eyes washed over the girl standing alone, taking her in from head to foot. She was dressed in Nike leggings so tight and shiny they clung to her spindly legs; the crop top she was wearing under her gilet offered no warmth against the biting cold wind that was blowing tonight; sturdy Nike trainers on her feet meant she could be problematic: she might be able to outrun him. She didn't move and he wondered if she was waiting to be picked up by some parent who would arrive in a 4x4, more than likely in their pyjamas and annoyed at having to leave the house. He'd give her five minutes, if no one arrived to rescue her, she'd be his practice girl. He wanted to make sure he got it perfect. Counting down the time on the clock it got to sixty seconds when a BMW pulled in front of the garage and mounted the pavement in front of her, hazard lights flashing. The girl stood up, crossing to the front passenger door and pulled it open climbing inside. He nodded, looked down at the clock and sighed, another thirty seconds and she'd have been his. He waited for another girl to cross his path, sure that soon enough one would.

ONE

Detective Constable Morgan Brookes was supposed to be on her weekend off. It was her birthday yesterday so her partner, Detective Sergeant Ben Matthews, had finished work at five instead of ten to come and take her out for tea. They were going to Zeffirelli's in Ambleside for pizza and a movie – it was early April and it wouldn't be too busy, not like in the warmer months. Morgan had purposely not eaten anything since lunchtime so that she'd be hungry enough to do the meal justice. Pizza was her all-time favourite and if she had to live on it for the rest of her life she would gladly do so with no complaint. Ben was in the shower now, and she was just lacing up the new bottle green Doc Martens that had been his birthday gift. She'd spent ages taming the curls of her copper hair and had perfected the tiny flick with her eyeliner; on her lips she was wearing the new peach coloured MAC lipstick Ben had bought her after she'd spent a hilarious ten minutes trying on the different colours and pouting virtually at herself online. She dressed mostly in black but was partial to a bit of bottle green because it suited her fiery hair so well. Ben had tossed his phone onto the bed on his way to the bathroom. It lay next to her and when it began vibrating, she glanced over at it. The screen flashed 'Withheld number' and she knew without a doubt that it was work. The power had gone off a couple of minutes ago and the light from the phone illuminated the dark bedroom as it pulsated. She had taken the candle from this room into the bathroom for him so he could see, and she was sitting in the dark, not in the least bit bothered by it. Morgan loved the dark, always had and power cuts didn't scare her at all. The phone was vibrating its way towards her, and she found herself tempted to ignore it, not because she didn't care but because she just wanted to spend a couple of uninterrupted hours with Ben. Her fingers ignored the fleeting thought that had flashed through her mind and reached out for the phone.

'Ben Matthews's phone, it's Morgan Brookes.'

'Sorry to bother you at home, is Ben available?'

The voice that she recognised as one of the call handlers from the police control room at Penrith didn't sound in the least bit sorry.

'He's in the shower, I'll get him. Hey, is there a power cut in Ambleside, do you know?'

She knew this was wishful thinking because there was a ninety per cent chance they weren't going to make it to Ambleside anyway by the tone of the call handler's voice.

'No, just Rydal Falls at the moment.'

Morgan paused. 'Is that why you're ringing? About a power cut?'

'Sorry, that would be a huge no.'

She opened the bathroom door, the steam lingering in the air clinging to her hair, and passed the phone to Ben who was standing there with a towel wrapped around his waist. Droplets of water dripping from his freshly showered mop of brown hair that needed cutting fell onto his chest. He was shaking his head, spraying her with warm water. She shrugged and he rolled his eyes. She knew he wasn't mad with her, but annoyed that he was being called back to work tonight. Thrusting the phone into his hands she backed away before her hair absorbed the steam and turned into a mass of frizz. She sat back down on the bed, listening to his conversation from the room next door.

'Where and who rang it in?... Is anyone in Barrow on call? Kendal? It's Morgan's birthday, I promised to take her out.'

Ben sighed. 'Okay, that's fine.' He ended the call, and she knew he was duty-bound to go to whatever the problem was. He came and sat next to her on the bed, smelling of coconut and lime body wash.

'It's okay, don't worry about it. I'll phone and cancel, we can go another time.'

He shook his head. 'It's not okay, Morgan, I promised we'd do something for your birthday.'

'It's not important, I understand that work comes first; it would be the same if I was on call. You know we're both married to the job and we wouldn't have it any other way. So, tell me what's happened?'

His damp fingers entwined with hers. 'I wish it didn't, but you could go without me. Why don't you phone Amy? I bet she'd love to go. Or Wendy, if she's not on call.'

Leaning over she brushed her lips across the side of his cheek. 'I could come with you.'

'Not this time, they've found a body in St Martha's church-yard, and it's your birthday weekend off. I can cope, super cop Marc is on his way and you are under strict orders to go and enjoy yourself.'

This time it was Morgan who let out a sigh. 'You really think I can enjoy myself wondering what you're up to and why you've been called out to a dead body in the middle of a power cut? I might as well wait in the car for you; besides it might not be as bad as they're making out and we might still make it to the restaurant.'

'I love your optimism, Morgan. How about you come with

me and if it's not likely I can get away then you have Amy or Wendy on standby?'

She nodded, knowing fine well that as much as she liked both Amy and Wendy, she didn't want to eat a romantic meal and sit in the dark cinema with either of them. If he wouldn't let her help, she'd rather go alone. The thought of St Martha's in a power cut made her shudder, she didn't like graveyards in the dark; watching too many horror films in her teenage years had given her an unhealthy dislike for them. The church itself was beautiful, but for her it would always be synonymous with the place she had to say goodbye to her loved ones: Sylvia and Brad were both buried there.

TWO

As Ben drove along the high street she stared at the shops and flats above them all in darkness. Some of the flats had candles burning in the windows, and she decided that life before electricity must have been grim. She thought about her aunt Ettie alone in the woods in the dark then realised that she probably wasn't in the least bit bothered by a power cut. She had more candles than the gift shop that sold them for her. Morgan hadn't spoken to Ettie for some time. Taking out her phone she sent her a quick text telling her to call if she needed anything. The outline of the church loomed against the inky sky, and there was a solitary police van outside, its lights on top of the van illuminating the darkness in red, blue and white, and its headlights were shining into the churchyard. She could see a tall figure standing next to Cain – poor response officer Cain, he caught as many rubbish jobs as she did. Desperate to get out with Ben to see what was happening, Morgan had to practically grip onto the soft leather seat with her fingertips to stop herself from moving. He got out of the car, and bending down he looked at her. 'Stay here, that's an order.'

She nodded; she would give Ben what he wanted until he

came back and asked her to help out. She loved that he wanted her to enjoy her birthday weekend, but it was difficult when she saw him heading out to a call without her. They were a team and always would be. He walked towards Cain and the tall guy, they spoke a few words and the tall guy held out his hand. Ben shook it. Morgan leaned forward, pressing the button on the window so it slid down, trying to hear their conversation. The night was cool, the air was frosty, and there was the gentlest of breezes. The muffled conversation didn't filter her way which was a shame. A car roared along the street, its full beam blinding her in the rear-view mirror, and she had to cup a hand across her eyes as it pulled to a stop behind Ben's car. She knew it was Marc before he even got out of the car. His door slammed, and then he was there, looking down at her sitting in the passenger seat.

'What's up? Are you ill or sitting this one out?'

'It's my weekend off. Ben said I was to stay put.'

'Well, we might need you all the same, so don't get too comfy.' He flashed his perfectly straight white teeth at her in a smile and, as he walked off, she caught a smell of that aftershave he always wore. She had no idea what it was called but it was expensive, that much she did know.

A few minutes later, Ben and Marc were suited up and heading towards the churchyard with torches. The tall man was still talking to Cain; he was fidgeting from foot to foot, giving the distinct impression that he didn't want to be here talking to the police. As soon as Ben and Marc were out of sight Morgan got out of the car; there was no point sitting here picking her nails when she could be of some use. Crossing to where Cain was standing, she heard him address the man as vicar and as she got closer Cain turned to face her.

'Morgan, this is the vicar, Theodore Edwards. He found the body.'

She realised that Cain didn't know she wasn't on duty and

didn't correct him; instead she held her hand out. 'Detective Constable Morgan Brookes.'

The vicar took her hand in his icy grip, his fingers so cold they chilled hers through to the bone. From what she could make out in the dark he wasn't very old, and his air of confidence told her he was comfortable with himself and probably easy on the eye. She imagined that he was the kind of vicar the old dears swooned over.

'Theo, just plain old Theo. Pleased to meet you, detective.'

'Plain old Morgan is fine.'

He laughed, the sound echoing around the area, and he cupped his hand across his mouth. 'Sorry, that was totally inappropriate. I realise this is not a laughing matter.'

Morgan smiled at him; she still didn't actually know what was going on, if this was an accident, sudden death, suicide or murder. 'We can all use a little humour, it helps us to cope.' She glanced towards the shadows dancing off the beams from the torches in the graveyard – they were a good distance from her. 'I know you've probably told Cain, but could you run me through it?'

He nodded. 'Of course. I'm afraid to say I'm a little ashamed by my reaction, Morgan. I was in the church when the power went out. I'm new to the area, I only transferred here last month. I got a little spooked, much to my embarrassment, and couldn't wait to get outside. When I did there was this awful stench.' He paused, crossed himself then carried on. 'I'm sorry that sounds heartless, I don't mean any disrespect. I honestly thought that there was a dead animal or maybe the drains had backed up, then I panicked and wondered if any vandals had disturbed a recent grave, you just never know.'

He stopped talking, lost in the memory, and Morgan thought about the boy who had once dug his own mother up after her sudden death and shuddered.

'Well, I foolishly continued walking in the direction and

thought that it was nothing to worry about. I couldn't see anything concerning and then the breeze blew the smell towards me, and I carried on past the last row of graves and that's when my candlelight picked out a single eye staring back at me from the ditch near to the hedge. I threw the candle I was holding in shock, which went out, and my phone died leaving me shrouded in complete and utter blackness. And this is where I show my true colours. I ran as fast as I could to the old people's home across the way, screaming like a teenage girl, and hammered on their door. I'm surprised they even opened it to me to be fair, I must have scared the staff and residents half to death.'

Morgan smiled, relieved it was dark and he couldn't see her. Theo Edwards was quite the storyteller. She bet his parishioners were captivated by his Sunday services. She glanced at Cain who she knew would also find this highly amusing. 'That must have been quite a shock for you, Theo. How are you holding up?'

'Apart from being frozen and feeling rather foolish, I'm much better than whoever that poor soul is.'

'Did you get a good look at the body? How did you know they were dead?'

'Morgan, that eye reflected in my torchlight told me everything I needed to know, coupled with the smell. I've seen a few bodies in my time.'

She arched one eyebrow, and he reached out to pat her arm.

'Dear Lord, this is sounding worse by the moment, I sound like I'm some hardened killer. What I meant is that I've been called out to a few parishioners who were dying or had recently died, to deliver the last rites to them. An unfortunate and sad part of being a priest, but it's nice to know that I can offer some comfort as they take their final breaths. You know what, I also think I should stop talking now because I sound as if I'm Dennis Radar's right-hand man.'

Morgan smiled; she knew exactly who Dennis Radar was. He, or rather his alter ego, BTK, was a sick, twisted serial killer in the US who had led a reign of terror that spanned thirty years before he was caught. What she didn't understand was why a parish priest would reference such a sick individual, and instantly her guard went up.

'I'm pretty sure you can return to the vicarage now, Theo, we don't need to keep you outside. You're probably in shock and a hot cup of tea will help you to thaw out a little. If we need you someone will come and see you there.'

'Really? Are you sure, that would be great, I can no longer feel the tips of my toes.'

Cain patted his shoulder. 'Absolutely, get yourself inside.'

Morgan asked, 'Are you staying in the vicarage?' She knew it was attached to the church, set back a little from the main road.

He nodded. 'Yes, I am, and if you need anything let me know. You're welcome to come for a hot drink and to warm your extremities if they get too numb.'

He walked away leaving both of them staring after him in silence.

THREE

Cain turned to her. 'I thought it was your weekend off?'

'It is.'

He smiled at her. 'Are you supposed to be out here?'

Morgan shrugged. When Theo was out of sight, she whispered to Cain, 'Wow, what do you make of him?'

'Poor bugger, we know how hard it is when we have to deal with a dead body. I bet he wasn't expecting that when the lights went out.'

'I don't know, Cain, there's something off about him.'

'How?'

'The way he just compared himself to BTK for one. How many priests do you think would know about him?'

'Everyone knows about him, Morgan, just like they know about Bundy and Shipman. They are the scourge of our society and people can't get enough of them. But if you think there's something off, I'll agree there is; you're our Supercop with a sixth sense for this kind of stuff.'

He laughed, and she smiled at him in the darkness.

'Morgan, what are you doing?'

Ben's voice shouted across to her, and she whispered, 'Shit.'

Cain whispered, 'Busted by the boss man.'

Marc answered for her. 'She's going to work the scene, aren't you, Morgan? I already asked her if she could make herself available.'

Ben's voice sounded tired as he questioned Marc. 'Really, you asked her as soon as you arrived?'

She walked towards their shadowy figures, putting an end to their conversation before it turned into an argument. 'Yes, I'm more than happy to, so what's happening, what can I do?'

Ben answered before Marc. 'I'm not happy about this, but fine. If you get suited up you could take a look at the body and give me your initial thoughts, and then would you go and take a full statement from the vicar?'

'Yes, of course.'

Cain shrugged at her. 'Happy birthday weekend.'

She nodded, how else was it supposed to go?

Getting dressed she grabbed a torch out of the front of Cain's van; he was leaning against the church gate.

'Amber is on her way to take over, just warning you.'

'Do you two not work together any more?'

'Yeah, sometimes but I try my best to avoid her because she drives me mad with her attitude. I told Mads if he kept pairing us up, I was transferring to Barrow. Obviously he didn't want to lose an officer of my calibre, so he tries to keep us separate.' He chuckled softly. 'Only kidding, we're too short staffed for them to let me move and I'd miss seeing you.'

'Cain, I would personally kick Mads's arse if he let you transfer. You are the best officer we have; you have no idea how relieved I am when it's you who calls in a job. I can guarantee it's genuine and not a load of rubbish.'

Cain reached out a gloved hand in the darkness and ruffled her hair. 'I'm not planning on going anywhere.'

Morgan shuffled away through the gate and onto the grass that crunched underneath her feet as she crossed towards where she could see Ben's shadow standing in the dark and trying not to stand on any graves. As she got nearer, she could make out the rugby shaped ball of her school friend Brad's gravestone and she pursed her lips, blowing him a silent kiss. The smell as she approached where Ben stood filled her nostrils and she grimaced; it wasn't quite as strong as she had encountered recently in Shirley Kelly's compact flat, but it wasn't much better. Ben's arm reached out to stop her going any further.

'There's a dip where the grass goes down, don't fall into the ditch.'

He shone the torch he was holding downwards, and she took in the partially covered body lying there. Some tiny pink flowers had been tossed onto the grubby sheet that had been wrapped around her.

'Oh God.'

'Exactly, I bet that's what the vicar said.'

She took in the bloated, blackened face with one eye partially open and the other a dark, empty hole. It was hard to say how old she was but Morgan would have placed her in her twenties, if she had to estimate.

'Where's the other eye?'

Ben shrugged. 'I'd say birds or some other animal has taken that.'

Her stomach lurched violently, her mouth filling with hot bile, and for one horrifying moment Morgan thought she was going to be sick all over herself. She tried to swallow back the acid as it burned her throat, whilst trying to take in deep breaths through her nose. She felt Ben's arm on hers.

'Are you okay?'

She shook her head. No, she wasn't, and this wasn't okay either. The air around her seemed to have thickened and she heard Ben's muffled voice through the ringing in her ears.

'You go speak to the vicar; we'll sort this out.'

Morgan turned abruptly, she didn't need telling twice, anything was better than this. She hurried towards the gates. Rushing past Amber who had just arrived, and stripping the scene suit off, she bagged it, took her notebook out of the glove compartment, then hurried towards the vicarage.

The house seemed far too big for one man to live in, rattling around in there in the dark. She hoped he had candles. Surely a vicar would have a never-ending supply of them to hand. Morgan stopped, sucking in deep breaths of frosty night air right down into her lungs, pushing down the bile. She would not be sick here, in the front garden of the vicarage, or in front of her colleagues. All the horrific crime scenes she'd attended had never made her feel this queasy before. It was the eyes. Reaching out her hand she pushed against the rough wall, holding herself up.

'Hello, are you okay out there? Do you need a hand?'

Theo's voice called at her from the darkness of the front door. Standing up straight, Morgan pushed herself towards his shadow. She wouldn't show her weakness to anyone, especially not him.

'No, no thank you. I'm good, is it possible to take a statement now whilst everything is fresh in your mind?'

'Of course, come on in. I've got a pan of water boiling on the gas cooker; the gas still works, thank God for small mercies.'

He stepped inside the blackness of his hallway, disappearing from sight. Morgan glanced back towards the church, where she could hear Ben's and Marc's muffled voices. Then she followed Theo inside. A single candle burned on a small table, casting a flickering glow over the large entrance hall. He was standing in the doorway to the room furthest away – it had to be that one, didn't it? Still, she followed him into a large, airy kitchen, a row of candles along the worktop illuminating the darkness. It was full of eighties orange pine cupboards and an old gas cooker that had seen better days, with two rings burning, shedding a little more light. He pointed to the small square table with three chairs.

'Take a seat. Would you like a mug of something hot to warm you up?'

She nodded. 'Coffee would be great, milk no sugar, thanks.'

He busied himself making himself a coffee too. Finally he turned around, passing one mug to her and placing the other on the table.

'I'll just grab some more candles so you can see what you're doing. I have a torch somewhere, I saw it when I was unpacking, but for the life of me, I can't remember where. It's a bit of a rambling house this, lots of empty and half-furnished rooms to get lost in.'

He disappeared, then came back with a bag of tea lights that he spread along the rest of the kitchen worktops and some on the table. Then taking a lighter from his pocket, he began to light them all. By the time he'd finished the room was much brighter. Morgan stared in awe at the oversized geometric orange patterns on the wallpaper. Sitting opposite her he laughed.

'It's ghastly, isn't it? I have no idea why the last vicar didn't redecorate. If I'm told that I have to stay more than a couple of months that's the first thing I'm doing, and I hate decorating with a passion, but it offends my eyes.'

She began to laugh, he joined in and suddenly he didn't seem quite so intimidating, if that was the word she was looking for. Picking up the mug of coffee she took a sip, the sickness had subsided, and she was suddenly grateful for it.

'Not much of a welcome for you. Why do you think you won't be here long?'

He laughed. 'I've had some awkward ones, but no, I've never come across anything like this. I guess moving around is part of my job; because I have no family or partner, they use me to fill the gaps in parishes where there is a desperate need for a vicar, and I get sent to lots of places. Which I kind of don't mind, but I really like it here so far, or I did until an hour ago. My heart is broken for that poor person, tossed in a ditch like a piece of rubbish. It is just so callous. They were a living, breathing being, no one deserves to be treated that way, it's so sad.'

Morgan nodded. 'It is. Are you okay to talk about what happened, give me a little background information about yourself?'

He smiled at her. 'Yes, of course, anything to help, although I'm not sure what else I can add.'

'That's okay, just take me through it again, but before we start can I have your name, date of birth and last address?'

He relayed the information then began his story once more, and this time Morgan wrote it down word for word, asking questions in between.

'Did you see anyone else in the church or the grounds?'

He shook his head. 'No, but then again I was walking around with my hand badly shaking and throwing the candle-light all over the place.' He stopped, his eyes opened wide. 'Do you think that whoever did this could have still been there, watching me?'

'No, I doubt it, the body looks as if they've been dead some time.'

'Then why has no one smelled or noticed it before? Why me in the middle of a blackout?'

Morgan paused; he was right. Why had no one noticed it before if the body had been there some time? Some of the graves had fresh flowers on them, so surely people visiting the grave-yard would have at least caught a whiff of it. Tomorrow she would take a look at the graves with the freshest flowers to see if she could locate family members and speak to them.

'What about CCTV, does the church have any?'

He chuckled. 'I believe that's a no; my last church was in the middle of Birmingham and that did because it was always getting vandalised. But I was assured before moving here that St Martha's had nothing of the sort, so there was no need for it. Which, if I'm honest, Morgan, was a huge relief. It's been quite an intense couple of years working in the inner city. So as much as I was reluctant to move away from the people and friends I'd made there, it's nice to come here and give my head some much-needed space. Slow down the pace a little. I want to make the most of it, take in the glorious views, explore the fells and villages, eat my body weight in scones and cakes. I've never had so many invites to afternoon tea.'

She smiled, refraining from telling him that he'd probably just moved to the murder capital of the north-west, which was probably far worse than Birmingham's inner city, but he didn't need to know that yet. He was sure to discover it for himself soon enough.

'Thanks, Theo, I don't think there's much else you can tell me. I'll leave you in peace.'

Swallowing the last mouthful of coffee, she pushed herself up off the chair, grabbed her notebook and pen. As she reached the front door, he called after her.

'So, what happens now, Morgan? My churchyard is a crime scene and it's the spring fete tomorrow, and while I don't want to sound insensitive, it's kind of a big deal. When I was told I was being sent here, I never imagined it would be such a busy parish, I kind of thought I'd be in for an easy time, you know, a few die-hard parishioners knocking on eighty turning up for a Sunday service. I didn't expect this sudden influx or the volume of people who attended my first service, or that they would be so keen to help out to raise funds.'

Morgan stared across the road at the retirement home with sprawling grounds. 'Maybe you could have it over there? I'm sure they'd be happy to let you set up stalls and the bouncy castle in their grounds.'

He peered across the road, his head bobbing up and down. 'You know, that might just work. Thanks, I'll go and speak to them in the morning and see if they'll let us relocate over there.'

'Good luck.'

He closed the door behind her, and she walked towards the gate. In the blink of her eyes the church and grounds were bathed in light from the spotlights that had been installed last year, and she felt a whole lot better as a low murmur from everyone signalled the return of the electricity supply. Rydal Falls in complete darkness wasn't as beautiful as you'd think, especially not when it kept such terrible secrets.

FOUR

The churchyard seemed far less eerie when Morgan returned. Wendy, the CSI, had arrived while she'd been in the vicarage and had chased Ben and Marc out of the grounds while she documented the scene, the bright flash from her camera lighting up the gravestones in quick bursts of light. As Morgan walked to the van where everyone was congregating, Ben lifted his arm to look at his watch, and then he looked at Morgan with an expression of misery and she smiled at him, shaking her head. As she got closer, she leaned in and whispered, 'I didn't want to go without you anyway.'

At that moment she felt her heart do that little fuzzy spark of adrenaline thing inside her chest, making her realise just how much she loved him. If it hadn't been for Ben taking a chance on her and believing in her she wouldn't be doing this now. She would never have had the chance to save Bronte, Macy or Evelyn, and she wouldn't have fought killers to make the world a better place. Remembering all the good she had done because of him, she felt a rush of love for Ben and pride in herself that was almost overpowering.

'What did the vicar have to say then?'

Cain answered for her. 'Morgan thinks it was him, so you should arrest him, and then we can have the rest of the weekend off.'

Snapping herself out of her thoughts she glared at Cain. 'I did not, I just thought there was something a little bit weird about him, and he compared himself to BTK which isn't exactly a great way to introduce yourself.'

Marc was watching her. 'BTK?'

'Bind, torture, kill – Dennis Radar, the serial killer.'

He shrugged. 'Should I know him? Is this relevant to the body?'

'No, not really. Well not unless we discover that the vic was bound, tortured and then killed.'

Cain, who was standing behind Marc, rolled his eyes at Morgan, and she had to look away from him. All of them were shuffling from foot to foot, and each time someone spoke their breath froze in the air.

Ben murmured, 'Christ, it's baltic out here. We need to get Declan here to take a look. At this point I'm unsure if it's male or female but I'm pretty sure it's suspicious. Whoever it is didn't wrap themselves in that sheet and lie in that ditch until they expired, but stranger things have happened so we'd better get confirmation. It's a pretty secluded area, and I think we can get a scene guard on until Declan can get here. Let's tape off the entrance to the church and wait for him inside the van with the engine running.'

Marc nodded. 'Yeah, whoever that is has been dead some time. We need to wait for the pathologist.'

Cain opened the van door, leaned in and rummaged around in a cardboard box until he pulled out a large roll of blue and white crime-scene tape. Morgan stood to the side with her arms folded across her chest, fingers tucked under her armpits to keep them warm.

'I think we should seal off this part of the street as well. If it's not suspicious then it won't matter, but if it is then someone had to get the body here and I'm pretty sure they would have used a car or a van – we all know how heavy a body is. Unless the killer is a contender for the world's strongest person, they would have had to get the body out of the vehicle, through that gate, which doesn't open very wide, and carry it across the grass and through the graves to get it to that ditch. There's a good chance they left some trace evidence behind, or we can pray that they did.'

Ben's phone began to vibrate. He nodded at Morgan before putting it to his ear. 'Declan.' He turned away, heading back to the church gate, where he had a brief conversation that ended with, 'Thanks, I understand.' He looked at them. 'He's already on his way to a body found in Preston behind a nightclub, so he won't be able to get here until the morning.'

Marc shrugged. 'Right then, as I said no point in us hanging around. Let's get enough patrols sorted to keep the cordon on and ask Wendy to tent the body until Declan can get here.'

Morgan whispered to Cain, 'What time are you on duty till?'

'Ten tonight, not too bad. Amber, however, is on until midnight.'

Marc began walking back to his car. 'Did he say what time tomorrow we can reconvene here?'

Ben shrugged.

'Oh, well give me a text. I have nothing on. I'll be here when you tell me.'

And with that he got inside his car, which was just outside of the tape that Cain had tied around the lamp post and fencing on the opposite side of the street. They watched as he began a three-point turn and then zoomed off out of the way. They all breathed a collective sigh of relief at his departure. Marc was not quite as unbearable as when he'd first arrived in Rydal Falls, but still a little full on.

'Thank God for that.'

Morgan grinned at Cain; Ben was also smiling.

'I know he's keen, but he takes over every time with no regard for what has already been done. It's so annoying.'

'I'm happy to stay, Ben, if you want me to?'

He shook his head at her. 'No, he's right, we need Declan to take a look first before we move them. I'll tell Mads to sort out the scene guard and we'll wait until we hear from Declan. The ball's in his court really.'

Morgan felt relieved. She could no longer feel the tips of her toes in this freezing weather. At this rate the body was going to be frozen solid anyway; at least that would make it easier for the undertakers to retrieve it.

'Cain, get in the van and warm yourself up. I'll tell Amber she can sit in the car too. No point in either of you getting frost-bite, is there?'

Cain didn't wait to be told twice and was already climbing into the van, the engine running, and he cranked the heating on to full. Waving at Morgan, he blew her a kiss and mouthed *Happy Birthday*. Pursing her lips, she blew him one back then walked to where Ben had parked his car, climbing inside to wait for Ben who was talking to Amber. When he did join her, he turned the ignition on and blasted the heater to warm them up.

'Blimey, it's so cold tonight. Hey, we could still go out for a meal you know. We've missed the cinema, but we can get food and a bottle of wine.'

'I'd rather go home, Ben, if that's okay. We can have a bottle of wine there, order a takeaway.'

Leaning towards her he kissed her. His lips were as frozen as her toes, but she kissed him back.

Ben began to turn the car around. Morgan stared at the floodlit church, its dark shadow casting down onto some of the graves, and she shuddered. There was something about churches that intrigued yet repelled her at the same time. Who was that poor person lying dead and decomposing in the grounds, and how had they got there? She felt bad that they couldn't do anything for them yet, but she made a silent promise that she would do everything she could tomorrow.

FIVE

Morgan drove Ben's car to St Martha's church, and this time the sky was pale blue with tinges of pink from the morning sun as it rose over Loughrigg Fell. There was a definite nip in the air, but it was going to be one of those glorious spring days, where you could be fooled into thinking it was almost summer, the warmth from the sun taking away the chill from the night before. Ben had slept all night without so much as snoring, while Morgan, on the other hand, felt like crap. At first glance she looked okay, her eyeliner was straight and her copper hair was contained in a neat bun on the top of her head, but she could see the tiny lines that had appeared around her eyes and the faint, purplish tinge to the skin under her eyes that had needed a generous amount of concealer to cover. She had lain awake listening to Ben's breathing, wondering who the bloated, frozen corpse had been and why, of all places, they had they been left in the church-yard. Had it been a present for the fairly new vicar and, if so, was someone targeting him? Or had it simply been a convenient place to dispose of a body? Her head told her it was, but her heart had other ideas: it wasn't as convinced that the new vicar was entirely innocent.

'So, what do you think?'

'Huh?'

She glanced at Ben realising he'd been talking to her and she hadn't heard a single word.

'About what?'

'Morgan, I knew you weren't listening. About this whole body in the church mess, what else?'

She shrugged. 'Hard to think anything when we know so little about it, boss.'

'Yeah, I suppose it is. I hope Declan is already on the scene when we get there, and we can get things moving.'

As she turned into the high street Morgan could see the cordon right at the end, the blue and white tape sealing off the far end of the street. Parked next to the police van was Declan's white Audi 4x4.

'Your wish is granted.'

'Bloody hell, that makes a change. What else should I ask for, the lottery numbers, someone to hand themselves in at the station riddled with guilt and wanting to confess?'

She smiled. 'An ID for the body would be good.'

Parking next to Declan's Audi they got out. He was already at the scene, and Ben pointed to the gate.

'Let's not keep him waiting.'

'Do you need me?'

'Yes, I do, and can you please message the boss?'

She didn't argue, happy to go back and look at the body in the daylight; somehow it made it less scary. She sent a quick text message to Marc then they both got suited and booted at the back of Ben's car and shuffled towards the officer standing at the entrance gates to the church. Giving their names Ben signed them in to the scene, and they walked across to where Declan was already crouched down looking at the body.

'Morning, both, thought I'd get here early and get started. I hope you're not offended I didn't wait for either of you?'

Ben shook his head. 'Absolutely not and morning, any thoughts?'

Morgan was staring down at the body. In the daylight she could see that the one hand sticking out of the sheet had painted nails that were chipped, and the fingers were long; although the flesh on them was grubby looking because they were starting to decompose, she decided that this was a girl, probably not much older than twenty at a push, and wondered if Declan would agree with her. The chopped hair and missing eye had turned her from a typical teenager into a scary-looking monster. Morgan's stomach was churning trying to comprehend what kind of monster could do such a thing and why? What was the whole point of this, why put them through such a terrible death then dump them here?

Declan shrugged. He was in the process of bagging up the one hand of the victim that had escaped from the sheet.

'Hard to say anything other than what a crying shame, this is just terrible. Discarded as if they're nothing more than a piece of trash.' He turned back to the victim and lowered his voice. 'Don't you worry, you are most certainly not and whoever did this is a wicked, wicked person. I'm going to take good care of you now.'

Morgan felt tears begin to pool in the corner of her eyes. Declan was such a nice man, so gentle and caring to every single victim that he worked with. She swallowed the lump in her throat.

'Do you know if they're male or female?'

'I'm swaying towards female, the fingers are slender, and the nails painted, but that's neither here nor there. What's with these flowers though? I can't really say more until we get the body back to the mortuary and unwrapped from this sheet. I don't want to disturb anything because I'm praying the dirty sheet is a treasure trove of forensics.'

'You and me both.' Ben sighed.

Morgan heard footsteps headed their way and turning saw Wendy approaching. She smiled over at her. Wendy was the closest person she had to a friend, apart from Cain who gave the best hugs, and Amy, her colleague who had been a detective much longer than she had. Morgan got on with most people, but she didn't seem to make friends any easier as she got older than she had when she was at school. She had always felt as if she was on the outside looking in on everyone else's friendships. When Wendy got close enough, she whispered, 'Thank you for the flowers, they're beautiful.'

Wendy beamed at her. 'You're very welcome, glad you liked them. I asked Alyson at Posh Flowers what you'd like, and she said they were more your style.'

'Well, she was right. I love them.' She thought about the box of flowers that had surprised her yesterday when there had been a knock on the door, all white and green. No pinks or gaudy colours, they were simple and elegant.

'Thought you'd want another set of pictures taken in the daylight, so I came straight here, and those flowers scattered on the sheet need bagging up before we move the body; they obviously mean something to whoever did this.'

Ben smiled. 'You thought right, thank you.'

They both stepped back to allow her to photograph the body, Declan pointing out specific areas he wanted her to snap.

A nearby door closed a little too loudly, the noise making both Morgan and Declan start. She looked around and realised that it was the door to the vicarage.

Leaving Ben, Wendy and Declan to it she walked back to the entrance gates in time to see Theo crossing the road and letting himself through the gates to the retirement home opposite. She slipped through the gap and hovered around by the police van, waiting for him to come back. She wasn't sure why, she just knew she needed to speak to him again. After a short time, he came striding back across the road, dressed in jeans and a thick, black woollen jumper, with a pair of Dr Marten boots that were identical to hers only much larger. He raised his hand, waving at her and she waved back.

'Good morning, Detective Brookes, you're up bright and early.'

His words grated on her, of course she was up early, there was an unidentified dead body in a ditch in his churchyard.

'Yes, serious murder investigations demand lots of late nights and early mornings.'

He chuckled. 'Yes, of course they must do. How silly of me to make such an ignorant comment. Thank you by the way.'

'For what?'

'For suggesting we move the spring fete over there.' He pointed towards the large mansion that had once been some lucky person's private dwelling. 'They were more than happy to accommodate us on such short notice. All is not lost, thankfully.'

'Good, glad to help.'

'Do you know how long the church is going to be out of bounds for? I'm afraid there are quite a few boxes and bags of bric-a-brac that I'll need to retrieve, along with the tombola prizes out of the vestry.'

Ben's deep voice answered from behind. 'Morning, vicar, I can get someone to escort you to retrieve what you need but I'm afraid it's going to be closed off for the foreseeable.'

Theo nodded. 'Of course, that would be very helpful. Thank you, Sergeant, I appreciate that.'

Morgan was hoping that Ben's offer of an escort to carry boxes of crap across the road didn't involve her, and she turned to glare at him. He shrugged at her and she rolled her eyes. The sound of a large vehicle driving towards them made her breathe a sigh of relief, here came the cavalry. A van full of task force officers could help Theo lug the boxes over there.

Theo smiled an impossibly cheery smile and headed back towards the vicarage.

'Back in a moment, just going to get the key to the church.'

Morgan lowered her voice. 'Saved by the men in black.'

The van doors opened, and a swarm of task force officers began to disembark. Their uniforms had not a drop of the fluorescent yellow that response officers had. Declan was watching them with a glint in his eye. 'They never fail to impress me, it's like an episode of *Criminal Minds* when they arrive. What a start to my day.'

She smiled at him. 'What now?'

'You can move the body. Let's get it out of this inclement weather, whoever it is has suffered long enough.'

Ben nodded then walked towards Al, the task force sergeant, to fill him in on what they needed. Morgan pulled her radio from her trouser pocket.

'Control, can you get the undertaker travelling, please?'

'*Roger that,*' came the reply, and she knew that within the next hour their Jane or John Smith would be on their way to Declan's mortuary, which had to be better than being left outside alone and abandoned to the elements.

SIX

Amy was sitting alone in the CID office when Morgan and Ben walked in, but there was no jacket slung on the back of Des's chair which usually signalled he was around.

'No Des?' Ben enquired, and Amy shook her head.

'His cat is ill, so he's taken it to the vet.'

Morgan found this revelation quite startling because she didn't know that he had a cat, or even that he was an animal person.

'On a Sunday? What's up with it?'

Amy shrugged. 'It's off its food, probably depressed having to live with him. I wouldn't be surprised if he fed it on vegan cat food.'

Morgan smiled. 'Poor cat, I hope it's okay.'

Ben was already at the whiteboard. Picking up the rubber he began to scrub the details off from the last case which had been left there. He carefully removed the copied photographs of Shirley Kelly and Emma Dixon, unpeeling the Blu-Tack from the back of them and putting them on Des's desk, which was the nearest. He wrote 'Jane/John Smith' at the top, then turned to look at Morgan.

'Not much, is it?'

'Well, we know very little, but you can put the vicar on there for a start. He found the body. I suppose there's not much you can do until we have some more information from Declan. Should I take a look at Missing Persons and see if anyone has been reported missing and not found in the last month?'

'Yes please. Amy, I'll have a coffee whilst I think of something for you to do.'

'Cheek of it. I'm busy, there's the robbery from the off-licence in Grasmere two nights ago. I'm checking the CCTV.'

'Sorry, my mistake, I thought you were shopping again.'

Morgan looked up from the desktop computer she had been logging herself in to. 'That's a bit strange, isn't it?'

'What?'

'How often do we have robberies in Grasmere?'

Ben shrugged. 'Not very, why?'

'Well, that body can't have been there for very long, some of those graves have relatively fresh flowers on them. What if whoever dumped the body robbed the off-licence on the way to dump it or after they had dumped it?'

'Why on earth would they do that? I mean if you want to get caught there's a pretty good chance of that happening, don't you think? And then what, we check their car and there's a corpse in the boot.' Amy laughed. 'Nah, that's a bit far-fetched.'

Frowning, Morgan shook her head. 'Not if they wanted to get caught or were messing with us. It might be a game to them, and we might be their entertainment. Just thinking out loud.'

Ben was staring at her. 'That would be a dangerous game to play, don't you think?'

Morgan sighed. 'Yes, it would but we seem to attract all sorts of killers. All the publicity, maybe they're wanting us to play along.'

His voice incredulous, Ben said, 'Where on earth do you get these ideas?'

Amy was walking around collecting days' old coffee cups from desks, and she laughed. 'Too much *Luther* if you ask me.'

'You can both laugh, I'm only stating the obvious. We've become infamous in the last year or so for the murders around here, and I'm worried it could get the attention of some deranged killer who thinks they're cleverer than us. I think we need to take a real close look at whoever committed that robbery.'

'Be my guest, do you and Amy want to go to Grasmere and talk to the shop owner?'

'Can't, boss, I've got an appointment this morning. Morgan, you can though, I can't see you causing too much trouble in Grasmere as long as you play nice.'

Morgan glared at her. 'What's up, is your cat ill too?'

'Ooh miaow. Nope, emergency doctor, I have a water infection.'

Ben's cheeks flushed red. 'Right, that's fine, you crack on with missing persons. Morgan, do you want to go then?'

She grabbed her jacket and phone. 'Actually, I do, thanks. I'll see you later.'

She walked out, glad to have something a little different to do and on her own as well, which was a rare luxury. She always ended up being partnered with someone and she didn't know if it was intentional on Ben's part because of her past history or whether it was just because they were such a small team. Either way she was glad of the freedom. As she reached the report writing room on the ground floor, she realised she had no idea what had happened in Grasmere: it was supposed to have been her long weekend off. She walked in looking for a friendly face to ask and saw Amber in the corner, not exactly friendly, but she'd do.

'Hey, can you print me off the incident report for the robbery in Grasmere?'

Amber nodded, rifled through a pile of papers next to her and plucked some out, handing them to her. 'I already had it printed. I did the initial enquiries before it got sent up to you lot.'

'Amazing, did you find anything worthwhile?'

She laughed. 'That would be a no, although the next job that came in after that was the body at the church, so I didn't have much of a chance before I got summoned over there.'

Morgan took them from her. 'Thanks, it's okay, I'm going there to speak to them now.'

She walked out of the station, noticing there were a couple of plain cars still parked in the yard. She quickly checked the app on her phone to make sure they hadn't been booked and chose the last one, which was free. It was a short but beautiful drive to Grasmere and she was determined to make the most of it. After she'd spoken to the victim of the robbery, she was going to call in to Sam Read Bookseller and grab a couple of books as well as a coffee, and maybe some cake. That was the best thing about working in the Lake District, all the shops were open every day because they relied on the many tourists to keep them thriving. If Des could take his cat to the vets, she could stop off at the bookshop.

SEVEN

Morgan parked the car, and as she fed her coins into the machine for a ticket she felt as if she was being watched, which was ridiculous, because no one knew who she was. Turning slowly, she scanned the cars and people who were milling around. Families, older people, no one obviously on their own. There was an ambulance parked in the far corner, but the cab was empty. Shrugging her shoulders she walked back to the car, sticking the ticket inside the front windscreen. The warmth from the sun radiated down the back of her thick, padded North Face jacket and she shrugged it off throwing it onto the passenger seat. Spring had definitely sprung, and it felt good deep down in her soul. She tucked her notebook into her trouser pocket. She had a thick, black roll-neck jumper on and she pushed up the sleeves a little, revealing the intricate petals and vines of her latest tattoo. Having a quick read of the report she'd taken from Amber, she knew the off-licence and the Co-op were the only shops in Grasmere which opened late and sold alcohol.

Walking into the tiny village she spotted Sam Read Book-seller on the corner and smiled. Her favourite shops were book-shops, closely followed by coffee shops and she spied the

Grasmere Tea Gardens a little further on near to St Oswald's church, which was separated by the River Rothay. She would pop in and pay her respects to William Wordsworth who was buried there, and his sister, Dorothy; in fact the whole Wordsworth clan had a plot there and it had been some time since she'd visited. The last time had been with her mum, who had bought her a book of Wordsworth's poems for her birthday. She had been fourteen and hadn't quite appreciated the sentiment, but she'd loved the graveyard full of beautiful headstones.

For a second, thinking about happier memories with her mum, the morning seemed near on perfect, and then she thought about the sad, decomposing body that had been left in the grounds of St Martha's and felt dreadful. Here she was enjoying a relaxing, leisurely stroll around Grasmere when an unfortunate person had been cruelly killed and dumped.

She reached the tiny off-licence, pushing the door open to the tinkling chime of bells. There was a woman sitting behind the counter looking down at her phone.

'Hi, Detective Constable Morgan Brookes. I'm here about the robbery.'

The woman looked up at her, nodding. 'Scariest thing that's ever happened to me, I crapped myself. I was on my own too, well I'm always on my own, it's not exactly a busy place. Most locals use the Co-op, it's cheaper than we are.'

'You're Ellen York?'

'I am. Did you look at the CCTV, do you know who it was?'

Morgan shook her head. 'Sorry, not yet. My colleague is reviewing it. I just wanted to ask you some questions.'

Ellen was wearing a black hooded sweatshirt with 'True Crime Squad' in big, pink bold letters on the front.

'Okay.'

'Did you get a good look at them, hair, eyes, skin colour, enough to give me a full description?'

'He was wearing a face mask; you know the kind everyone

wears because of Covid? When he first came in, I had to look twice though because it wasn't like the usual ones you see, it wasn't a disposable one. It was black and it had a mouth on with sharp teeth on it. It was horrible, if I'm honest, made me jump a little. He had a baseball cap pulled low over his eyes too. I knew from the first glance at him that he was up to no good, gave off a real bad vibe. But I ignored it and told myself not to be stupid. A lot of people still wear their masks around here, not everyone, but it really stood out. He hovered around for a few minutes looking at the bottles of wine, and I just wanted him to grab one and bugger off.'

'Were there any other customers in?'

'No, a couple had left a minute before he came inside. I reckon he'd been waiting for it to go quiet. We shut at ten and this was almost ten to. So then he grabbed a bottle and brought it over to the counter. I smiled at him, you know, good customer service and all that, scanned the bottle and the next thing I know he's waving a bloody big knife in front of my face. I almost dropped the bottle I jumped that high. He told me he wouldn't hurt me if I gave him the cash out of the till.'

'What did you say?'

'That he was in for a shock; everyone had paid by card.'

Morgan couldn't stop herself from smiling. 'How much was in the till?'

'Thirty-four pounds and eighty-one pence, not worth his petrol or time and effort to get here. Anyway I grabbed the cash and threw it on the counter. He never said another word. Scraped it into the palm of his hand with the knife, picked up the bottle and told me if I rang the police or screamed for help, he'd come back and cut my vocal cords out.'

'What did you do?'

'Screamed as loud as I could and rang the police. Bloody idiot, he was going to kill me for thirty-four quid, he could sod off. I watch all the true crime documentaries and they tell you to never do what a criminal tells you.'

'You're very brave, were you not scared he'd come back inside?'

'Stupid more like, I ran and locked the door after him. My hands were proper shaking. I couldn't turn the key, but I did in the end. I was fuming by this point and I know it seems daft, I didn't know you could be scared and angry at the same time but I was, I was like honestly raging. If he'd come back, I think I'd have smashed him over the head with a can of Strongbow.' She pointed to the stack of cider on the counter with vivid yellow 'reduced' stickers.

'Can you describe him to me?'

'He was tall, around six foot. Stocky, but not fat, he looked as if he worked out but liked a drink and he had a bit of a beer belly, but not massive. His jacket looked tight on the tops of his arms as if they were muscly. Couldn't see his hair much. I think he shaved his head, but like I said he was wearing a hat. His eyes though were dark, like really dark. The kind you see on the serial killer documentaries, you know what I mean? Proper Ted Bundy eyes.'

Morgan nodded; she knew exactly what Ellen meant, some of the worst serial killers had the blackest of eyes. 'It must have been terrifying for you.'

'Yeah, it was. I watch this kind of stuff on YouTube all the time, all I kept thinking was this was just like a documentary. Can't believe it happened to me, you know. My mates thought it was cool. I told them I was cool with it but between you and me I'm not. I'm scared to be in here. I've got my phone with me in case he comes back. I'd have phoned in sick, but I need the money. I'm going on holiday soon and can't afford to sack this off.'

Morgan guessed that Ellen was maybe a couple of years

younger than her, but not much. She reminded Morgan a lot of herself.

'Why are you still on your own? Are they not getting extra staff in?'

'Yeah, after five no one has to work on their own any more, and they let me work a day shift until I feel better. So, it's okay really, they're nice bosses.'

'Where are they?'

'Benidorm, back on Friday. They didn't feel as if they needed to rush home for thirty-four quid. Don't really blame them either to be fair.'

'Sorry, did you already say if he took the wine with him?'

'Yep, he was wearing gloves though, so it wouldn't have mattered if he hadn't. I didn't see where he went. I didn't follow him because I'd locked the door. I told the copper who came to see me, Amber, all of this already.'

'I know, I'm sorry, it's just better for me to hear it direct from yourself. Did you give a statement?'

'I did, and CSI came and did their stuff. It was quite exciting.'

'What about his voice, did you recognise it? Was he a local?'

'It was quite deep; I don't think he was from around here, sounded a bit more like he was from Yorkshire way or maybe Lancashire, or maybe I'm just guessing and haven't got a clue.' She laughed and Morgan grinned at her.

'It's difficult, isn't it? Reliving an awful experience, you start to question yourself and what you saw. I do it all the time.'

'Have you been robbed too?'

'Not exactly, but I've been in horrible situations. The main thing is you're okay. We'll do our best to catch him. And if you think you recognise him, or anyone comes in the shop who has a similar build and gives off bad vibes, make sure you ring the police and get someone here straight away.'

'Do you think he's going to come back?'

'I can't say, Ellen. I just want you to be very aware that it's a possibility and to take every precaution that you can. What about the couple that had been in, did you recognise them? I could do with speaking to them.'

Ellen laughed. 'Good luck with that, I think they were French. They were having an argument in some foreign language anyway. I didn't understand a word they were saying. And thanks, I will. I told you I watch true crime shows all the time on YouTube.'

Morgan fished a card out of her trouser pocket, and passed it to the woman.

'Ring me if you think of anything else or need to talk.'

Ellen stared down at her name. 'Morgan Brookes, I've heard of you. I thought your name sounded familiar. You're amazing, you hunt serial killers and are so cool. I can't believe you're in my shop, someone needs to make documentaries on *you.*'

She smiled. 'I'm not sure amazing is the right word, but thank you and I'm being serious, Ellen, you watch yourself okay.'

She nodded. 'I will, thanks.'

Morgan left her before she asked her if she could snap a photo with her. She supposed if the woman liked true crime, she was going to have heard of her with the number of murders there had been around here. It left her feeling unsettled though, as if she was an open book for anyone to read.

Closing the shop door gently she looked up and down the street. The few shops and businesses that had CCTV had handed copies over. She wandered around trying to figure out why someone had chosen to rob a shop in the middle of a village. It didn't make sense, this wasn't the sort of area that had people desperate enough to carry out such a crime, unless it was a travelling criminal. Most of the locals could afford a bottle of wine even if it was pricey. Something wasn't right about it and the fact that the robbery happened and then the body was dumped, the calls coming in after each other was suspicious. She headed towards the church, hoping to lighten the heavy load that was pressing down on her.

EIGHT

Morgan was sitting on the terrace of the café across the river from St Oswald's, sipping her latte and throwing pieces of her sandwich down onto the floor for the two jackdaws that had practically become her two best friends in a matter of minutes, when her phone began to vibrate. The warmth of the sun on her face and the sound of the river bubbling below her had lulled her into a false sense of security, and she'd momentarily forgotten all about why she was here. She somehow knew it was Ben before she even looked at it.

'Hello.'

'Are you busy? How did you get on?'

She looked across the river at the group of school children all in matching uniforms being pushed in the direction of Wordsworth's grave by a harried looking teacher.

'Nothing really. No I'm not busy, just got myself a latte. Do you need me?'

Her fingers crossed he would say no, then she could browse the bookshop at her leisure.

'Yeah, sorry. Declan is ready for us; I can get Amy to come with me after her doctor's appointment.'

'No, it's fine. I'm heading back now, just reliving some teenage memories. It's such a quaint village, isn't it? Just the right number of shops and tourists. Do you want a sandwich bringing back?'

'I'm good thanks.'

'I'm still thinking that the robbery and dumping of the body are linked. Nothing has made me change my mind on that front. I've got it: the robbery was a distraction. He knew that the police would get called to the shop, so there was a good chance there wouldn't be any on active patrol in Rydal Falls, so it might have been a decoy.'

'Yes, that's a good shout, if you think that it's connected then that's good enough for me. Even though it was risky I can see the logic in it. See you soon, drive safe, Morgan.'

He ended the call. She looked at the two black birds that were now sitting on the railings directly opposite her. Breaking the rest of her savoury cheese sandwich into pieces she whispered, *it's your lucky day, bon appétit.* Then she threw the pieces over the railings onto the grassy bank behind them. Downing the rest of her coffee she left the happy birds and the bustling café to head back towards the car, glancing wistfully at the bookshop and promising herself she'd come back after they'd caught the killer.

Ben was pacing up and down in the office when she walked back through the door. He looked at her, the frown on his face instantly melting away and turning into a smile.

'You look happy.'

She grinned. 'I am, I had a lovely hour wandering around lots of happy memories of that place. It's just a shame they weren't happy at the actual time and instead of enjoying the time there with my mum I'd looked at it as if I'd been tortured for the afternoon.'

'Isn't that standard for moody teenagers? I doubt your mum would have expected any other reaction.'

'I suppose so, but if I'd known how little time I had left with her though, I would have put a smile on my face and really savoured every minute. I never got to buy any books either and I love the little bookshop there.'

'Ah, coffee and memories, no wonder you're smiling. You're so easily pleased. I'm sorry you never got to go to the bookshop, I'll make it up to you.'

She shrugged. 'I know you will, and aren't you glad I'm so easily pleased?' Winking at him she walked towards him and gave him the briefest of hugs.

'Come on then, let's get to the mortuary and see if we can figure out what happened to that poor victim. Did Amy have any luck with the missing persons reports?'

Ben leaned over Amy's desk, picking up a couple of printouts and passing them to her. She looked down at the pictures. There was a woman in her fifties, short, bleached blonde hair with long black roots, glassy eyes that signalled she was either high or drunk, and a flower tattoo that ran along the side of her jawbone. 'Ouch, I bet that hurt like a bitch.'

Ben nodded. 'I bet it did. I don't think it's her. I think whoever it is, is much younger. Look at the other one.'

She did and sucked in a deep breath. This was a pretty teenage girl with long, silky blonde hair. She had almond-coloured eyes and an almost perfect pink pout.

'Where is she from?'

'Blackpool, seventeen-year-old Shea Wilkinson, which is why she wouldn't necessarily come to our attention.'

'It can't be her, can it?'

Morgan was praying to God that that bloated, rotting corpse with shorn hair and one eye missing wasn't this beautiful young woman she was looking at.

'I'm going to say that I hope not, but she's been missing for around four weeks.'

'Where did she disappear from?'

'Last seen hanging around outside an Odeon cinema on a leisure park in Blackpool. She'd been waiting for a lift home, but her sister was late getting there, and she was nowhere to be found.'

A cold fear began to snake its way up Morgan's spine at the terror of someone taking this beautiful girl. Had she been kept for four weeks? And then killed and brought to Rydal Falls?

'You can read the misper report on the way to the mortuary, get up to speed with everything they have or haven't done to locate her up to now, she's our case now her body has been found here.'

The coffee Morgan had enjoyed earlier felt as if it had turned to acid in her stomach, leaving a bitter taste at the back of her throat. She didn't want to call it or wish such a dreadful death on Shea Wilkinson, but deep down in the pit of her stomach she knew that the post-mortem results would prove that this was her. She didn't say it out loud; Ben always teased her about her ability to predict when disaster was about to strike or already had. Instead, she clutched the papers in her hand and followed him out to his car.

The one-way system around Lancaster was pretty quiet for a change and they reached the hospital car park much sooner than Morgan would have liked. She had read the actions listed on the report. Shea's phone had been pinged and had been located on the central reservation of the M55 heading towards Preston. CCTV had shown her leaving the area on her own, with her hood up, walking towards McDonald's. She should have been caught on camera near there, but the camera had been offline. All of her friends had been spoken to and all the businesses in the area visited. There had been no further sightings of her once she had left the line of sight of the camera near to the cinema. It listed her clothing: black gym leggings, black T-shirt, black Nike trainers, belly button piercing, two gold hooped earrings, no tattoos.

'She was clearly driven away from the area; did they not do ANPR checks at the time of her disappearance?'

Ben shrugged. 'Does it say that they did?'

She bent her head and carried on reading despite the growing sensation of sickness inside her stomach; she wasn't a good passenger at the best of times. She couldn't see any ANPR records. Ben parked the car and she stumbled out into the car park, taking in gulps of fresh air as she tried to quell the sickness that was forcing its way up her throat.

'You okay, Morgan? You look like you're going to puke.'

She nodded, looking around frantically. There was no way she was going to throw up in a hospital car park. Inhaling deeply through her mouth she took some deep breaths, until the sickness dissipated.

'You okay now?'

She stuck her thumb up and he patted her arm, and began walking in the direction of the mortuary entrance. She followed him, wishing for the first time that he had asked Amy to accompany him, because she didn't know if she could face looking into the eye of that dead girl if they proved it was Shea. Folding the papers, she tucked them into her trouser pocket and walked briskly after Ben. How had her morning gone from pleasant to this?

He was already inside chatting to Susie with her raspberry-coloured ponytail when she caught up to him.

'Morgan's feeling a bit peaky, travel sickness.'

Susie nodded emphatically. 'Oh, I get travel sick all the time, were you on your phone? It's the worst thing ever. This one time I was sick on a school trip to Blackpool Zoo and the only thing they had was a carrier bag full of holes. It was dripping all over.'

Morgan felt her stomach lurch as her mouth filled with water, and Susie stopped talking.

'Sorry, too much detail, do you need to go be sick?'

She shook her head once; Susie took this as a sign to keep chatting.

'Hey, what books have we read this month, peeps? Ben, you go first.'

Ben laughed. 'None, unless you count the Screwfix catalogue. Ask Morgan she's a voracious reader.'

Susie nodded appreciatively. 'So, what did you read last?'

'*Verity* by Colleen Hoover and *The Book of Accidents* by Chuck Wendig.'

'Ooh, *Verity* is a bit disturbing but great. I haven't read the other.'

'Susie, book club is over. Stop holding up my guests of honour, we have work to do.' Declan was leaning against the door of his office, dressed in navy scrubs and white wellington boots. His hair in a cap, he still looked as dashing as ever. As she got closer to him, he peered at her.

'Are you ill, Morgan?'

'Car sick.'

'Is that it, because I don't want your germs if you have a sickness bug, and I definitely don't want you puking all over my clean mortuary floor. If you'd rather sit this one out tell me now and you can make yourself comfortable in my office.'

For a split second she wanted to say yes please, I do want to sit this one out. But she stole a glance at Ben, and she didn't want to worry or let him down. And she wouldn't let down Shea, or whoever this poor soul was.

'I'm good, I swear if I feel sick, I'll leave.'

Declan's eyes narrowed as he scrutinised her expression trying to read her thoughts.

'Permission to enter granted then. Come on, you two always cause such a fuss. That miserable bugger from Whitehaven, when he comes, never so much as passes the time of day with anyone but at least we get on with it.'

Morgan had no idea who he was talking about, but Ben laughed so she gathered that he did.

NINE

The air inside the mortuary was even cooler than usual. As she stepped inside a shiver ran down her spine and she wished she had worn something warmer, then she remembered she was wearing the thick, black roll-neck jumper which was the warmest one she owned. Maybe she *was* coming down with something. Or maybe she was dreading this post-mortem. Staring at the black body bag on the steel table she didn't know if she was able to do this again.

'Are you scribing, Morgan, or do you want me to do it?' Ben whispered into her ear.

'I'm okay, I'll do it.' She knew it would give her a chance to not watch every single cut and dissection if she was busy writing everything down. Wendy walked in followed by Claire, the Barrow CSI. She smiled at them.

'Two for the price of one, can't be bad.'

Ben nodded. 'Claire, thanks for coming. Wendy, you too.'

Neither of them replied, they were getting paid to be here, they were too polite. Wendy caught Morgan's eye, and she mouthed *you okay?* She smiled and nodded at her then looked away. Declan was fiddling with the pale blue Roberts radio he had plugged in on the opposite side of the room. He settled on a station that was playing retro noughties songs and All Saints began singing 'Take Me to the Beach'. Morgan realised that at this very moment she would give anything to be sitting on a beach and not in this freezing cold mortuary about to watch another innocent victim be cut open to find out how they had been killed.

When everyone was ready, they cut the yellow tag from the body bag. Susie began to slide the zip down and the smell of decomposition began to seep out of the bag. The air in the room, which reminded her of the chlorine that clung to your nostrils when you entered the swimming baths, was instead beginning to smell of raw sewage as the thick, heavy vapour from the body escaped. Susie carried on, not even flinching. Morgan however found herself almost choking on the stench. It had taken her by surprise, even though she knew the body was decomposing she'd thought the frigid, cold air last night may have frozen it somehow. Ben shifted from foot to foot, cupping his sleeve across his mouth and nose. Declan smiled to himself, then began to assist Susie to roll the victim from the bag. Once they did that and Wendy had photographed her, they rolled the faded grey sheet from her body, carefully spreading it out onto a table to check for any trace evidence. A belly bar with two pale pink stones rolled onto the floor. Claire picked it up with some tweezers and bagged it up, then Wendy and Claire worked diligently photographing. It was Claire who spoke first. 'There are a few hairs on here, be nice if they're from the killer and we get a DNA match.'

Wendy nodded. 'Wouldn't it?'

Morgan was too busy staring at the greenish-blue marbling across the now bloated body lying on the steel table in front of her. It was female and the piercing jewellery confirmed her fear that this may be Shea, who had a belly button piercing. The bloating from the stomach gas and decomposition must have pushed it out of the hole. The long hair from the photograph was no longer present; it had been chopped off close to her head.

Morgan glanced at Ben. 'I think it's her.'

Declan looked bemused. 'Who?'

'Shea Wilkinson, a missing teenager from Blackpool who was last seen four weeks ago.'

No one said anything, all of them hoping that it wasn't Shea.

'Does she have any scars or distinguishing features, Morgan?'

'An appendix scar that's quite recent and a scar below her left elbow that's old.'

Declan picked up the victim's left arm, turning it slightly to peer at the skin around her elbow. 'There's a bit of slippage, but I can see a scar.' He pointed to the area just below her elbow. 'You may be right, Morgan, but I'll carry on and we'll document everything in order.'

Morgan felt her shoulders sag, the weight of Shea Wilkinson's world pressing down on her. Her parents, her family, her friends – all of them were about to be sent imminently to a living hell from where there was no escape.

TEN

It was confirmed that the grotesquely bloated decomposing body was that of seventeen-year-old Shea Wilkinson. Susie had managed to fingerprint her, and they matched to the prints on file for fourteen-year-old Shea who had assaulted a teacher at school and been arrested. The appendix scar was present too. Declan had been sombre throughout the entire procedure which had taken four hours. Samples had been taken from the vitreous humour inside her eye to check for alcohol. Her mouth and oesophagus had been swabbed, and her stomach content checked, which had almost caused Morgan to vomit when the gas had been released. There was nothing left inside it except the blue liquid. Liver samples had been taken to send off for toxicology, blood samples were also taken. Declan had confirmed that her eye had been scavenged by a bird as there were grooves in the wound that matched that of a beak. Her feet were bare and there were traces of sandy soil on the heel of her left foot, consistent with her heel hitting the ground first.

'She tried to run away, barefoot. You can tell by the soil where it's compacted on her heel and the balls of her feet. Samples will be sent off to a forensic botanist and a soil scientist to study, and they could potentially determine where she was killed or running away from her killer. At least you may get a location, which should be a big help.'

They were sitting in Declan's office, Morgan struggling to stop the tears that kept pooling in the corner of her eyes from leaking down onto her cheeks.

'It's horrendous, there is no doubt about that. Her cause of death was the blunt-force trauma to the back of her head. Caused by an object similar to a ball pein hammer; but there was also evidence of her wrists being tied together by the indents in the skin.'

Ben's tone was hushed, as though Shea could hear them discussing her from the other room. 'How long was she kept alive before he killed her do you think?'

Declan shrugged. 'Time of death isn't exact at the best of times, you know that. It's hard to say, especially with the level of decomposition. The samples of maggots and pupae casings will help narrow it down, but a rough estimate I would say she's been dead around three weeks.'

Morgan looked up at Declan. 'But she went missing four weeks ago.'

He was nodding. 'Whoever took her kept her for anything up to a week before she was killed.'

'Oh my God, that's awful. She must have been so scared, bless her.'

'It may have only been a couple of days; her stomach contents were well digested which tells me he kept her long enough for that to happen. He cut her hair, too, so you need to figure out why he would do that.'

'Her poor family, are they going to have to identify her like this?'

Declan shook his head. 'I wouldn't do that to my worst enemy, let alone her parents. We have a positive ID from the prints and scars, plus we've sent DNA off for comparison.'

Ben's knuckles were bunched into two hard fists that he kept pounding softly against the side of the leather chair he was sitting in. He stood up, reached over and shook Declan's hand.

'Thanks, we'll be in touch if there's anything else. I better phone Marc with an update.'

He turned and walked out of the room, leaving Morgan still seated. Declan lowered his voice, 'I don't think he's coping too well with this one, Morgan. You better keep an eye on him.'

Standing up she nodded. 'I don't think any of us are, Declan, but thanks I will.'

She walked into the long corridor that went on forever, expecting to see Ben at the far end, but he was nowhere in sight. Morgan hurried along it, desperate to get out of the hospital and into the fresh air where the sun was shining and everything was alive, not stone-cold dead. She reached the car they'd arrived in, with no sign of Ben. Not sure if she should go looking for him or give him some space, she decided to get inside and wait, glad she had the keys. Despite the warmth of the sun on her pale cheeks she was frozen to the core. Turning on the engine she fired up the heater and blasted warm air around the car. The radio turned on, mindless chattering about the latest movies filled the car – it was a welcome distraction. She was worried about Ben, felt sickened at what had happened to Shea and wasn't sure how they were going to face her parents. The door opened, jolting her from being inside her own mind, and she looked at Ben. He was clearly distraught, the skin around his eyes reddened where he'd rubbed it. He didn't speak, she didn't look at him a second time, and reaching out her cold hand she took hold of his, squeezing it, then put both her hands back onto the steering wheel. They were going back to Rydal Falls to figure out how to find the bastard who had done this before it happened again, because if there was one thing she did know: he wouldn't be able to stop now he'd started and unless she could stop him it would happen again.

ELEVEN

Des had dropped his cat off at his apartment and was now sitting in the office cradling a mug of coffee and savouring the peace and quiet. He was sifting through the list of jobs: robbery at Grasmere, dead body in the church grounds at Rydal Falls. A cold shudder ran down his spine at the thought of yet another body in this place. It was getting a bit much, too many murders in such a short space of time. He'd come to work here expecting an easy life, maybe a few robberies, rural thefts, the odd burglary, nothing too taxing or strenuous on the old brain. It had been okay as well until Morgan had joined the team. He knew he was being ridiculous, but he couldn't help himself. He thought she was bad luck and he dreaded being paired up with her even for the briefest of time. The office door opened and in walked Ben and Morgan, and he smiled at them.

'How's your cat?' asked Morgan.

'Think it's got some kind of virus, nothing serious though.'

'That's good, you must be relieved.'

He nodded. 'Where have you been?'

'Post-mortem for the woman found in the church.'

Des was glad he'd taken his cat to the vets now; he'd rather pay out eighty quid than have to go watch a PM on a Sunday afternoon.

Ben looked sombre; it must have been bad. The DI walked in, and a few moments later so did Amy. Ben had disappeared into his office and when he saw the others, he came back out.

'We need a briefing, should we meet in the blue room in ten minutes?'

Four heads nodded simultaneously. 'Good, I need to speak to Blackpool CID and inform them that the victim is Shea Wilkinson, they may want to send someone down I suppose, it depends on how busy they are. They can go pass the death message on to her parents then, before anything gets leaked. I want the family informed before we do anything else. No one here is to speak to anyone regarding this until the message has been received. Is that understood?'

'Yes, boss.' They all murmured, and Des wondered why Ben was being so touchy. Another day another body, shouldn't he be used to this by now? He kept quiet though, not wanting to make him angry in case he paired him up with Morgan. He'd rather work with Amy and her sarcastic mouth any day of the week. Ben went back into his office followed by Marc, who closed the door behind him.

'What's wrong with him?'

Morgan looked sad and for a moment he realised just how young she was. She was doing a tough job, had been through some even tougher moments and was still here, sticking it out when she could have asked to go back on Response. He felt a sudden, grudging respect for her and made up his mind not to be so unkind to her.

'Shea Wilkinson is, or was, only seventeen; she was taken from outside a McDonald's on a retail park in Blackpool a month ago.'

A look of shock crossed Amy's face, and he was sure his own echoed it.

'Jesus that's awful, how did she end up here?'

Morgan shrugged. 'That's not the worst. Declan thinks she was kept alive for up to a week after she was taken. You should see the body. You would never guess she was a lively, pretty teenage girl. She looks like some creature dragged out of the Black Lagoon.'

Des shook his head. 'That's not good, not good at all. Why here, why not kill her and dump her in Blackpool?'

'I guess that's down to us to figure out.'

All three of them stood up, making their way to the blue room ready for the briefing. Des was the last out of the door. He turned to look back at Ben and Marc deep in conversation, wondering just how much work this case was going to be and if there was a chance Morgan would end up fighting for her life again. He hoped not – surely it wasn't supposed to be like this? They should be the ones chasing the bad guys and not the other way around. The killers should be scared of them – he wasn't supposed to be the one who was living with the continuing fear that at any moment it might be one of them.

TWELVE

The blue room was almost full to bursting: task force officers were leaning against the wall because all the other seats were taken. They were waiting on Ben and Marc to start the briefing. Wendy was there, along with Claire, who was staying on to help out. Mads was chattering away, his mug of coffee almost empty, and he looked around for someone to go and refill it. Morgan didn't make eye contact with him because he was sure to ask her and she had no plans of ever going back to brewing up duties. The three stairs that led down to the blue room creaked loudly, signalling the arrival of Ben and Marc. Everyone sat straighter and stopped talking, ready to listen to what they had to say. The whole station held Ben in the highest of regards, but Marc hadn't reached the same respect yet because he was still finding his feet and settling in. They entered and headed to the front of the room, where Marc sat down leaving Ben standing.

'Thanks everyone for being here, this is a tough one but we're here to make sure we do everything that we can to put this to bed. We're here regarding Log 009 of last night in relation to the body found in the church grounds of St Martha's. Myself and Morgan attended the post-mortem and we can confirm the body is that of seventeen-year-old female, Shea Wilkinson.'

Gasps filled the small room as Ben continued, 'Shea went missing from somewhere near the McDonald's on White Cross Retail Park in Blackpool after a visit to the Odeon cinema with her friends. She was waiting for a lift home from her sister, and her friends decided to walk, leaving her there alone. Her sister was late, and Shea began to walk towards the entrance to the retail park. She was picked up on camera leaving the cinema and passing McDonald's, then there are no further sightings of her. The other cameras are not working.'

Al, who was sitting next to Morgan, whispered, 'Well, there's a surprise. Do they ever bloody work when we really need them to?'

She turned her head slightly to look at him and shook it, no they didn't, at least most of the time. Sometimes they struck lucky and got nice CCTV evidence, but not often.

Ben continued, 'A Family Liaison Officer and a couple of detectives from Blackpool police are on their way to pass the death message as we speak. This case is our priority, nothing else is taking over unless there's a possible connection between them. I want all our efforts concentrated on finding this killer because—'

Marc stood up. 'Because we don't believe that this is an isolated incident or that it is his first.'

Everyone stared at him, mouths open.

He continued, 'It may be that this is his first time dumping a body in our neck of the woods, but I suspect that this is not his first murder. Why? He's too confident, too self-assured. He took a girl from a retail park in a busy town, for Christ's sake. Kept her captive somewhere for a number of days and then drove her body to Rydal Falls to dump it.'

All eyes looked towards Ben who was nodding in agreement, and he continued, 'Petals were found scattered on top of her and soil samples taken from the soles of her feet were sent off to be tested. We think she tried to run away from him, but he caught her. Until those results come back, and I'm praying that they do give us something to work with, we have no clear idea of where he kept her captive. There are countless barns and empty buildings around this area, well off the beaten track, which means...'

Morgan spoke up, 'That he's local or knows the area well. And if he's not local he's been coming here either for work or on holidays. I suppose he could have used Google Maps but I have a gut feeling it's someone who knows the area. He could live in Blackpool, or maybe he was there for work too.'

'Thanks, Morgan, we have a lot of work to do. I want you and Des to go to the church, have a look around. Speak to anyone who lives nearby, see if you can find me a witness to someone in a car or van hanging around near to the entrance. Amy, I need you to go through the CCTV footage that Blackpool have sent over in case they missed something. Al, I want the whole area of the church and grounds searched again for the murder weapon which Declan thinks is a ball pein hammer, one with a round end.' He waved a printout of the kind of hammer he was talking about in the air, then turned and tacked it to the whiteboard. 'I want the inside of the church turned upside down if you have to. A church is a pretty good place to hide a weapon, check underneath all the pews, altars, wherever you think. Wendy, Claire, if you can be on standby in case anything is found in the search that would be very much appreciated.'

They both nodded. Des stood up and so did Morgan. She didn't question Ben putting her with Des, but she did wonder why. The pair of them didn't get on too brilliant, but for Shea's sake she would do everything asked of her because she wanted to find this killer before he had the chance to strike again.

· · ·

They sat in silence all the way to St Martha's. When they arrived the narrow street was jam-packed with cars double parked all over the place. Des tutted loudly.

'What the hell is going on? Isn't this supposed to be sealed off, it's a major crime scene?'

Morgan cringed. The church fete was in full swing across the road in the grounds of the retirement home. There was still a line of blue and white police tape strung across the road nearer to the church, and a PCSO was guarding the scene. As the car crawled towards the church, Morgan recognised the PCSO: Sam had her arms tucked inside her body armour, looking frazzled as she steered a couple of old ladies away from the church towards the fete. She waved. Morgan felt terrible that she hadn't told the vicar to cancel it. What had she been thinking? Ben was going to have a heart attack if he saw this mess.

'Unbelievable, I mean who gave them the go-ahead to continue with this shambles? Christ, look at that, they're everywhere.' He slammed on the brakes as two old women stepped right in front of the car, arms full of books and cakes.

'Blimey, this is terrible. I thought it was going to be a few stalls, maybe ten people turning up so I said to move it across the road, but this is like a circus.'

She lifted her phone to her ear after dialling Ben's number.

'*Yeah.*'

'You're not going to believe what's going on down at the church.'

'*Well, I'm not because absolutely nothing should be going down, it's a crime scene.*'

Morgan felt the blood pumping in the temple at the side of her forehead, pulsating in time to the terrible music that was being played over some tinny loudspeakers. She closed her eyes, inhaling deeply but before she could tell him Des had taken the phone from her.

'Boss, this is like Notting Hill Carnival. The church is still sealed off and there's a PCSO stopping anyone getting in, but the retirement home is just crazy busy.'

'On my way. Make sure no one has access to the church or grounds please.'

Morgan looked at Des. 'I didn't know.'

He nodded, a grin on his face. 'Well, you may finally have fallen from grace after this disaster. There's no way the boss is going to let you off with this mess. Never mind, shit happens. I suppose you know that more than any of us.'

He was enjoying it. He stopped the car in front of the tape and got out. He was already crossing the road towards the entrance gates of the home. She turned to Sam. 'Oh my God, this is crazy.'

Sam sighed. 'Tell me about it, you'd think the Queen was here. I've never seen so many people, and I don't think for one minute they're here just for the church fete, the nosey buggers. They know something bad is going on and they're here to gawp. I'm sick of telling them not to duck under the tape; honestly some people are just stupid.'

'Thanks, Sam, I'll get someone to come give you a hand.'

'Don't bother, there's only me and Tina in until two. She's guarding the church grounds in case they try and climb over the wall.'

Morgan nodded as she turned to walk across to the fete. Her heart had sunk to the bottom of her Docs like a lead ball. There was a woman sitting at a table guarding the entrance.

'Fifty pence, please, lovey.'

Morgan patted her pockets, but she didn't have any cash on her – she rarely carried it. Her phone was her usual method of payment. Before she began to explain that she was here on police business she heard a deep voice behind her.

'Joyce, we don't charge the good officers of the law who are here to do a job. It's okay, Morgan, you can go in.'

She turned and smiled at Theo who was beaming at her. Joyce on the other hand was leaning forward and staring at her intently.

'You're a police officer?'

Morgan saw that her shirtsleeves had risen up, her tattoos peeking out from underneath them. Joyce was giving her a once-over that would have made a prisoner blush as she took in her messy bun, winged eyeliner, rolled up black trousers and Doc Marten boots.

Theo saved her the trouble as he stepped forward. 'She is, one of our finest and you're holding her up from doing her job.'

When he put his hand on Morgan's arm, his fingers were like ice, and she shivered at his touch as he led her past the small, rickety pine table that Joyce was sitting behind and into the car park. Leaning close to her ear he whispered, 'Sorry about that, Joyce is a shrewd businesswoman.' He chuckled loudly, and she pulled her arm from his grip.

'I don't have cash on me, thanks.'

He nodded. 'No one does really, we've all gone contactless, haven't we?'

A loud screech trilled through her ears. 'Morgan.'

She turned and was hit abruptly in the middle by a child, small for her age but stronger than she looked, as her arms wrapped around her and squeezed the life out of her. Looking down she grinned to see the back of a familiar head. Macy's face was pushed into her midriff. She wrapped her arms around the kid, squeezing back. Theo was grinning at them both.

'You have a way with people. I think they like you, Detective Brookes.'

She laughed; Macy was still hugging her.

'You know I wouldn't say that I do, but I guess I have a special bond with the people whose lives I've helped to save.'

He looked at her, his head tilting slightly, eyes open wide.

'Well now I'm going to need you to expand on that because that is a very interesting concept.'

She felt heat rushing up her throat and cheeks. 'Maybe one day. Macy, you can let go now, that was the best hug ever.'

Macy was grinning at her. 'It was, that's good.' She turned to look at the vicar. 'You should Google her, she's a real-life superhero, aren't you, Morgan?'

Morgan laughed, her cheeks now resembling an overripe tomato. 'Shh, don't give my secrets away, Macy.'

Macy stood there, flexing her arm muscles. 'She has a black cape and mask she wears like Batman but only it's much cooler.'

Theo let out a hearty laugh, and Morgan was mortified. She spied Macy's mum rushing towards them and breathed a sigh of relief.

'Hi, Morgan, I'm so sorry, I didn't realise Macy was terrorising you. Macy, leave her alone she's busy. Why don't you go sell some cakes or something.'

Morgan watched Macy's mum smile at the vicar, the warmth in her eyes and pinkness of her cheeks radiating towards him, and wondered if everyone had a crush on him, because there was no denying, he was charming and good-looking. Joyce was enthralled by the goings on just behind her table and was watching it all going down intently.

'I better go check on her. Make sure she's not fiddling anyone and giving them the wrong change. It's great to see you, Morgan, you look really lovely.'

'Thank you, she's doing great, isn't she? It's lovely to see you both.'

If Joyce was enjoying all of this, Theo was absolutely enraptured by it all, one eyebrow was arched quizzically at Morgan. She smiled at him but there was no way she was telling him what that little exchange was about. Macy was tough and had managed to survive being abducted by a killer who had kept her locked up in his sister's bedroom for days. If he wanted to know, he would have to find out from someone else. It wasn't her tale to tell.

A woman's voice yelled, 'Vicar, can you come over here?' So loud it could be heard over the screeching kids and awful music playing by the bouncy castle.

Theo smiled at Morgan, shrugging. 'Sorry, my flock calls, maybe we could catch up later and you can tell me what kind of superhero you are? I'd be very interested to know.' He winked at her. She didn't speak and he turned, striding across the car park towards the table at the far end, leaving her inhaling a cloud of his aftershave, something subtle yet attractive.

She stopped herself. What was he? some kind of Pied Piper? Did he weave some magic over everyone he spoke to, so they fell under his spell?

'What you think about him then? Serial killer or nice guy?'

She jolted, turning to look at Des who was standing next to her with a paper bag in his hand.

'He's okay, certainly different for a priest. Why do you ask that?'

'Bit of a coincidence, isn't it, new priest in town, there's a power cut and he stumbles across a rotting corpse in his churchyard.'

'I'd say it was more a case of unlucky.'

'You tell me, why would some guy as good-looking as him give it up to be a servant of God? He must have women falling over his feet on a daily basis. It's like torturing yourself, why do it?'

'He's not Catholic; he hasn't sworn a vow of celibacy.'

'Ooh and you'd know this because?'

'Because it's a Church of England church, Des, it states it quite clearly on the noticeboard over there outside the church.'

'I think you like Father Theo. Don't let the boss know and don't let it get in the way of the investigation. Just because he's a vicar it doesn't mean that he isn't capable of doing awful things.'

She frowned; she had felt exactly the same last night. Hadn't he aroused her suspicion with his references to BTK? She had said as much to Cain, so why was she feeling all defensive about him now? She didn't know; maybe it was the way he managed to charm everyone around him. A small voice in the back of her head whispered *just like Ted Bundy*.

THIRTEEN

Morgan left Des, who was taking his bag of freshly made fruit scones back to the car, and wandered around. So many locals having a nice time when there was a dead girl in the mortuary, it didn't seem right. How long had Shea lain in that ditch whilst everyone went about their business? She spied a familiar grey-haired woman in the distance, but even with her back to her she knew who it was and hurried towards her. Reaching the stall with the small jars of home-made teas, baskets of crystals and beautiful smelling candles she paused, waiting for her aunt to turn around.

'Ettie.'

'Morgan, where have you been? It's too long, how are you, dear?'

Ettie stepped out from behind her wooden trestle table and wrapped her arms around Morgan, pulling her close. Morgan did the same. Ettie smelled of lavender, rosemary and lemon. She smelled like family, the only family she had left, and a sadness passed over her smile at the distant memories of the life she'd led that had brought her to this point.

'You smell so good, I've missed you.'

They stayed that way, wrapped in each other's arms for a couple of minutes, neither wanting to let go.

'And you smell of Chanel perfume with a touch of sadness. What's wrong, Morgan?'

Morgan pulled away from her, amazed at how her aunt could read people so well.

'It's complicated.'

'It always is with you. Tell me, is that handsome boss of yours around? Although I don't know if I've quite forgiven him for making me spend hours in that police cell.'

'Not today, he's really busy, we have a serious case ongoing.'

'That poor soul in the church, I heard about that. I also heard that you had moved in with him and are getting along splendidly.'

'You did?'

'You should know that just because I live out in the middle of the woods that I still find out all the gossip, also underneath that sadness I can tell that you're happier than you've been in a long time. If that's because of Ben, then he's forgiven. I want you to be happy, dear, you deserve the world. How is that insomnia?'

'Thank you, he does make me happy. Insomnia's much better, I rarely wake up now unless I get a phone call from work.'

'Then that's all you need, no more of my Find Love tea for you. It's worked a treat.'

'What, I thought you gave me Sleep Well tea to help with that?'

'I did, but I made you a special blend with some Find Love thrown into the mix. I hadn't done that before so I was a little bit sceptical that it would work. It has and I'm relieved you're sleeping better and with a kind, loving man by your side.'

Morgan laughed. 'Ettie, I can't believe you did that.'

'Pft, sometimes we all need a little push in the right direction. You two were going to get together at some point, it just steered you the right way.'

'Well, what have we here? Do you two know each other well?'

Theo's loud voice boomed into her ear, and she turned to look at him suddenly feeling protective over her aunt.

'We're old friends. I buy Ettie's tea; it's wonderful to help you sleep.'

Ettie nodded, she didn't say a word.

'I should try that. I tossed and turned all night after that little discovery. I felt terrible when my alarm went off.'

He picked up a jar of tea, but Ettie took it off him.

'That's not the right tea, you want this one.' She picked up a jar and passed it to him.

'Thank you, what do you do with it?'

'Steep some in the hot water in a teapot, then strain it into a cup or mug, whatever you prefer, an hour before bed. It's all natural ingredients picked from my own herb garden.'

He looked at Morgan and winked. 'I am impressed, how much for this one please?' He began to dig in his trouser pocket for some loose change.

'It's on the house, a welcome gift for our new vicar. If it works and you like it or need to buy more, you can pay for the next jar.'

'Thank you, that's very kind of you. I will let you know how I get on, this is all very interesting. I really like all this New Age stuff; you know the church is too hung up on old traditions.'

He pocketed the tea and began to wander over to the next stall. Ettie whispered, 'New Age, it's called witchcraft and it's older than his precious church.'

Morgan laughed. 'I don't know about him yet; he seems okay but...' Her voice tapered off.

'But? That's a big but.'

'He found the victim last night and there's something about

him... don't let him know you're my aunt. At least not until I have him figured out.'

Ettie nodded. 'Anything you say, dear, that's between us anyway. I wonder if his church would agree with him drinking tea made from an ancient woodland kitchen witch.'

Morgan laughed, her head thrown back. She noticed Des staring at her from a distance.

'I better go, take care, Ettie.'

Ettie pushed a small jute bag into the palm of her hand. 'Obsidian, Smokey Quartz, Amethyst and Black Tourmaline for protection. Keep it with you, it will help ward off the negative energy and keep you grounded.'

Leaning forward, Morgan brushed the soft crinkled skin on Ettie's cheek with her lips, at the same time pushing the bag of stones into her pocket.

'Thank you, I shall treasure these. I still have the others you gave me by my side of the bed.'

Ettie nodded her approval. 'You can never have too much protection.' She winked at her, a large grin on her lips.

'What's in those jars?' A woman with four kids in tow asked loudly.

Ettie turned to speak to her, and Morgan slipped away, crossing the car park to get to Des who was waiting for her next to the ancient St John's ambulance that had seen much better days. The guy with green combat trousers on and a first aid kit slung over his shoulder was chatting to him. When she reached Des, he turned to her. 'Ready?' She shrugged, not quite sure what she was supposed to be ready for.

'Yeah, are you?'

Des turned back to the big guy. The man didn't look that much older than her and she wondered how he'd ended up working this on his own. 'Hope you have a good one, no major emergencies.' Then he walked away, heading towards the gates. Morgan caught Des's arm.

'Have you asked inside about CCTV?'

'No, have you?'

'I'll go do it now, where are you going?'

'Back to see which houses look onto the church, see you across the road.'

Morgan felt a hot, prickling sensation on the back of her neck and she slowly turned around to see who was watching them. Theo was leaning against the side of the ice-cream van now, and he lifted a hand and waved to them. The first aider was also staring in their direction, but at least he had the courtesy to look embarrassed and turned away. Unlike the vicar who was now licking the biggest ice-cream cone drizzled in chocolate sauce she'd ever seen.

She turned away and walked towards the entrance to the home, where the doors were propped open and there was a group of residents sitting in chairs and wheelchairs all watching the goings on. An old man resting his forearms on the top of his walking frame smiled at her. 'You have an admirer; he can't take his eyes off you.'

She laughed, turning to see who he was talking about, but Theo was now talking to a group of women, and Des was nowhere to be seen.

'I don't think so.'

The old man shrugged, and the woman next to him in a periwinkle two-piece suit with cropped grey hair and large hooped earrings shook her head.

'Don't listen to him, love, he's away with the fairies. Aren't you, Jacob?'

Jacob smiled a toothless grin at her, and she smiled back, squeezing through the gap to get inside away from all the people. There were far too many here for her liking; she preferred being alone.

Her eyes took some adjusting to the gloomy entrance hall which was so big it spanned the entire length of the home. There were arched doorways leading into a variety of lounges and a dining room. There was a large oak reception desk halfway along the hall and she headed towards it. There wasn't anyone manning it, but there was a brass bell with a small sign that said, 'ring for attention', so she did and the loud ping echoed around the downstairs. This must have been the most elegant, beautiful house at some point. There was a grand, sweeping staircase to the side of the desk.

A woman in a lavender uniform came running down from the first floor, her blonde hair spilling out of the ponytail and her cheeks red.

'I'm sorry, it's been crazy. I have no idea why the supervisor said the church fete could go ahead in the grounds. We're short staffed and I'm trying to juggle taking the residents outside to have a look with caring for the ones who are bedbound.' She looked at Morgan, who was smiling at her, and sat down. 'And I'm due to finish very soon. Sorry, I shouldn't be moaning at you. Can I help? You're with the police, aren't you?'

'Don't worry, you probably needed to get that off your chest, it can't be easy. How did you know I was police?'

'You're dressed a bit too smart to be browsing a glorified jumble sale on a Sunday afternoon. Are you here about the body in the church? It's so sad, poor soul.'

'You'd make a good detective, that's very observant of you.'

'I watch all the detective shows on TV, nothing else to do on a nightshift in-between changing wet beds and toileting people.'

Morgan smiled at her. 'It must be a hard job.'

She nodded. 'It pays the bills, but I do love the residents, well most of them. Some of them are a bit of a pain, but you know that's just people in general.'

'Has anyone asked about CCTV footage? I'm wondering if

you have any cameras that look across at the car park in front of the church?'

'Theo did, the vicar. I told him that we have cameras all around the outside of the building because we sometimes get residents that can wander off. Even though we try and keep them safe, some of them are like cat burglars: they escape out of windows and doors open for only a split second.'

Morgan felt that familiar feeling of uneasiness at the mention of Theo's name. Why was he asking about cameras? What was it to him?

'There is one on the front gates, but it only covers the actual entrance. Look, come around here and I'll show you.'

Morgan stepped behind the desk where there was a monitor that showed the entire perimeter of the building and grounds. The nurse pointed to the small square of screen that showed the entrance gates. She was right, it really did only cover the gates. She felt deflated.

'I'm sorry, I guess you were hoping that we may have captured the vehicle of whoever it was murdered that poor person.'

'Yes, I guess I was. Thank you for showing me though, it's very much appreciated. I didn't catch your name.'

'You're very welcome and it's Milly Blake.'

'How old are you, Milly, if you don't mind me asking? Just for my notebook.'

'Eighteen next Saturday.'

Milly beamed at Morgan, and she couldn't help but smile back.

'Are you having a party?'

'You bet I am, we're having a sixties night here for the residents and my family and friends. I've been organising it for months. I figured that I might as well bring a bit of fun to this place and liven it up. We've got a disco and a karaoke booked;

all the residents have been giving me their favourite songs so we're going to make up a playlist.'

'That sounds brilliant. I bet they'll love it, that's very kind of you.'

'Ah, we're short staffed as it is and I'm always at work or covering for someone when I'm not. I thought it might be the only way I get to have a party.'

Morgan grinned at her. 'Thanks again, have an amazing birthday.' She was almost at the door when Milly shouted after her.

'Hey, you should come. Bring that dishy bloke you're with. I saw you both from the bedroom window. Is he single? He looks like he could do with livening up a bit.'

She laughed. 'He is single, I'll mention it to him. Thanks.'

Walking out of the doors she couldn't help smiling to herself. She'd never particularly noticed if Des was dishy. Each to their own, she supposed as she headed out of the entrance gates. She still couldn't shake the feeling that someone was watching her but this time she wasn't going to turn around to see Theo standing there. She wouldn't give him the satisfaction of knowing that he was bothering her.

FOURTEEN

Ben's car was parked next to the plain white Corsa she and Des had arrived in. Neither of them were anywhere to be seen. Sam pointed towards the church. 'They went inside.'

'Thanks, are they suited and booted?'

'Not this time. Ben said he was about to release this part of the scene. He's having one last look around, and he said there was no point in keeping the road closed off because it was going to cause chaos when all these cars try to leave. I think he's still keeping the church sealed off though and the grounds.'

'I suppose that makes sense.'

Morgan ducked underneath the tape, looking at the church in daylight. It was such a pretty church even if it was terribly spooky at night, especially in a power cut. Instead of going inside she made her way to where the victim had been discovered, to get the names off nearby gravestones where fresh flowers had been laid recently. There were five: she wrote down the name of the person who had died, then read the inscription for a mention of a husband, wife, mother, father and noted them too. When she'd written them down she turned to look at Brad's grave; her old schoolfriend was on the last row that overlooked the ditch. There was a bunch of with-ered, brown, dried-up flowers and she was sure they were the ones she'd brought him a couple of months ago. Taking a moment to stare at his photograph she kissed two of her fingers, pressing them against his face. Then bent down and pulled out the dead flowers, taking them to the wire bin near the back of the church. Des and Ben were standing there watching her and she felt a rush of heat as her chest and throat began to burn, wondering how long they'd been watching her. Dropping the flower stalks into the bin she crossed towards them.

'Anything inside?'

Ben shook his head. 'Task force are giving it one last look when they can get the van down here. Are you okay, Morgan?'

She nodded. 'Of course, I was just saying hello to Brad.'

'Any luck with the CCTV?'

'The retirement home has a camera on the gates, but it liter-ally covers the gates. It doesn't stretch out onto the road or capture the parking area outside.'

'Damn, that's a shame. Any other cameras?'

'We haven't checked yet.' She lowered her voice. 'I think we need to take a closer look at Theo.'

'The vicar? Ben looked at her, mildly confused. 'Why?'

'I don't know, there's just something about him. The whole time we were over there chatting to people I felt as if he was watching me. Like he couldn't take his eyes off me, and it made me a bit uncomfortable.'

Des laughed. 'Maybe he fancies you, Morgan. You might be his type, and you said yourself, he's not taken a vow of celibacy.'

She glared at him. Why was he this rude especially in front of Ben? 'Why don't you go eat your scones, Des?'

He laughed even harder, shaking his head, and walked off towards the car. She waited until he was inside and out of hearing.

'He's talking utter rubbish by the way, he does not fancy me.'

Ben had a bemused expression on his face. 'Well, I couldn't blame him if he did, but Des is being an idiot. Ignore him, one day he'll grow up into an adult like the rest of us. What do you want to do about Theo then?'

'I think we need to bring him in.'

'Why don't we do a full background check on him first? Speak to the people who knew him from his last parish and make sure he wasn't under any investigation there for anything. We could always get him to come in for a formal statement and put him through the whole custody experience, but I'd rather we checked for any intelligence on him. It's a bit tricky bringing in the vicar when he's new to the area and, by the looks of it, is gaining a whole new fan club of followers.'

She nodded, happy that Ben agreed with her. 'What if he has an outhouse or shed at the back of the vicarage that he's kept her in?'

'Hopefully the soil samples will be able to tell us where exactly she was kept. They've been fast tracked and we should have the results in seventy-two hours with a bit of luck. If they pinpoint this area, then we will bring him in and get a search warrant for the vicarage and any outbuildings. As it stands we don't have enough evidence to point the finger directly at Theo. Have you had enough of working with Des for today? I can send him back to the station to start the in-depth checks on Theo.'

Although she didn't want to admit defeat and let Des get away with being an arsehole, she had indeed had enough of him.

'Yes, I have.'

He smiled at her. 'Then I'll go tell him the good news. He's probably as fed up with you.' Ben winked at her and walked towards the car where Des was waiting.

People were starting to leave the fete now, large groups of

families, the scouts and what looked like a busload of pensioners. Morgan slipped back into the church grounds, keeping to the side of the wall that was the boundary between the church and the vicarage. Once she was at the far end, way past the vicarage, she looked around, no one was watching, and then she apologised to the large tomb with a concrete coffin above the ground and stepped onto it, hoisting herself onto the drystone wall. Her boot finding a footing, she pressed it into the gap and clambered to the top so she was peering into the back garden of the vicarage. There was a run-down shed with a broken door that was hanging off, that wasn't any good. She looked around and at the far end saw a small stone building with no windows. It had a sturdy door and she thought *bingo*.

Ben was talking to someone, so she jumped down quickly, going over on the ankle she'd sprained a while ago on the slippery slope of the roof of Rydal Caves. Grimacing she tried not to put too much weight on it and found herself limping back towards the entrance of the church, where Ben was making polite conversation with Theo. It seemed as if that man was everywhere, he was more omnipresent than God. Ben frowned at her limping towards them but said nothing. Theo, on the other hand, looked concerned.

'Have you hurt yourself, Morgan? How on earth have you done that? Would you like to come inside and soak your foot in some cold water?'

He smiled at her, a big knowing, cheesy smile, and she shook her head.

'I went over on it looking into the ditch where you found the body last night. No, thanks, it's okay, it will be all right in a few minutes.'

He turned away from her back to Ben. 'Like I said, anything I can do please let me know, and if that poor soul's family needs to speak to someone, then don't hesitate to send them my way. I can help ease their pain in their time of need, it's one of my finer traits.'

Ben nodded. 'I will, the road is opening up now and it should ease the flow of cars leaving the fete. It looks like you've had a great turn out, lots of coppers for the church funds. The church, however, is still out of bounds I'm afraid, just for a little longer, but as soon as we release it, I'll make sure you know straight away.'

'Thank you, Ben, that's great and very much appreciated. Morgan, you take care and look after that foot.'

He turned, walking towards the vicarage, leaving them looking at each other. Ben grabbed her elbow. 'Come on, let's get away from here and you can tell me in the car how you really hurt your ankle.'

He led her to the passenger seat and she got inside, then he went to tell Des he was good to go.

Des began the slow crawl to get past the hordes of pedestrians that were slowly sauntering up the street. The knackered old ambulance came out of the entrance gates and followed behind Des's car.

FIFTEEN

Milly walked out of work towards the gates. There were still people packing up the stalls from the fete and the place was madness. She had said her goodbyes to the residents who were still sitting watching everything from the main entrance; with nothing much else to look at they had passed their day pleasantly. Before leaving she'd run back inside to grab some of the tartan woollen throws they kept on the back of the lounge chairs to put over their knees. She didn't want them catching a chill before one of the afternoon staff realised it was getting cooler and they should be brought back inside. The vicar was standing by the gates saying goodbye and thanking everyone, and as she walked past him, he reached out and grabbed her arm.

'Thank you for coming.'

'Oh, I was there by default.'

He arched an eyebrow at her.

'I was at work.' She pointed to the large mansion behind her, and he laughed.

'Of course, I'm sorry I'm terrible with faces. You're...?'

He stopped and she knew he hadn't the faintest idea who she was, even though she knew him, but that could have something to do with the fact that he was the second good-looking bloke to have come into her life today. There wasn't much choice around Rydal Falls. She'd always liked older men, and that copper had been a bit tasty too.

'Milly, Milly Blake, I'm a health care assistant.'

'Yes, you are. I'm sorry, Milly, I spoke to you earlier about the CCTV. Did the police get everything they needed?'

She nodded. 'As much as there was.'

'Good, that's good.'

He still had hold of her elbow, and she looked down at his hand, not wanting to seem rude by pulling away, but at the same time wishing he'd let go of her. She was tired and wanted to go home, shower, put her pyjamas on and pour herself a vodka and cherry cola. Maybe light a candle and watch a bit of TV; she loved the ones where they found people their dream home. It gave her the motivation to turn up for work despite the envy that always accompanied it. She didn't want to live with her parents forever. He seemed to realise that he was keeping her and let go, smiling that big white smile that made his eyes crinkle and the women swoon at his feet. Theo was an absolute dream boat: the crisp white collar he wore at his throat, against the velvety black of the shirt, paired with the faded jeans he had on, and the boots, made him the sexiest vicar she'd ever seen. Pulling her bag up onto her shoulder she stepped away from him and smiled back.

'Have a good evening, Father, I hope there's not too much cleaning up to do.'

With that she turned her back on him, hurrying along the high street desperate to get home. She was having ungodly thoughts about Theo, that hot shower was probably going to be a stone cold one if she didn't snap out of it.

She turned off the still busy high street onto Cloisters Avenue, as it was the quickest way to get to her parents' detached house that overlooked the river. She wished she'd driven to work now; she was hot and getting stickier by the minute. A cool breeze and the sound of gurgling water signalled she was near to the riverbank, and she smiled. This was her happy place, she loved to sit and paddle her feet in the cool water on a meltingly hot summer's day. Usually there were families picnicking or fishing, lots of kids whenever the sun shone, but they must all have been to the church fete because it was deserted, just how she liked it. Crossing the side of the road with pavements and the few houses dotted along it, she walked on the grass instead, staring down at the fast-flowing water. She didn't see the man leaning against the trunk of one of the ancient oak trees dotted along the riverbank; he was too far in the shadows. Instead, she picked up a large stick and launched it into the river, something she'd done since she was a small child, and, smiling, she watched as it began to move along the water like a small ship on its way to another world where she didn't have to mop up old people's wee or clean up after them. Not paying a slight bit of attention to the path in front of her, she knew it like the back of her hand, had walked it more times than she could count, her foot connected with something hard, and she felt herself tripping. She couldn't stop even though she flung her arms out to try and balance herself. Landing with a loud thud and an even louder 'Ugh', she had landed heavy on her stomach, managing to wind herself.

'Are you okay? I watched that happen. I would have tried to catch you, but I was too far away.'

Her eyes watering, her breathing hitching, she glanced up at the man standing over her. Recognising him, she grimaced with both pain and embarrassment.

'Yes, what an idiot.'

He reached down his hand, she grasped it and let him pull her to her feet.

'I have no idea what I fell over.' As she said this she turned and saw that someone had placed a large wooden log across the

full width of the path. How had she not noticed that? Her
cheeks were burning with shame.

'Bloody kids, or teenagers. What if I was an old woman, I
could have broken my hip and lain there for hours.'

She felt a cold shadow cross over her as he stepped closer,
blocking out the sun. He was taller than her. Turning her head,
she heard the whoosh of something in the air, then something
hard and heavy connected with her head with a loud crack and
she blacked out instantly, falling back into his arms.

SIXTEEN

Morgan had noted all the names on the gravestones in the back of her pocket notebook whilst Ben was talking to Al, who was about to send the search team into the church. There were four gravestones near to the ditch which had fresh flowers. The task was time-consuming and would probably add nothing to further their investigation, but she couldn't ignore the fact that the people who left the flowers may have seen someone hanging around recently. She made her way back to Ben.

'I have some names to check out, see if we can trace the relatives.'

He nodded. 'That's great, do you want to crack on with that? I'll wait with Al to see if the search comes up with anything.'

'Yes, I can do. I'll go see if Theo has any parish records that might help.'

Over at the retirement home the stalls had all been packed away, and there was a stack of boxes containing the remnants left behind that no one had wanted. She couldn't spot Theo anywhere. Ettie was loading up the small van she had bought a while ago, and Morgan rushed to help her with the last couple of boxes. Once they were safely inside and the door shut, she asked, 'Have you seen the vicar?'

'He left some time ago. I assumed he'd had enough and had gone back to the vicarage. He could charm the birds down from the trees that man, no wonder it's been such a good turnout. I was expecting a few stalls and not many people. It's been crazy, my teas have almost all sold, along with a lot of my crystals.'

'That's great, worth your coming then?'

'Definitely, but the highlight was seeing you, dear.'

Morgan laughed. 'And mine was seeing you. I better go and see if I can find Theo, I need to speak with him.'

Ettie didn't say anything, but her eyes were staring deep into Morgan's, and she sighed. 'I hate to tell you this but beware of the wolf in sheep's clothing. There is something about that man that unsettles me. I've been watching him. Can you take someone with you? I don't think you should be alone with him.'

'You find him odd too? Don't worry, Ben's over at the church along with some armed officers, I'll be fine.'

'I find him strange. If you're sure, Morgan, but be careful?'

'I promise I will, he's probably all talk and no action.'

'I hope you're right, dear.' Ettie kissed her cheek. 'Don't leave me waiting so long for you to visit next time. I'm not getting any younger you know and you're all I have left.'

Morgan patted her aunt's arm. 'I won't, take care, Ettie.'

Morgan wandered towards the entrance to the retirement home, where two nurses were wheeling the patients who had been watching back inside.

'Excuse me, have you seen the vicar?'

They both shook their heads, and Morgan thanked them. It wouldn't hurt to check out the vicarage. For all she knew he may have gone back there for a stiff drink after his busy afternoon.

The sun had dipped behind a bank of clouds that covered the entire sky and cast a dark shadow across the driveway to the house. A chill ran down Morgan's spine, but she kept on walking towards his front door, knocking as loud as she could; she had no idea if he was inside or not but she didn't want to hang around for ages if he wasn't here. There was no reply. Pressing her ear against the door she listened for any signs of life inside, but there was none. She wondered about checking out the rear garden in case he was around the back. Looking around to see if anyone was watching her, there was no one, she hurried towards the back gate.

It was taller than Ben – a faded, arched wooden gate that had once been painted a dull red. She twisted the metal latch, surprised when it turned easily. She had expected it to be bolted from the other side or too rusty to work properly. Pushing the gate open enough for her to squeeze through, she called, 'Hello, Theo, are you here?' Silence was the only thing that greeted her. Standing there unsure what to do, her eyes scanning the overgrown garden, she spied the stone outbuilding she had seen earlier. She was torn: did she go and have a look to see what was inside or did she do things properly and see if they had enough evidence to bring him in for questioning? Morgan knew exactly what she should do, but it didn't stop her. Before she knew it she was striding purposely through the overgrown grass towards the small stone building. The door was painted the same dull red as the gate. She wished there was a dirty window she could peer through but there wasn't. She reached out and tried the latch, but this one didn't move; it was stiff and there was also a rusted lock beneath it.

'Morgan, what are you doing? I'm not inside there.'

Her hand dropped to her side, and she felt the hairs prickle on the back of her neck. Turning to see Theo she waved. 'Haha, I guess you're not. Sorry I was just being nosey. Can I have a word, Theo? If you're not too busy.'

She walked back towards him, *stupid, that was really stupid, Morgan*, berating herself. She smiled at him as she got closer, and, interestingly, he didn't smile back this time and she wondered if she'd pushed him too far. His cheeks were flushed and he didn't look as calm and collected as he had earlier. He opened the back door which led into the kitchen, where she paused, thinking about her promise to Ettie not to be alone with him. Ben and Al were nearby though, and knew she was with Theo, so she followed him in. He pointed to the same chair she had sat in last night, and she sat down, looking at the garish orange wallpaper. Finally, he spoke.

'It's even worse in daylight, isn't it? What were you looking for, Morgan?'

'You, I wanted to ask if you knew where the parish records were for the graves in the churchyard.'

'Why would you want those? I'm assuming they'd be kept in the vestry; I don't have them here I'm afraid.'

'I wanted to speak to the families who had visited recently to lay flowers on the graves near to where you found the body.'

'That's a good idea, let me see if I can help you. Do you have the names of the deceased?'

Taking her notebook out of her pocket she flipped to the page where she'd written them down and then stopped. She wasn't sure about Theo and she realised that she may be putting them in danger if they had seen something.

'Ahh, it doesn't matter anyway, we can't do anything at the moment. I'm sorry for bothering you. I forgot they're still searching the church and it's out of bounds. Maybe you could let me know when the church has been released and I'll come back to have a look with you.' She took a business card out of the small plastic pocket of the protective cover her notebook was tucked inside and slid it across the table towards Theo.

He picked it up and glanced down at it, then stuffed it into his jeans pocket.

'Of course, anything to help.'

Morgan stood up. 'Thanks, I'll leave you to it.'

She walked towards the front door, a chill settling over her shoulders that didn't seem to want to leave, and a crawling sensation rising up her back. She knew that he was staring after her, watching her walk out of this house, and she didn't turn around.

SEVENTEEN

If Morgan had felt flustered in Theo's company, then it was nothing compared to the look on Ben's face. He was on the phone to someone, and it didn't look as if it was going too well. She pointed to the car, and he nodded, then turned away from her. She didn't wait around to find out what was happening, deciding she could ask him later. She was going back to the station to do a check on the names: Facebook and the police intel system should give her what she needed. The sun was setting fast, the air much cooler, and if it was anything like last night, pretty soon there would be a definite chill in the air.

The station was deserted. Sunday teatime, so everyone was out on patrol or at home eating their tea. Task force were still at the church, even Mads had gone home and he was always here. She walked across the atrium, her boots tapping across the freshly polished floor. She took the stairs two at a time and when she reached the second floor, was surprised to see Marc sitting behind the desk in his office. Looking up from his computer he lifted a hand and waved at her, and she waved back expecting him to jump up and come question her, but he looked back down to whatever he was doing and she felt relieved. Passing the kitchen, she switched the kettle on before going into the office to see who wanted a brew. Amy was there, Des wasn't.

'Where's Des?'

Amy shrugged. 'Your guess is as good as mine. I thought he was with you?'

'He was, he bought himself some home-made scones and left with them.'

'He bought cakes and didn't bring them here?' Amy said in disbelief.

Morgan smiled. 'Well, I don't know if you can class a scone as a cake, but yes he bought some.'

'The greedy pig has probably gone home to eat them before coming here so he didn't have to share them. Sums him up totally that, pretending he's a vegetarian and a health freak then eating crap behind our backs.'

'Do you want a coffee?'

Amy nodded. 'How did you get on at the church, anything?'

'Not before I left. I spoke to the vicar, Theo, a couple of times; he's weird.'

'He's a vicar, isn't he supposed to be weird?'

'No, you can't say that. Just because religion isn't your thing it doesn't make them weird.'

'He's fit though, isn't he? I saw pictures of him when I was doing the usual checks. His face is plastered everywhere online. I mean did you ever see *The Thorn Birds*? I watched it years ago – that vicar was handsome and had an affair.'

'He's not a Catholic priest, he's allowed to have a partner.'

'Is he? Bloody hell, why did I not know this?'

'Amy, I think there's something off about him. What if he killed Shea?'

'Nah, he wouldn't be so bold as to pretend to find her body if he had, that's next level.'

Morgan went to make two coffees; she wasn't so sure. It

would be too easy though, wouldn't it? if he was the killer and was blatantly walking around right in front of their noses, parading himself as a man of God when, really, he was the devil's spawn. Passing Amy a mug she took the other and sat down at her desk, logging on to the computer system. As soon as she was in, she pulled up the Quick Address System and typed in each surname to see if there was a match; Rydal Falls wasn't the biggest of towns. There were three Millers, two Steiners, two Marshalls and one Troughton. She noted down the addresses and then ran their names through the intelligence system to see if she could find any information on them or phone numbers. There was nothing apart from Stephanie Marshall who had been arrested driving OPL – over the prescribed limit of alcohol. There was a phone number on her record and Morgan rang it, not really expecting an answer but thinking nothing ventured, nothing gained. Most people didn't answer calls from the police station because they showed up as unknown or number withheld. Sipping her coffee she almost spat it out when a voice said, '*Hello.*'

'Oh, hello. Sorry to bother you, my name is Detective Constable Morgan Brookes. I'm following up some leads and wondered if you had any relatives buried in St Martha's?'

There was a slight pause before the voice replied, '*As a matter of fact I do, my mum and dad are buried there. Why are you asking?*'

Yes, Morgan, why are you asking? 'A body was discovered in the churchyard and I'm trying to trace anyone who has visited in the past week. Have you been there recently?'

'*Well, yes, it was Mother's Day. I always take flowers then.*'

'Did you notice anyone hanging around, or anything that was out of the ordinary?'

'*What, like a dead body?*'

'Yes, I suppose so.'

'*No, I did not and if I did, I would have phoned you lot.*

*What kind of a person do you think I am? I wouldn't ignore
something like that, poor bugger.'*

'You didn't notice anyone in the area, any vehicles?'

'Not really, but then again, I had no reason to, did I?'

'Thank you for your time, if you do think of anything can
you give me a ring?'

*'Yes, but I honestly don't think I know anything that could
help.'*

She hung up, leaving Morgan staring at the notepad on the
desk. She'd written 'Mother's Day' and underlined it three
times. She felt bad: she should have taken the time to buy
Sylvia a bunch of flowers and she hadn't even thought about
it. Looking at the notepad she thought, one down, three to go:
the names on the grave inscriptions had all belonged to women
except for the one which Stephanie Marshall's mum and dad
shared. She took her desk diary out of the drawer and flicked
through the pages until she came to the weekend of the
twenty-sixth of March, last weekend. The church must have
been busy. There would have been a service on the Sunday
and then people visiting graves to lay flowers for their mums.
Shea couldn't have been there then; someone would surely
have noticed her. So, what did that leave? Monday to Saturday, who had the means to get a person who was clearly dead
out of their vehicle and into the ditch? Who knew about the
ditch? It had to be someone who either visited the churchyard
or was associated with it. She wrote a list: Theo Edwards, a
gardener perhaps, and all the other people who had brought
flowers for their mums, the churchyard had looked a lot
brighter than usual, with the pretty bouquets dotted around.
She'd need to visit them all, see if anyone was the right age –
anyone elderly could be ruled out because whoever had
carried Shea was fit and strong. Carrying someone who was
alive was difficult enough but a dead body was almost
impossible.

The door opened and Marc walked in. He nodded at them both.

'Where is everyone?'

'Ben's still at the church, no idea where Des is,' Amy answered.

'Any updates?'

'Nope, sorry.'

He flopped down onto Des's swivel chair. 'We need something, a link, a lead, some forensics, a helping hand from God.'

Morgan smiled at him. 'I think the forensics should help narrow down the crime scene because at the moment we have the place where she was abducted from and the dump site, but we don't have a murder site yet. Hopefully the soil analysis will steer us in the right direction.'

'Yeah, let's hope it does because we're kind of at a stalemate with it all until we get something to work with.'

He stood up, a long sigh escaping his lips, and left them to it.

Amy was looking at her. 'Well, if the big chief has no idea, then we're screwed.' She picked up her phone, calling Des. It went straight to answerphone.

'Don't you think we don't know what you're doing, Desmondo. I know all about the scones, you greedy pig. Why don't you get your arse back to work and share them around?' She hung up.

Morgan laughed. 'He's definitely not coming back now.'

'I know, but I had to let him know we know, or it would simmer away all day making me madder.'

Morgan carried on with her searches, linking the names on the graves to the local addresses and then running them through the intelligence system to see if anyone had a criminal record that might flag them up. There was absolutely nothing; she was going to have to go and visit the addresses.

'If Ben comes back tell him I've gone out on enquiries. He knows what I'm on with.'

'You're leaving too, I'll be lonely.'

'No, you won't, you're just mad because there's no cake.'

'True.'

The first address wasn't far from the station. She spoke to Mr and Mrs Troughton who had been to the cemetery together; they hadn't noticed anything. It was the same with Miss Miller who was pushing eighty herself, and Mr Steiner who answered the door with a toddler in one of his arms, a plaster cast on the other. He looked flustered but told her it was his gran who he'd taken flowers for and no, he didn't see anything out of the ordinary. Dead ends, all of them. She'd been hoping for something, a suspicious male, a dodgy van that was out of place. Whoever their killer was he seemed to fit in, or he put Shea there in the early hours of the morning when the streets were deserted. Morgan sat in the car with her eyes squeezed shut. She had a headache beginning and if she didn't take painkillers soon it would be a nightmare to get rid of.

EIGHTEEN

Her phone began vibrating. Reaching out her hand, she didn't look at the screen.

'Morgan.'

'Where are you.' Ben's voice was breathless.

'Just been to visit Benjamin Steiner on Adelaide Street.'

'There's a missing girl.'

Morgan's eyes opened and she sat forward. 'From where? How long?'

'Milly Blake, she should have been home a couple of hours ago. Her dad went to look by the river because he said she liked to spend time there. They live opposite it and he found her bag discarded on the footpath, no sign of Milly.'

'Milly, I know that name. Where am I going?'

'Riverside Gardens. A big white detached house on Riverside Road.'

She turned the engine; how did she know that name? Milly, of course, she'd been talking to a Milly in the retirement home a couple of hours ago. A shiver ran down her spine. Milly had been due to finish work soon. Oh God, she prayed that it wasn't the pretty, chatty teenager who was going to turn eighteen in a few days, but there was a lump in the back of her throat and a heavy feeling in her stomach that betrayed the hope she was feeling.

She knew Riverside Road, it had been by the riverbank where her biological father, Gary Marks, had hunted his victims back in the nineties. She shuddered, her school friend, Jess, had been hit by a truck down here in the middle of the night, her body left broken like a rag doll as she'd bled to death on the cold, unforgiving road. And now this. It was still dusky, the night hadn't quite drawn in, and someone had taken a seventeen-year-old girl from the riverbank, leaving her bag behind.

Parking behind Ben's car she jogged along the path to where he was standing next to Cain. Just the sight of the pair of them eased her fears a little but not a lot. Ben pointed to the path. There was a large log that had been placed across it and next to that a pink, shimmery backpack.

'The bag has been moved slightly by Milly's dad. He picked it up to look through it and check it was hers. Inside is her phone and purse with her driving licence, bank card and twenty-pound note.'

'Not a robbery then?'

Ben's head moved from side to side. 'Cassie is on her way with the dogs, Brock and Caesar; she's going to search for a lead in case Milly has fallen into the river or hurt herself.'

'Where's Milly's dad?'

Cain answered. 'Amber has taken him back to the house to wait for an update. He's wanting to get a search team together, family and friends to walk the riverbank in case she's fallen in the water.'

Morgan looked at the heavy piece of wood and discarded bag, then she scoured the area. 'She's not here, I don't even think she's in Rydal Falls unless...'

'Unless?'

'What if the vicar has her? He has that stone outbuilding where he could keep her.'

'I don't know, Morgan; he was hanging around most of the day. I talked to him not too long ago to tell him we were releasing the scene and he could have his church back. I don't know if he'd have had enough time to follow Milly then lure her to his car and take her back to the vicarage without any of us noticing, and where the hell is Des?' Ben was exasperated and she wished she could give him an answer.

'Maybe not. I'm sorry, I don't know where Des is; I haven't seen him since he left the vicarage earlier.'

Ben tutted, walking towards the dog van that was parking up to greet Cassie.

Morgan looked at Cain. 'What do you think?'

'I think that we need to kick arse and find Milly before something awful happens to her.'

She nodded. 'It had to be someone who either knows her or was watching her today. Did they follow her home? But if they were behind her how did they know she'd come this way and put that log in the way? Or was it someone hanging around hoping for a lone female to walk along by the riverside?' She shuddered, this was too close to home, too reminiscent of what Gary Marks had done all those years ago. Did whoever took Milly know about him and his heinous crimes? She found herself staring along the riverbank. It was so pretty, if you could separate it from its tragic history.

'Maybe we're jumping to conclusions, Morgan. She might have fallen over, dropped her bag and someone gave her a lift to the hospital.'

'Have we checked the hospital?'

Cain began to talk into his radio, asking the control room to check with both Westmorland and Furness General Hospitals. They were the nearest, Lancaster was a possibility but that was much further. Both she and Cain walked away from where they were standing to let Cassie and Brock have a clear area to search. Brock was out of the van and straining at his leash. Morgan walked over to the van. She could see Caesar's huge black nose squished against the metal cage. Cassie set off with Brock, and Morgan patted Caesar's nose through the mesh, whispering, 'If they don't find Milly, will you help me? I bet you could do it, couldn't you, boy?'

He stared at her with his huge, chocolate brown eyes, and she wanted to smoosh her face against his.

'He might bite you,' Ben commented from behind her. She turned to him, shaking her head.

'He wouldn't, we're great friends, aren't we?' To confirm this, he let a great drool of goo out of the side of his mouth.

'Gross.'

'Shh, he's got feelings you know.'

'So have I, I also have major heartburn. Should we go and speak to Mr and Mrs Blake?'

Morgan didn't want to, but she knew that she must. It didn't matter how many times she had to deal with grieving relatives or worried parents, it never got any easier. He stepped away from the dog van and she followed him, her head down. She had a sudden urge to grab Ben and pull him close, but she wouldn't, not in public and especially not here.

As if sensing her need he turned to look at her, and his eyes met hers. 'Are you okay with this, Morgan?'

She nodded and he whispered, 'I don't know what I'd do without you.'

Briskly crossing the road, they walked to the detached house just a little bit further on from where Milly's bag had been left. They reached her house and walked through the gates, and Morgan nodded in appreciation at how beautiful it was. It was painted an icy white, with grey windows, a nice modern touch

on an old house. The front door was ajar. Ben knocked and
stepped inside, and she followed him. The house reminded her
of the Potters' house. That house had been renovated and was
beautiful inside, despite the fact that there had been a
murdered family in the cellar. Amber appeared. She looked
relieved to see them and waved them towards the room she'd
just stepped out of. Inside was a tall man, pacing up and down.
A woman with her back to them, with a mass of grey hair in a
bun on the top of her head, was staring out of the window
towards the police activity opposite. The man looked to be in
his late forties. He was running his hand through his thick head
of dark brown hair.

'Have you found her?' He stared at them; his eyes wide in
desperation. The woman, who Morgan had assumed was
Milly's gran, turned around and she realised she was much
younger than she'd placed her.

'Please, tell me you've found her. I can't, I can't possibly get
through the night if you haven't found my baby.'

The man crossed to the woman, pulling her close. 'Of
course, they'll find her, Stella, it's what they do, it's their job to
find people who have gone missing.' He looked at them both, his
eyes pleading with them to say yes.

Ben nodded. 'We're doing everything that we can to find
Milly. Has she ever not turned up before? Could she have
changed her mind and gone to visit a friend?'

'And leave her bag on the footpath with her phone and
purse inside it? Don't be ridiculous, she's obviously hurt, maybe
dazed and disorientated. She just wouldn't leave her personal
belongings for anyone to find.'

'Matthew, they're just trying to help.'

'I spoke to a Milly earlier, at the retirement home, and she
was telling me about her party. Does Milly work there?'

Stella and Matthew both turned, their eyes fixed on her,

making her feel uncomfortable. Even Ben was looking at her as if to say *and...?*

'Well, I think it was Milly. Do you have a recent photograph of her so we can be sure?'

Stella nodded then picked up her phone and scrolled through, passing it to her. Morgan looked down at the photo of the girl from earlier; she was grinning at the camera with a raised glass of fizz in her hand. Morgan gave a quick nod at Ben, passing the phone to him.

'We're doing everything that we can, the dog is out there now. If there is a scent of her it will pick it up.'

'*If* there's a scent? Of course there is going to be a scent of her, she can't be far. She didn't have a car; she hasn't just vanished into thin air.'

Morgan felt bad for Ben, who seemed to be digging himself into a hole. She realised that Matthew and Stella were not going to be happy with anything other than the full facts. There was no point trying to make them feel better because the truth was Milly may well have disappeared into thin air if the person who took Shea had taken her too. It was a tough call to make. How much did you tell them without actual proof that this was the case? Morgan spoke. 'If she got into a vehicle and was driven away then I'm afraid there isn't going to be much of a trail. We're not saying that she has, but we can't rule it out at the present moment. I'm sure you would prefer that we cover every eventuality and follow up any possible leads instead of being single-minded and just focusing on the riverbank.'

Matthew was staring at her and she knew he was trying to decide whether she was worth listening to. 'How old are you, Detective?'

'That's irrelevant, Morgan has lots of experience working missing persons and serious crimes.' Ben was sticking up for her, but she didn't need him to.

'I'm twenty-six, Matthew, I've worked several high profile

murder investigations and each time with a positive result. I don't give in easily, even if it means putting my life on the line, which is exactly what I intend to do to find Milly. You have my word that I will do everything in my power to bring her home safely, you have to trust me on that.'

He nodded; Stella put her arm on his. 'Thank you, Detective, we appreciate that. I just want to know that she's okay and not lying injured somewhere needing our help. I couldn't bear it if she was.' Her voice broke before she finished her sentence, and Matthew turned to his wife, holding her closer, his eyes no longer cold and hard; they were melting pools of tears ready to flow down his cheeks any moment.

'We need a list of her friends, where she likes to visit, boyfriend, anybody who she might contact.'

Stella nodded, pulling away from her husband, glad to be doing something to help. It's always the women, thought Morgan, they're always the ones who know everything. The men don't ever have much of a clue where their kids are or who they hang around with.

'Let's go into the kitchen and we can sit down. Would you like a cup of tea?'

Ben nodded for Morgan to follow Stella, and he stayed with Matthew. A few moments later, as she was sitting on a blush pink bar stool at the kitchen island which was almost the same size as an actual island, she heard the front door close. Ben had left her to it; she didn't blame him because this was difficult for them all and she knew he'd rather be out there running the search team. Stella was busy making a tray of tea; finally, when the boiling water had been poured into the pot and the milk jug filled she turned around, placing it on the smooth, white granite surface in front of her. Morgan smiled at her, thinking of Ettie and how she liked to make her own blends of tea, serving them to her on a similar tray, always with a slice of cake.

'Sugar?'

'No, thanks.'

Stella lowered her voice, looking around to make sure Matthew wasn't listening.

'Please tell me if you think something bad has happened. I can't take it if you give me false hope. Matthew is not very good with anything remotely upsetting. We lost our two-year-old, years before we had Milly, and he never got to grips with his grief.'

'I'm so sorry to hear that, it must have been devastating for you both.'

'He drowned in the pond, at our old house. We were arguing over something so stupid it wasn't even worth the time and effort. I had put Luke down for his nap, and we hadn't heard him come back down the stairs. The kitchen door was ajar because I had been out there gardening. I hadn't closed it properly behind me; we were arguing. I didn't even know that Luke had slipped outside. I didn't even know he was dead. I went upstairs to check on him and his cot was empty, the door open, my heart almost broke free from my ribcage. I screamed his name; I searched the house, and Matthew, who had been about to drive away back to work, was getting in his car when he heard me. He came running back inside and it was then that he noticed the kitchen door.'

Stella let out a loud, hitching sob and buried her head into her hands. Morgan reached across and gently patted her arm. Stella wiped her eyes on her sleeve, then looked at Morgan.

'That's why he won't accept that she's not in the river. We were stupid enough to let our baby drown and he's never got over it.'

Morgan's heart had felt heavy before and now it felt like a lead ball had lodged inside of her chest. She couldn't imagine the pain and grief they had been through and now this.

'I'm so sorry for your loss. That must have been the most heartbreaking thing you've ever gone through. Thank you for sharing that. It wasn't your fault though, Stella. It was one of those ridiculous series of events that can end in complete and utter tragedy that had nothing to do with you.'

Stella looked deep into Morgan's eyes.

'Thank you, that's really sweet of you but we both know that we were at fault. Our stupid argument ruined our life forever. We were never going to have any more children and then one day I began to throw up every time I smelled coffee in the morning and along came Milly. We worship the ground she walks on. She is such a darling girl, so kind and caring. I often wondered how we were blessed with another chance at parenting, when we so badly screwed up the first, and I swore that this time I would never, ever take my eyes off her.'

'Milly is almost eighteen, you can't keep her wrapped up in cotton wool forever. She is going to want to have her freedom, her friends, her life.'

'Where is she? She would never in a million years go off like this if something bad hadn't happened.'

Morgan sipped at the tea, not wanting to tell Stella what she was thinking: it would probably cripple her for the rest of her life.

'I don't know at this moment, but I will find her.'

Stella bowed her head. Her fingers reached out to Morgan's, and she wrapped them around hers, squeezing them tight. Morgan opened her notebook and picked up her pen.

'Who are her closest friends?'

Stella began to list the ones she knew. There weren't many but there were enough to be getting on with.

'Would it be possible to take a look at Milly's bedroom?'

'Why? She's not up there I can assure you.'

Morgan reached out for Stella's hand, gently holding it.

'I know she isn't; I like to get a feel of the person I'm looking for. It really helps me connect with them.'

Stella nodded. 'First door on the left. I can't go up there at the moment. I think I might fall apart completely if I do.'

Up the stairs, opening the door Stella had told her to and stepping inside a large room, it smelled like freshly baked cakes, and she noticed the vanilla frosting candles on her bedside drawers. The room was large and airy, the whitewashed walls had pastel pink picture frames on them, and Morgan stared at the photos of Milly, her parents and friends. There was a large double bed with a glittery pink throw over the white cotton duvet. Milly liked pink and sparkles; she was the complete opposite of Morgan. She noticed a sparkly notebook on one of the bedside drawers and picked it up. It was an action plan for Milly's party, with her guest list and the playlist of all the songs the residents had asked for at the home. Morgan stared at it. Milly was a nice girl, one of those reliable, caring girls that would help anyone who needed it. She was throwing a party to celebrate her birthday and including all of the old people she looked after; there weren't many seventeen-year-olds who were that caring. She closed the book, took a look around and whispered, 'I'm going to make sure you get home for your party, Milly. I promise I'll find you.'

Leaving her bedroom as she found it, she went downstairs to the kitchen where Stella was staring into her teacup. She couldn't waste any more time here: she needed to be doing something to find Milly. Excusing herself she left Stella where she was.

She passed the lounge where Matthew was standing with his back to her as he stared out of the large French windows trying to keep track of the police activity.

NINETEEN

Brock had lost Milly's scent not too far away from where her bag had been discovered. Ben, Morgan and Marc were huddled together trying to decide what they needed to do next.

'Look how near she was to her house.' She pointed to the house only a hundred metres away. 'She almost made it home, this is so unfair.'

Marc nodded. 'I know, we'll find her.'

Morgan hoped that they would before anything awful happened to her. It was Ben who had begun pacing the path back from where she must have walked. He stopped dead in his tracks turning back to face them.

'Just say that her friend picked her up, she forgot her bag. Maybe put it down for a moment, saw the car and forgot to grab it. There is a chance she's safe in someone else's house not aware of all this fuss. We can't rule it out until all her friends have been spoken to.'

She tilted her head, arching one eyebrow at him just the way he did to her occasionally. 'Rubbish, you know that's not what happened. I agree we need to speak to her friends, but we can't afford to waste time ignoring the obvious.'

'Someone find Des before I really lose my shit with him. I want him and Amy as well as any available patrols checking out that list of addresses. You and I will go back to the retirement home and see if she went back for something.'

'Can we also check on Theo?'

'Yes, if it makes you happy, we will pay him a visit too. Al is going to coordinate this search; this is his area of expertise not mine.'

As if by magic a grey Skoda parked next to Cain's van and out got: Al and three more officers. They waved at them. Marc would fill them in on what was happening and what needed to be done.

Ben drove the short distance to the retirement home, short in a car but a bit of a trek by foot. He crawled along so they could both look out for Milly. The gates were wide open and he drove straight through, though the front door was locked, which Morgan was relieved about. Something awful was going on and it seemed to be centred around this area. She would hate for anything to happen to the residents in the home. She rang the doorbell with a camera on it and held up her warrant card, so whoever was on the desk could see. A crackly voice said, *'How can I help?'*

'Police, we need to speak to you about Milly Blake.'

There was a click as the door release was pressed, and Morgan pushed the door open and stepped inside with Ben close behind. She walked down the large hallway towards the desk she'd been chatting to Milly at only a couple of hours ago. There was a much older woman in a dark blue uniform sitting there.

'What about Milly, is she okay?'

'Detectives Brookes and Matthews. I'm afraid she's been reported missing.'

The older woman's eyes widened, and her jaw slackened as a look of confusion crossed her face. 'How, I mean where has she gone? She only left a few hours ago. Who has reported her missing?'

'Her father, he found her bag discarded on a path by the riverside with her phone and purse inside, and there has been no sighting of Milly. Did she come back here or mention if she was going anywhere after work?'

The woman held up her hands. 'Whoa, you'll have to slow down a little bit. Back it up and say that again, slowly, so I can understand.' She pointed to a tiny hearing aid tucked inside her left lobe. 'I caught some of that, but not all.'

'Has Milly been back here since she finished work?'

'No, she has not. I have been on the desk monitoring the chaos that the vicar brought down on us at short notice.'

Morgan glanced at Ben. 'Has Theo been here since?'

'No, he left before most of the clearing up was done. That man can charm the songbirds out of a tree, but he was nowhere to be found when we needed him to give us a hand with his mess.'

She felt the hairs rise on the back of her neck. 'He didn't stay to finish clearing up?'

'No, are you deaf too?'

Morgan ignored her sarcasm. 'Do you know if Milly would have gone to visit anyone from here who we may not have the address for?'

She shrugged. 'I doubt it, we're all much older than Milly and the friends she does have that work here are all on the late shift. They're currently putting our overexcited residents to bed.'

Morgan forced herself to smile. 'Could you please go and ask them if they know where Milly might be?'

The woman sighed but turned and went up the stairs. When she came back down, she was shaking her head at them.

'I'm sorry, neither of them spoke to her before she left they have no idea where she is.'

Ben looked around at the large hallway and staircase behind the desk. 'If Milly gets in touch with you, it's imperative that you phone the police to let us know.'

'Where is she? This isn't like her to cause such a fuss, she's a lovely, quiet girl. Everyone loves her to bits. She's so kind and considerate towards the residents, even when they're being downright pains in the arse. If you find her, can you let me know? I'm Amanda and I'm on until midnight.'

'Honestly, we don't know but someone will be in touch when she turns up.'

They turned away from her, Morgan trying her best not to break into a run and sprint across the car park to the vicarage. They got outside and Ben grabbed her arm. 'Just a little reminder we have nothing to suggest that he's involved in any of this. We're just paying him a courtesy visit, that's it, unless he has her tied up and gagged in the kitchen.'

'I know, but it's kind of creepy, isn't it, how he fits the bill perfectly, especially when he compares himself to Dennis Radar.'

'He can call himself Hannibal Lecter for all I care, we need concrete evidence before we can take any action if there's any to be taken. I know you're concerned, Morgan, but don't let it get personal, he has no past convictions to give us that extra push we need, so we have to tread carefully.'

She stopped, glancing at Ben. She knew he was right, of course he was, but she had this feeling that everything wasn't as great with the charming Theo as he made out. They walked along the path to the vicarage. Slowly. The air was so still you could cut it with a knife. It was silent too, no birds, no traffic, no screams for help. Before they could knock on the large, wooden door it opened and Theo was there smiling at them. He'd changed out of his black shirt and dog collar, and was wearing a black hooded sweatshirt with the *Stranger Things* logo on the front and a pair of jogging bottoms.

'My, you two can't keep away. Can I help you?'

Ben spoke. 'I know, there's a lot going on at the moment. We're searching for a missing health care assistant from across the road. Her parents reported her missing over an hour ago, and we're just checking to see if anyone has seen her.'

His face paled in the yellow light from the bare bulb hanging down in the hallway. 'But that's terrible. Who is it, and how do they know they're missing?'

'Milly Blake, she was there today helping out.'

He held up a hand. 'Please, I know who Milly is. She's that dear, sweet, helpful girl who I've been speaking to, and the way she is so wonderful to the residents. She was fussing around them all afternoon taking care of their needs.'

'She is, have you seen her and what have you been speaking to her about?'

His dark eyes turned to look into Morgan's, and she felt as if he was staring down into the depths of her soul, probing deep inside, looking for something.

'Well, I saw her this afternoon several times. I spoke to her about the body in the church to ask if the cameras may have covered the entrance, so I could let you know if they did. I was trying to be helpful. This is awful, what can I do to help? Would you like to come in for a cup of tea whilst we figure out what to do?'

Ben stepped forward. 'That would be great if you don't mind.'

Theo's eyes opened wide; *you weren't expecting that, were you, Theo?* Morgan's mind whispered to her. He nodded, stepped back and turned, letting them follow him inside.

'I could really do with the toilet if that's okay, it's been a bit hectic.'

He pointed up the stairs. 'Third door along.' Then flicked

the switch so they were bathed in the same watery yellow light. She looked up, there were no lampshades anywhere. Theo smiled. 'Yes, as well as not paying to get this place decorated, the last vicar was also very scrupulous with their money and took all the light fittings with them.'

She smiled at him. 'At least it gives you a good excuse to decorate.'

He led Ben down to the kitchen, and she hurried upstairs. Glancing behind her to make sure they weren't waiting for her, she began to listen at each door for any signs of life behind them. There were five doors, and not a peep came from any of them. Her heart sinking, she went into the bathroom, flushed the chain and washed her hands, looking around. It was stark like the rest of the house. It was going to take some doing to turn this place into a home.

As she went downstairs Ben was walking back towards the front door.

'Rain check, we need to get back to the scene.'

Morgan followed him to the front door, confused but not saying a word. They stepped out into the cold night air.

'Sorry to bother you, thanks.'

Ben was heading down the path and through the gate back to his car, she followed.

Once they were inside the car and the vicarage door closed she breathed out a sigh.

'What's that about?'

'We could hear you creeping around upstairs, the bloody floorboards were creaking. That was embarrassing, Morgan. Did you find anything?'

'No, I only listened.'

'There were no signs of anyone being inside that house

other than him. He didn't have enough time to take her. Can you phone Des again?'

She dialled Des's number and heard his voicemail kick in immediately. 'He's turned his phone off.'

'What? Why has he done that? He's still supposed to be on shift.'

She shrugged. 'Who knows why he does anything, he's not exactly the keenest copper in Cumbria, is he?'

'Maybe not, but we need him and he's taking the piss.'

A horrible thought ran through Morgan's head. 'We haven't seen him since earlier, and he saw Milly. It's a bit strange how he left to go back to the office and now she's vanished without a trace.'

Ben jerked his head in her direction. 'I don't even want to know what you were about to say, don't say it. What's wrong with you? It's like you're on high alert.'

'I am on high alert, Ben, girls don't just disappear into thin air. We don't live in the middle of the Bermuda Triangle.'

He began to drive faster than normal.

'Where are you going?'

'To find Des, and if he finds out that you were pointing your finger at him...'

'What, how would he find out? He wouldn't unless you told him.'

She felt anger and betrayal at the way he was talking to her, how he was putting Theo and now Des first, ignoring her input, and her insides were a seething mass of knots. They didn't speak all the way to Des's house, which was on the opposite side of Rydal Falls to where Ben lived. He stopped the car and got out, but Morgan didn't move. He leaned inside. 'Aren't you coming?'

'No, I'll let you speak to him.'

He shrugged, shutting the door and walking down the tiny path that led to Des's grey front door. Ben knocked so loud she could hear it through the car window. No lights came on, no one answered the door. He hammered on it, then she watched as he took out his phone. Jabbing his finger at the touchscreen she knew he was raging. Getting out of the car she walked to where Ben was standing with his phone clamped to his ear.

'Where the hell is he? His car isn't here.'

'Does he have a back garden, could he be around there?'

'No, it's a terraced house, he has a small backyard that's just about big enough for his cat to go pee in.'

'Any sheds out there?'

Ben turned to stare at her with a look of horror on his face.

'No, at least he didn't last time I was here. There's not a lot of room.'

It didn't stop him from racing to the end of the street to go into the back alley and locate Des's back door. He found it. There was an empty bin outside. He turned to Morgan. 'Des wouldn't leave his bin out, he is too particular; he wouldn't want it cluttering up the back lane.'

He rolled it over to the back door, leaned it against the wall and climbed onto it. Morgan grimaced, but held it still so Ben didn't fall and break his ankle.

'No shed, a bicycle, a couple of planters, no sign of life.'

There was a miaow as a cat pushed its way out of the cat flap in the back door. It stared up towards Ben who turned and jumped down off the bin.

'His cat's there.'

A thud as the super large white cat jumped up onto the wall where he'd been momentarily leaning. It was staring down at them both.

'That cat is watching us.'

Ben smiled. 'I know, I should have it on my team, it probably works harder than Des. Seriously though where is he? I don't understand, I mean he's not the hardest worker, but he's usually not this much of a slacker.'

His anger had dissipated into frustration, and he reached
out his hand to stroke her cheek. 'I'm sorry for snapping at you,
it's just been a hell of a day. There was no need for that.'

'You're forgiven, just. I'm not trying to be awkward. I'm
trying to think who could have taken Milly. In my mind Theo is
still a good suspect and as for Des.' She shrugged. Did she think
he had it in him to do something so heinous? Probably not, he
was too lazy for one, but it didn't explain why he had vanished
into thin air right at the same time a girl had been abducted,
did it?

'I know and I snapped because I don't want to look at the
possibility of one of my team having any involvement in this
case. Maybe Des and Milly ran away together, wouldn't that be
something?'

Morgan smiled. 'It would be better than what I was thinking, that's for sure.'

They walked back around to the car, and Ben gave the
house that was still in darkness another glance. 'I'll come back
in a little bit and see if he's home, maybe he felt ill and has taken
himself off to bed or the doctors.'

TWENTY

They went back to the station, cold, hungry and frustrated beyond belief. They hadn't spoken a word to each other on the short journey. Morgan was exhausted. She felt as if she could lie down and close her eyes for a week. Everything seemed heavy: the responsibility of finding Shea's killer, locating Milly and a lack of caffeine were making her entire body feel sluggish. She could barely lift her boots to climb the stairs, each one felt like a mountain. She half expected them to walk into the office to see Des in his default position, feet on desk as he leaned back on his swivel chair with his fingers clasped behind his head. Morgan's headache was well and truly in full swing now. It had taken a grip whilst she'd been sitting with Stella and wasn't about to let go. She rifled through her desk drawers to no avail. She didn't have any painkillers. Glancing at Des's she knew that he would – he was a major hypochondriac, always popping pills, vitamins and anything that would keep him healthy. She felt bad for doing this, but she didn't think he'd mind her borrowing a couple of paracetamols. Opening the middle drawer, where she knew he kept his pharmacy, she spied a red box of ibuprofen and popped two pills out of the blister.

Amy walked in, took one look at her and asked, 'Are you looking through his drawers?'

She shook her head, sending a blinding pain along her eyebrows, then stuck her tongue out with the two white capsules sitting on it.

Amy nodded. 'Let you off, and where is he anyway? He's not answering his phone not even to me.'

Morgan dry swallowed the pills, and Amy clapped.

'Whoa that's hardcore, even Des can't dry swallow and he pops pills like a pro.'

'We went to his house. He's not there, it's all in darkness.'

'That's odd, if he's not here and he's not at home I don't know where else he could be.'

'Neither do we.'

Ben, who had been making coffee, walked in with two mugs, handing one to Morgan. 'Want one? And how did you get on?'

Amy shook her head. 'I've been to her three closest friends' houses and none of them have seen or heard from her today, but they said that's not unusual when she's working. They were all chatting last night in a group chat they have on WhatsApp about Milly's party; there was nothing remotely unusual about it.'

Ben nodded. 'So, we don't think she's suicidal? She never talked about being depressed?'

'I asked them that and they laughed and said Milly was the least likely person ever to do something like that.'

Morgan spoke, 'We didn't ask her parents if that was a possibility.'

Ben turned to her. 'I did. When you took her mum out of the room, I asked her dad, and he was adamant that she wouldn't do that. Besides if she had gone into the river, I think we would have found her by now. Lowland Search and Rescue are working their way along the riverside and Rydal Water.

Don't forget the dog didn't pick up her scent by the riverbank either, it stopped on the roadside where it's likely she got into a vehicle; but we've covered the suicide angle so it can be ticked off the list unless we find anything that points to that.'

'What are the odds on Des doing a disappearing act the same time a girl goes missing? You don't think they've gone off together, do you, like he's having some kind of mid-life crisis?' Amy was being serious; there wasn't a hint of a smile on her face.

'Actually, when I was talking to her, Milly commented about the good-looking guy I was with, and I laughed it off. What if she was serious? What if Des picked her up and they've gone off together somewhere?'

'Morgan she's not even eighteen. Surely even Des wouldn't go for someone so young.'

'She's very attractive. What if she was talking to him and they arranged to meet? He might not have realised just how young she is.'

'That doesn't explain why she'd leave her bag behind with her purse and phone inside it.'

Amy shrugged. 'What if she was in the throes of passion and forgot about it?'

'What, with Des?'

Ben was shaking his head, and Morgan looked at him. 'Younger girls do find older men attractive. Not that I'm stating the obvious or anything.'

Amy let out a giggle that she tried to stifle with the palm of her hand.

'Yeah, I guess they do, and older men definitely find younger women attractive so touché, Morgan.'

'What are we going to do?'

'Put an ANPR marker on Des's car. I have no choice but to follow this up. We can't ignore the obvious: he was in the same place as Milly who told you she thought he was attractive and now the pair of them have disappeared. Hopefully Des is just having a momentary lapse of judgement and the pair of them will turn up soon, but...'

'Lapse of judgement? If he's gone off with a seventeen-year-old I'd say he's completely lost it, boss. He could have just come back here and shared his cakes out, then gone home for a cold shower. Why cause all this fuss?' Amy actually looked bewildered.

'Maybe they sneaked off together, not realising that Milly leaving her bag behind was going to cause all of this fuss.'

She shrugged. 'He's an arsehole, if he has.'

Ben nodded. 'He definitely is, but I don't think he has.'

'Where is he then, if he hasn't? And, in Des's defence, Milly is only a week away from her eighteenth birthday.'

'That's the million-dollar question, Morgan. If we knew that we wouldn't have a search team out scouring the riverbanks and area.'

Morgan squeezed her eyes closed. 'I think that we're getting confused or led away from the fact that a girl is missing and we have the body of another in the mortuary. Let's forget Des could be involved for now, unless we find out he's recently been on a trip to Blackpool.'

Ben flashed her a look that she hadn't seen before, a combination of anger and dismay all rolled into one neat little ball. It didn't stop her. She knew that Ben and Des had worked together for quite a few years, but she couldn't forget that she'd worked closely with Taylor, believing him to be her friend when he was actually her murderous biological brother.

She stood up, walking across the room to the board, and picked up a marker. On it she wrote, 'Shea Wilkinson and Milly Blake both seventeen, both missing from the area where they live, blonde hair.' She closed her eyes trying to remember what colour Milly's were. She had greenish-blue eyes; she had no idea about Shea's without looking at a photograph, because she was missing one when they'd found her and the other had been covered in a milky white film. Both girls were slender; she tried to think of other similarities. Long hair: Shea on her photograph had long hair and Milly's had been in a high ponytail but it had been long. She stopped writing, turning to Ben and Amy.

'Whoever this is, if the cases are connected, which I think they are because the similarities are too much, then he has a type.'

Ben nodded. 'He likes them young, but not too young. They both have long blonde hair, both late teens.'

'Both beautiful,' added Amy. 'Or at least Shea was before this bastard got hold of her.'

'We need to focus on Milly. If it's the same guy who has her then she only has a matter of days before he kills her. We also need those soil samples back to give us a clue as to where he took her and kept her. I wonder how long they'll take?' He glanced at the clock on the wall; it was almost nine.

Morgan knew what he was thinking. 'Declan won't be at the mortuary now unless something has come in.'

They had been working nonstop with very little to eat or drink, no wonder she had a headache from hell. The door opened and in walked Marc looking as deflated as they did. He looked at the board and shook his head.

'Are you seriously thinking these are connected?'

'We can't rule it out, sir,' Ben answered.

'I honestly thought the rumours were just that, rumours about this place. I had no idea I'd moved to murder central. How long have we got to find this girl?'

'If they're connected, a few days, hopefully.'

'And if they're not?'

'Then we don't know, sir, but the odds on them not being connected are very low. You just have to look at the victim profiles to see the similarities.'

'How do we stop this from happening again? Put out a press

release warning all seventeen-year-old blonde-haired girls not to go out alone?'

Morgan stood up. 'Yes, if we have to that's what we will do. I'd rather we made a statement and warned the public, so they know there's a monster, stalking the streets.'

He nodded. 'Nothing from the scene, search and rescue didn't find a body or injured girl. It looks like we're focusing on the theory she was taken or got into a car willingly. Any update on boyfriends, male friends?'

All three of them looked at each other, unsure whether to mention Des. It was Amy who broke the silence.

'Sir, we can't find Des and Morgan said that Milly told her she thought he was attractive.'

Marc stared at her in disbelief. 'Are you saying that one of my officers may be responsible for this?' He waved his hands in the air. 'Where the hell is he?'

'I doubt very much that he is. I think this is just an unsettling coincidence, but at the same time I don't want to blindly ignore the obvious. Until we find Des, I think we need to focus on locating him.'

'What about his phone? Goddamit and his radio? Don't they have GPS in them?'

Morgan glanced at Ben. 'Yes, of course they do. Sometimes the signal can be a bit sketchy around here because of the terrain, but yes.'

She couldn't believe that not one of them had even considered this. They had been too focused on trying to convince themselves that he couldn't possibly be involved in Milly's disappearance and hadn't been thinking straight. Marc left them to go to his office and speak to the Force Incident Manager up at headquarters.

TWENTY-ONE

All three of them waited in silence for Marc to return. None of this would be passed over the airwaves as every officer carried a radio set. At least not at this moment in time. If things exploded then they would, but even then they might switch to another channel to keep things from getting out of control and stop the gossiping, because if there was one thing that coppers were good at it was gossiping amongst themselves. Ben knew that they couldn't afford for this to get out, and he prayed they were clutching at straws and that there was no way, shape or form that Des was involved in this. Yet, at the same time he had this niggling feeling in the pit of his stomach that maybe this time Des's vanity and desperation for some female attention may have got the better of him. He didn't see that there would be any way back from this if he had done a runner with Milly Blake. There would be an internal enquiry, the Police Standards Department would be involved because this had happened in work time, and PSD were not known to be forgiving in these kinds of situations.

The door opened and they all turned hoping it was Des: it

was Marc. 'His radio set is in the station somewhere; his phone is going to be pinged as soon as they get the all-clear.'

Morgan crossed to his desk, pulling out the drawers where his radio was sitting not even turned on. 'What if we're wrong and he's gone home feeling poorly?'

'We went there remember? The house was empty.'

'We didn't go inside though, did we? What if he's fallen over or had a heart attack, it happens, doesn't it?'

'You want us to put his door in?'

'I don't see we have a choice; he may be in need of medical assistance.'

Amy was already standing up, pulling her jacket on.

'I know where he keeps a spare key.'

Ben and Morgan turned to stare at her, and Ben shook his head.

'And you only just thought to tell us this because?'

'Because you two were going to get the whammer and smash the shit out of his front door. He's going to be furious enough when he finds out what a fuss there is. Imagine his face coming home to see his own front door has been put through and us all trampling through his house?'

'I suppose you have a point,' Ben answered.

'I always have a point, it's a shame no one listens. Come on, let's go take a look and make sure he hasn't had some kind of allergic reaction to the giraffe milk from the health food shop.'

Morgan smiled; Amy relentlessly made jokes about Des's one attempt to become a vegan to impress a woman at the gym whom he'd dated a couple of times. Des hated them; the others found them amusing. Marc was watching them as they filed out of the office, and Ben was expecting him to tag along.

'Are you coming, sir?'

He shook his head. 'No, I'll leave that in your capable hands. I'll hold the fort here in case we get a call to say Milly has turned up.'

Ben didn't try to persuade him otherwise; it would be nice to not have him breathing down his neck. He was getting better and fitting in more, but Ben still didn't trust the guy a hundred per cent, especially not with a situation as delicate as this.

TWENTY-TWO

Every bump on the road sent shockwaves of pain radiating through Milly's head, causing a wave of nausea to rush from her stomach to her throat. She couldn't be sick because she couldn't open her mouth to let the stream of hot liquid spray out. She was curled on the floor of a car or van, she wasn't sure what, but at least the blanket underneath her took some of the impact. She had no idea where she was or why she was on the floor feeling queasy with a throbbing pain in her head that was far worse than the sambuca hangover she'd got on her seventeenth birthday after drinking shots with her best friends. She had no idea who had hurt her or why, it was all a bit fuzzy. She knew she'd been walking home and had almost reached it when... The van turned a corner, throwing her against the metal panel where she hit her head again, silver stars floated across her iris, then she blacked out once more.

The next time she was able to open her eyes she realised how still she was. The van wasn't rumbling along what had felt like a pothole filled dirt track, and her bruised body wasn't rolling around. She lay there, trying to figure out what had happened for someone to do this to her, but she couldn't. Blinking furiously, trying not to cry, she wondered if she could get free of the ropes binding her arms together. Although she couldn't see them, she could feel the roughness biting against the tender skin of her wrists. A sob wrestled its way up from her chest, but it died in her mouth because the tight band of material that was cutting her circulation off made it hard to breathe or make any noise that wasn't muffled. Someone had hurt her, she knew that much, someone had bundled her into a van and driven her God knows where? She knew all about stranger danger, had listened intently to the PCSO who used to come into primary school to give them their yearly school talk about it. In fact, she used to go home and have nightmares about it. She closed her eyes, wishing she was back in school where all she had to worry about was actually not worth the worry in the first place. If Davey Adams was mean to her the teacher used to step in and put a stop to it. She wondered if anyone was going to step in and put a stop to whatever this sicko had in mind. She also wondered if this was the grown-up Davey Adams, even meaner and more twisted than the seven-year-old one who'd made her life a misery back then.

She lay there wondering how she was going to escape and get out of this mess, because it was a mess, when the van doors opened and a rush of cool night air came towards her. It was dark outside, and there was a dark shadowy figure standing staring at her. She stared back trying to figure out who it was. Did she know this person? Whoever it was had a really misshapen head, it looked deformed. He stepped inside the van and she felt a wave of panic wash over her. She tried her best to scream as he bent towards her, but the sound was muffled. He was lifting his finger to his lips, which she thought couldn't be real – they were long slits of red with tiny black stitching along them, and his eyes exactly the same. Milly tried to push herself away from him, but the sudden movement caused her head to swim, and she felt herself drifting away as the head wound he'd caused came into contact with something hard.

TWENTY-THREE

Des's house was still in darkness when Ben pulled up a little further down the street. He jumped out followed by Morgan and Amy.

'Where does he keep a spare key? There's no plant pot and anyone could find it.'

Amy walked over to the window, where she placed her hand underneath the deep sill and felt around until her fingers touched the shiny tape. 'Stand in front of me, I don't want his neighbours to see he keeps one duct taped under here.'

Ben looked at Morgan, but they did as she asked, standing so she couldn't be observed as she bent down and peeled the key from its place.

'I bet his insurance company love him. He might as well keep the front door open,' Ben whispered.

The key was stuck to the thick silver tape, and Amy ripped the tape off and inserted the key into the lock.

'I don't know if I feel right about this,' she whispered. 'Should we knock first?'

Ben leaned forward and pounded on the door with his

curled fist. They waited a few seconds; no lights turned on and there was no sign of life.

'Should we ask his neighbours if they've seen him?'

Ben turned to Morgan. 'If he doesn't trust them with his spare key, I doubt they get on well enough to know when he's coming and going. Open the door, Amy, and let's get this over with. If he's ill then we can get him some medical help.'

'Yes, boss.'

She turned the key and the door opened effortlessly directly into the front room of his house. Ben stepped inside first, shining his phone torch around to locate the light switches. Turning on the lights all three of them stepped inside, closing the door.

'Des, are you here?' Ben hollered.

There was no answer. The house was sparse to say the least. In the front room was a desk with a laptop and chair. A shelf above it with a few books on. Morgan looked at them, recognising some of the titles but not all of them. *Self Esteem for Men, Positive Thinking, The Power of Now, The Secrets of Success.* A wave of sadness washed over her; she gave Des so little time thinking that he was always looking down on her when maybe he was just lacking in confidence and found her a bit much. Amy joined her, shaking her head.

'Well, he needs a refund on those, he's still a miserable bastard.'

Morgan smiled and she felt a little better. Ben was in the kitchen where the cat from earlier was miaowing loudly at his feet.

'Aw, boss, you've made a friend.'

It was rubbing against Ben's trouser leg, and he looked terrified.

'Tell it to go away, I don't like cats.'

Amy laughed. 'You tell it, it seems to have taken a liking to you and I'm allergic to them, so I'm not going near it.'

Morgan looked for its food bowl, which was empty, then she opened cupboards until she found a stack of small cans of expensive cat food. Opening one she spooned it into the dish, and the cat began rubbing against her then dived into its food, forgetting about the pair of them.

'Aww, see it was just hungry. Des can't have been home if the bowl was licked clean and it's starving. I think that cat is the closest thing he has to a best friend.' Amy wandered towards the stairs, opened the oak door that was tucked away into the corner of the room and yelled, 'Des, are you up there?'

She didn't wait for an answer; instead, flicking the switch she ran up the narrow staircase to check the bedrooms. Morgan looked at Ben. Amy was the closest out of them to Des, and it didn't seem right that they all went trampling up there. They heard her go into the rooms above, turn on lights then turn them off again. She came back downstairs.

'He's not here. His bed is made, and he must be some kind of clean freak because there isn't one item of clothing thrown on the floor or over the back of a chair. Did he have that book about decluttering by Marie Kondo on that bookshelf? Because this is possibly the most boring house I've ever been in.' She laughed at her own joke, then stopped. Ben and Morgan didn't look that amused. 'So, now what? He's not here, we've fed his cat, and we still have a missing girl. Let's not waste any more time here.'

'Bollocks,' said Ben as he walked towards the front door.

Morgan followed him. 'What about his cat?'

'What about it? It's got food and water; there's a cat flap so it can go out for a crap. What else does it need?'

'It's owner, human companionship?'

'If you're suggesting that we take it with us, Morgan, then absolutely not. Bloody hell, I can't think of anything worse. Des is bound to turn up soon, he can't have gone far. I mean he's probably got a new bird and is round at her place, for all we know. Which in all honesty is very likely, don't you think?'

She shrugged; she wasn't sure what was going on with Des but if he was messing around in work time causing all this fuss, she was going to be the first to give him an earful. She didn't say it to Ben, but there was that sinking feeling inside her that told her something was wrong, and she didn't know if Milly Blake being missing was something to do with him or not but it was there, hovering around like an old friend waiting for her to let it out and tell her *I told you so.*

TWENTY-FOUR

The sombre trio got back into Ben's car as his phone rang.

'Hey, they've pinged his phone and it comes back to within a one-mile radius of St Martha's church where the body was found last night.'

'You're joking right? He's still there when we've been wasting our time looking for him?'

'I'm just the messenger, Ben, I thought you'd want to know. I guess he wasn't home?'

'No, just his cat.'

'Do you want me to get a patrol down there to go look for him, or do you want to head there?'

'We'll go look for him, thanks, Marc. Any update on Milly Blake?'

'I'm afraid not, we seem to have drawn a blank. Without her phone it's impossible to locate her. We both know what a godsend location trackers are when it's something of this nature.'

'That they are, they make our life a lot easier.'

He hung up. 'I gather you heard the gist of that conversation?'

Morgan was sitting next to him. 'Yes, did we leave him

behind? But wouldn't he have gone home by now or phoned us
for a lift back to the station? Hang on, he was in his car, maybe
he broke down and his phone died.'

Amy let out a small laugh. 'Sounds like it's the perfect
excuse for him to sit and stuff his face with those scones and not
have to share them.'

Morgan felt a little better, all this fuss and he was probably
waiting on roadside assistance to come tow him home.

Ben drove slow along the high street looking for Des's car.
They reached the church with the small patch of tarmac outside
suitable for a few cars.

'We're looking for a black Audi A3, he's only just bought it.
I don't think he's going to be very happy if it's broken down
already.'

Amy chortled. 'We'll never hear the last of it. Where is he, I
can't spot him or his car?'

Ben stopped the car. 'Morgan, do you want to have a walk
around and I'll drive down Church Lane, Church View and
back around?'

She got out, standing for a moment. She had spent more
time here the last twenty-four hours than she had at Ben's. The
retirement home was lit up against the dark night sky, lights
blazing in all the windows. Morgan could see the huge cut-
glass chandeliers hanging from the high ceilings in both
lounges. There was a definite nip in the air again tonight
although it wasn't quite as frosty as last night. She turned to
look at the church. She'd rather be inside the home across the
road than about to go into the churchyard once more. Last
night it had been a circus, but tonight she was completely
alone. Pushing open the black cast iron gate she stepped
through into the grounds. She turned on the torch on her
phone so that it illuminated the graves directly in front of her.
Where are you, Des? If he was here, wouldn't he be sitting
inside the church where it was warmer? Or maybe he'd just

dropped his phone earlier in the day, and he wasn't here at all. Still, she grabbed hold of the huge iron ring on the door and twisted it. It was locked tight, it didn't budge, and Morgan let out a sigh. No Des in there then. She needed to check the grounds, just in case, God forbid, he'd had a heart attack. Walking around the side of the church she realised that the lights weren't on tonight. After last night's power cut they had come back on illuminating the pretty church and grounds, but it was complete darkness tonight. A cold shiver ran down her spine. Why was it so dark? Moving her phone from side to side as she walked forwards, she found her feet heading towards the ditch where they had found Shea's body last night. She felt a sinking feeling inside the pit of her stomach for Shea and her family who were going to be devastated for the rest of their lives. Forcing her feet to move forwards one foot in the other she called out, 'Des, Des.'

'What are you doing, Morgan?'

The voice was so close to her that her feet almost leapt from the ground. She turned to see Theo standing a few graves behind her.

'Jesus Christ, oh God. I'm sorry, you scared me to death.'

Her phone torch was shining onto his face, and he lifted his arm shielding his eyes.

'You did a pretty good job of scaring me, why are you calling Des?'

He stepped closer, and she stepped back without even thinking about it, her survival instinct kicking in. He was dressed from head to toe in black, with that woollen hat pulled down over his ears.

'You're going to catch your death out here, come inside for a coffee and you can tell me what on earth you're doing.'

Her head shook. 'I'm good thanks, it's really busy. We're looking for...'

'Morgan, everything okay?'

She felt her shoulders relax at the sound of Ben's voice. 'Yeah, I was just checking.'

Ben came towards the pair of them, the look of concern on his face all but thawing her frozen insides out.

Theo turned to look at him. 'Is everything okay?'

Morgan thought she heard a faint buzzing sound, and she turned to see where it was coming from.

'Yeah, sorry, Theo, we have an AWOL detective and a missing girl, and we're all a bit fraught and tense.'

'Shush.' She pointed in the direction of where Shea's body was found. 'Can you hear that?'

'No, sorry, what is it?'

The noise stopped, and she hurried towards the ditch behind the last row of graves. Her boots crunching on the crisp grass, she reached the ditch and held her breath, afraid to look into it in case Shea's badly decomposed face was there, staring back at her, but she did. The buzzing had stopped, and she couldn't see anything. Wishing they were in a police van with a dragon light, she shouted to Ben, 'Ring Des's phone.'

He obliged, taking his phone out and crossing the grass to stand with her. There it was again, the faint buzzing sound that a phone makes when it's been turned on silent. Walking slowly along she stopped and shouted, 'Down there, it's down there.'

About to clamber down to retrieve it Ben lurched forward, grabbing her arm.

'Why is his phone down there?' Turning to Theo, he shrugged. 'I'm sorry to do this to you again, but I need to clear this area and have it searched.'

A look of disbelief crossed the vicar's face. 'Of course, whatever you need. I'll go back inside. If I can be of any assistance, then let me know.' He glanced at Morgan who looked away; she found his stare far too probing. They watched him head back towards the gate when she called out to him, 'Why are the lights not working?'

He turned back towards her. 'I don't know, that was why I came outside, to take a look, and I saw you.'

'Oh, right.'

He left them to it, going back to the vicarage, when they heard the sound of his front door close.

Amy came walking through the gates. 'What's happening?'

'Morgan found Des's phone, it's down there.' Ben pointed into the ditch shining his own light down onto it. The phone had a spider web of cracks all over the glass back and was badly damaged; it had either been dropped or maybe even stood on.

'Where's Des?'

'I don't know. We need to search the area just in case.'

Neither Morgan nor Amy had to ask what he meant; they were on high alert now because there was no way he would have been anywhere near this ditch and dropped his phone without retrieving it. Something was going on and they needed to figure out what it was and fast.

TWENTY-FIVE

Just like that, St Martha's church was once again closed off to the public whilst a full search of the area was conducted. Ben waited by the church doors with Morgan; Amy was waiting outside for Wendy to arrive and stopping anyone from coming in. This time it was discreet, there were no police vans with their blues and twos illuminating the church. No fluorescent yellow uniformed officers. A couple of Al's task force officers all dressed in black were conducting the search. They had no clue as to what Des was doing, if he was involved in Milly's disappearance or if it was something else. What if he was in danger too? They hadn't really considered it. The very fact that his phone had been found in the ditch where Shea Wilkinson's body was discovered didn't bode well though. He had little reason to be wandering around in there. Morgan watched as the three officers walked through the graves at a snail's pace. She whispered to Ben, 'What about inside the church?'

Ben reached forward and tried the cast iron door ring; it didn't turn – it was locked up tight.

'We're going to have to get Theo to let us in.'

'I don't like it; he's been involved in all of this from the start.

Finding Shea's body, chatting to Milly today, disappearing around the time she left work and now we have no idea where Des is or why his phone was in that ditch.'

'You want to bring him in for questioning?'

'I don't see how we can't. Should I go ask him to open the door for us? What if Des and Milly are inside, injured?'

Ben stared at her. 'Then you can say that you told me so.'

She shook her head. 'What pleasure would I gain from that? I don't want to be right. I just want to find them.'

Going briskly through the gate, she walked down Theo's path to the vicarage for what felt like the tenth time in twenty-four hours. This time he didn't come to the door to greet her. The house was in darkness. Morgan curled her fingers into a fist and rapped her knuckles against the glass pane. She stepped back, not wanting to be too close to him if he opened the door. There was no sound from inside. She waited a few seconds then hammered on the door. Nothing, twice now she'd been here today and got no reply. But she'd seen Theo go inside. It was starting to really bother her, and she turned to walk back to Ben. Almost at the gate the hairs on the back of her neck began to prickle as if she had walked through an invisible electrical force. A fear so cold and hard pressed down on her shoulders she needed to turn around and see what was causing her to feel this way, but she couldn't. Stopping in her tracks she inhaled a deep breath: *you are not afraid, turn around.* She whipped around and stared into the darkness. Looking at the blacked-out windows of the vicarage, she thought she saw a shadow step away from the upstairs window, a split second. Screwing her eyes up she stared at the window to see if it happened again. After a few moments she turned and walked away, closing the gate behind her.

Ben was pacing up and down. The night air was getting icier by the minute, and he had his hands tucked into his pockets. As she approached him, he studied her, his voice low.

'What's the matter?'

'Nothing, I'm just giving myself the heebie-jeebies. He's not answering the door.'

Ben looked down at his watch. 'I've only just sent him home and it's almost nine on a Sunday night, where would he be?'

'Gone to pick up pizza, some people get to eat regularly, but he knows we're here. He said to knock if we needed anything. He might be in the bathroom.'

He laughed a little too loudly and stopped himself. 'Well, you can blame Des for this missed meal.'

'I will, don't you worry. Seriously though, where is Des? Do you think he's in trouble or do you seriously think he could have something to do with Shea and Milly?'

A task force search officer, Steve, walked towards them. 'Nothing except the phone. What do you want to do about it?'

'Wendy should be here any moment; I want it photographing in situ then it can be bagged up and taken back to the station. I want it fast tracked to the mobile phone unit up at headquarters.'

'We'll wait for Wendy if you need to get off. No sign of that young girl from earlier either. This is all a bit of a mess, isn't it?'

Ben nodded, and Morgan thought to herself *you have no idea.*

'Are you sure, Steve?'

'Positive.'

'Thanks, that's great, I'm frozen.'

Morgan wasn't kidding. Her fingers and toes were almost as numb as last night.

They walked back to Ben's car; Amy followed them.

'Right, plan of action?'

'Station, hot drink, review what the hell is going on with Shea, Milly and Des, food, get someone to locate Theo and speak to him then home for a couple of hours kip. I'll get Marc to authorise the overtime and pay for the food. I think we're going to have to draft in some help. I'll speak to DCI Claire Williams from the Murder Investigation Team and see what she advises, maybe Barrow CID or Carlisle can send a couple of detectives our way to help out.'

Amy side-eyed Morgan, who knew that Ben was feeling the pressure if he was going to be asking for extra help.

TWENTY-SIX

Marc didn't just authorise the overtime; he took everyone's order and went to collect the Thai from the newly opened Bam Siam Restaurant himself. By the time he came back with bags of delicious aromatic food even Morgan, who had been feeling a little strange, found her stomach growling and desperate to tuck into her container of chicken pad thai. They ate in silence, needing the fuel to keep them going for as long as it took. When they were full and the containers with any leftovers packed away for tomorrow's lunch, Ben looked up from the Force Policy Book he had on the desk in front of him.

'I think because it's a substantial amount of time since anyone has heard from Des we are going to class him as a misper along with Milly Blake. Now the question is whether they have eloped together, or something more sinister has happened. We're currently waiting on forensic samples to come back from Shea Wilkinson's bare feet. I'm going to stick my neck out on a limb and suggest that once these come back, we will have a primary crime scene. We need to know how Shea got from Blackpool to Rydal Falls. How she was transported and where she was kept for a few days until she was horrifically murdered, and where she was murdered.'

He closed his eyes for a few seconds, and Morgan felt bad for him, wanting to reach out to him, but that was out of the question. When he opened them, he smiled at her, conveying in his own way he was okay.

'I think that the person who abducted, then killed Shea has taken Milly because it's too much of a coincidence. They are both similar ages, both pretty with long hair, both taken when they were alone. So, whoever the suspect is has to have been watching them.'

'Or he's opportunistic, right place, wrong time kind of thing.'

'I don't know, Morgan, what are the chances of him being by the riverside when Milly was walking along there? He either knew that she walked home that way, or he followed her. Whichever it is, that makes him highly organised.'

Morgan let out a small gasp. 'He had to have been at the spring fair at some point to have seen Milly. He must have a vehicle to have transported her from the river. We know that the CCTV isn't working on the outside of the retirement home, but what about the high street cameras? We need to check out all the vehicles that entered and left the area.'

Amy was shaking her head. 'I hate to say this but there are only two obvious suspects if you ask me and both of them are nowhere to be found tonight.'

Ben stood up. 'Des and Theo the vicar? Do we know if Theo has a vehicle? I want ANPR markers put on both their cars, and the cameras checking to see if either of them passed through the camera on the main road out of here. Boss, what do you want to do about calling in some help?'

Marc was staring out of the window down at the car park. 'I don't think we need to look for Des's car, isn't that it down there?'

He was pointing to the car park out the front of the station which was for visitors' use and not police officers or staff. All three of them rushed towards the window to peer down into the darkness, and, sure enough, sandwiched between two plain white hire cars was Des's Audi.

Ben turned, rushing towards the door, muttering, 'The bloody idiot.'

Amy, Morgan and Marc weren't far behind him. He took the emergency fire escape stairs that weren't supposed to be used, and they all followed. At the bottom was a fire exit. Ben pushed the metal bar and the door flew open. He was at the car before the others were out of the door. He peered into the dark interior and saw nothing, no Des, no sign of life, no anything. He let out a frustrated sigh, placing his hand on the bonnet to see if it was still warm. It wasn't, it was stone cold which meant he hadn't driven it for some time.

'How did we miss this? Where the fuck is he?'

He tried the handle, and it opened easily, and there was no mistaking the metallic odour of blood. 'Has anyone got a phone on them? Mine's upstairs.'

Amy passed hers across. He pressed the torch button and shone it into the shiny interior of Des's new car and saw a dark pool of liquid on the driver's seat. It was a congealed mess. As he shone the light higher there were splotches of the brownish blood spotted all over the cream leather interior. Amy realising exactly what she was looking at cupped a hand over her mouth.

'Oh God, whose blood is that? Des's? Where is he? He must be badly hurt if he's bled that much.'

Marc nodded at Ben. 'Right, let's have you both upstairs phoning all the hospitals you can think of. I want you to find his next of kin and see if he's been in contact with any family members. Ben and I will sort this out, is that okay?'

Morgan couldn't tear her eyes away from the blood that was spattered everywhere. 'Yes, boss.'

'Good, take Amy with you.'

She looked at him. 'Yes, okay.'

Grabbing Amy's elbow, she pushed her away from the bloodied mess and towards the side entrance of the station. The food that had tasted so amazing ten minutes ago was now sitting heavily in her stomach, churning away and threatening to come back up. Amy for once was speechless, her face had lost its rosy glow and she looked as if she was about to pass out. Swiping her card to get back into the station she kept on pushing Amy towards the lift, not trusting her legs to make it up the stairs without her knees buckling underneath her. This was how it felt to be on the outside peering in. How many times had it been Morgan who was in danger? It felt far worse watching this unfold. How had Ben dealt with the frustration, the fear that it was too late, that he couldn't save her from the monsters that stalked the streets of Rydal Falls? They hadn't saved Shea and they had no idea where Milly and Des were. Did Des need saving or was he the one that Milly needed saving from?

TWENTY-SEVEN

It was chaos outside in the car park despite the lateness of the evening. Sundays were usually blessedly quiet with not much happening at all. Now there were floodlights surrounding Des's Audi. The on-call CSI from Barrow had driven up with a DS from Barrow, who was assessing the scene with Ben and Marc. Cassie had turned up with Brock to search the area in case Des was injured and had stumbled away from his car on foot leaving a trail of blood. Both Morgan and Amy were leaning against the glass watching it all.

'What do you think?' Amy asked in a voice that was much softer than normal.

'I don't know what to think. I'm hoping that he isn't badly injured and lying somewhere needing medical attention, but at the same time I have a bad feeling about the fact that both he and Milly are missing.'

'Yeah, I know. I don't think he's a killer though. You know when people on those crime documentaries say, "but he was such a nice guy"? I know he isn't the most charming guy around, but he's okay when you know him. I'd never peg him as some creepy dude who would abduct teenage girls and kill them.'

Morgan took a moment to answer because she didn't see him the way Amy did. Was that because she didn't know him as well as she did, or because he didn't like her a whole lot? She was finding it hard to answer her, not sure what to say because anything she would say might upset her.

'We never really know anyone, do we?'

'What's that supposed to mean?'

'Nothing, just thinking out loud. Look at Taylor, he was pretending to be someone else. His whole life was a lie and we believed it.'

Amy didn't answer her. She pressed her face against the glass to get a better look at what was happening. 'Should we go back down and help them?'

'Help who?' Ben had opened the door, and they hadn't even realised they were so intent on watching what was going on.

Amy turned to look at him. 'You.'

He walked inside followed by a man around the same age, his sandy blonde hair a little ruffled as if he'd been running his hands through it. He reminded Morgan of Ben who would do the same in stressful situations.

'This is DS Will Ashworth from Barrow, he's going to be leading this investigation.'

The man smiled at them with such warmth in his eyes that Morgan instantly felt her shoulders relax.

'Hey, sorry to invade your investigation but you know how it is when it comes to dealing with one of our own, it has to be investigated from an external source so they can't say there was anything untoward if, God forbid, it has to go to court. I'm hoping we can find Des quickly and make sure he's safe, bring him home.'

Amy glared at him. 'I don't know why we can't just crack on

with it. We're a pretty good team. We don't need your help, no offence, sir.'

'Will, not sir, and I am fully aware of what a brilliant team you are. It's not my decision to step in or Ben's. It's the force policy to ensure there is no misconduct, Amy. I'm not here to take over. I'm here to help.'

'Yeah, well have you had any experience running these kinds of investigations?'

Morgan looked across at Ben whose expression was one of pure horror at how rude Amy was being.

Will nodded. 'Actually plenty, for a while Barrow was the murder capital of England before you thankfully stole our title. I've run a few major investigations, so yes, I know what I'm doing.' He turned to Morgan and smiled. 'I've heard a lot of good things about you, Morgan. You remind me of my wife, Annie. I bet you two would get on like a house on fire; she's been through some tough times.'

Morgan smiled at him, her internal person radar telling her he was a good guy and meant well. Amy was still glaring, and when he looked away, Morgan elbowed her in the ribs gently. She glared at Morgan instead, shrugging her shoulders.

Ben sat down, leaving Will standing. 'Over to you.'

'The dog hasn't picked up Des's scent apart from in and around the car, so he hasn't stumbled off injured. There's no blood trail, nothing for the dog to go on.'

'Then how did his car get here?'

Will continued, 'If he'd driven it here bleeding that profusely, there would be a trail, yes?'

They nodded.

'Unless, of course, it's not his blood. We'll know more in a few hours, as the samples are being fast tracked to Chorley Forensic Science lab. At the moment I'm not a hundred per cent as to whose blood it is, but I'm keeping my mind open.'

'What can we do?' Morgan asked.

'Go home and get some rest. I'll take it from here and if anything turns up I'll personally ring you to come back.'

Amy shook her head. 'Yeah, like we can just go home and have ourselves a hot chocolate then go to sleep. Forget it.'

'Amy, there is very little you can do right now. I'm on call. I've been home since three this afternoon; I've taken my son, Alfie, to the park and spent time with my family; I've had my tea and I've been snoring in front of the TV for a few hours. I'm ready to go, trust me on this. I will keep you informed if something turns up. I know how hard this is, I've been there so many times.' He stopped talking as if he was about to give too much information away, and Morgan noticed the flash of pain across his eyes as if he was remembering the stuff he'd been through.

Ben stood up. 'Amy, go home. You're going home even if it's just a couple of hours, it's an order.'

She nodded. Her eyes downcast she grabbed her bag and coat then walked out.

He turned to Morgan. 'You are too.'

'What about you?'

'I'm okay, I'll stay.'

Will shook his head. 'You go too. I can manage and if I can't then I'll ring.'

Ben looked torn; she knew he would have a hard time walking away, but if Will was to run the investigation wasn't a lot he could do.

'What about Shea Wilkinson and Milly Blake?'

'Shea is still your investigation; you can continue with that tomorrow. Milly and Des, I'm convinced, are both tied together from what you have told me.'

'You'll take both of those?'

'Absolutely, go get some rest.'

'Everything you need is in my office; the policy book is on my desk for Shea should you want to take a look. There's a file in there too, but everything is on the system.'

'Thanks.'

Morgan pulled on her coat and noticed Will gently clamp Ben's shoulder to reassure him. She liked him, he seemed genuinely nice and caring.

Ben nodded and followed her out of the office. They walked down the stairs in silence and out into the rear yard.

When they were in the car Morgan took his hand in hers. 'He seems okay.'

'Yeah, he's been through some tough stuff. I've only worked with him once before, but he's good. He'll sort this mess out, find Des and Milly.'

'Are you okay with it all?'

'What, the whole my officer is missing and there's pools of blood in his car or the fact that I can't even run the investigation?'

'Both.'

'I feel bloody useless. I'm furious with Des. What is he playing at? and I'm heartbroken for Shea, worried sick about Milly, and I think I'm going to throw up.'

Morgan, who was driving, pressed the green exit button for the gates to release and they took forever to open, but once she had nudged Ben's car through the gap, she put her foot down, purposely not looking across at Des's car which was being uplifted onto a recovery truck to be taken away for forensic tests. She wanted to get Ben home before he was sick all over the interior of the car.

TWENTY-EIGHT

Ben's phone was vibrating underneath the pillows somewhere. Morgan forced her eyes open; they felt as if they had glued themselves shut. Ben was dead to the world; he didn't even flinch. Feeling under the pillows she grabbed it.

'Ben's phone.'

'Happy Monday morning, Morgan, that's a bit of a mouthful before coffee. Where's the big guy?'

She blinked, pulling herself up, and glanced at the clock not quite believing it was almost seven.

'Why are you always so happy, Declan?'

'Because life is beautiful, and you should know that more than anyone.'

Standing up she crept out of the bedroom wanting to leave Ben as long as possible before waking him. He'd come home last night and had thrown up in the downstairs toilet, barely making it before the Thai they'd eaten had been brought back up.

'I know, I do. It was a long day yesterday; did you hear about Des?'

As she said that she rushed downstairs, putting him on loudspeaker so she could check Ben's messages and see if there were any updates on him.

'*No, what about him? Has he gone Buddhist this time to impress a new bit of stuff?*'

'He's missing, along with a seventeen-year-old girl.'

'*Nooo way, have they gone off together?*'

There were no messages or missed calls from anyone on Ben's phone. She took it off speaker and pressed it to her ear.

'We don't know, it's all very up in the air at the moment. We found his car in the front car park at the station. There was a lot of blood on the driver's seat.'

Declan was quiet whilst he processed what she'd told him. '*Is he hurt?*'

'We don't know what's going on. Ben's been taken off running the investigation because he's one of us. What did you ring so early for?'

'*Erm, blimey, Morgan, you've completely thrown me. What did I ring for? Oh, yes. I know, the soil samples came back from the forensic botanist, and I wanted to make sure Ben got the email. It makes for some interesting reading. When sleeping beauty wakes up can you make sure he reads it? But I'll tell you now anyway. Basically there were traces of sand, shells and, wait for this, some pollen spores from a plant that is only found in one place in the entire country. Petals of the same plant from Walney Island had been thrown on top of the body; the email narrows down a specific area, but I think that's where Shea was taken and kept before she tried to make a run for it. Bless her, so sad.*'

The kettle was boiling, and Morgan's eyes were fixed on the bubbles as they fizzed and popped inside of the clear glass jug.

'Walney? That's in Barrow. Why would he take her from Blackpool, drive her all the way there and keep her for a few days, then kill her and dump her body here a few weeks after she was dead?'

'*As you well know, that's not my remit. I'm just the messen-*

ger. You two are the quiz masters. So I'll leave that in yours and Ben's capable hands. Let me know how you get on and if Des turns up.'

The line went dead, and she felt a warm pair of arms snake around her middle as Ben held her tight from behind. He buried his head in the nape of her neck, kissing the skin and whispered, 'Morning, beautiful.'

She held on to his arms, relaxing back into him and wishing they could go back to bed. She sighed turning to face him. He looked dishevelled, and she couldn't have loved him any more even with a five o'clock shadow and dark circles under his eyes.

'Any news? I woke up thinking that last night was one of those long, never-ending nightmares you sometimes have then I realised that it wasn't and we're in a huge, bloody mess.'

'Nothing on Des, but that was Declan. He said that the soil sample results are in, and Shea was on Walney, or at least that's where she tried to run away from. There were pollen samples from a plant that's indigenous to Walney Island and nowhere else.'

He pulled away from her, confusion in his eyes. 'How? I don't get it.'

'Whoever took her must have kept her on Walney.'

She passed him a travel mug of coffee, and he leaned against the counter. She took a sip of her own and sighed. Ben's coffee machine was the next best thing to heaven.

'It's kind of ironic.'

'What is?'

'Shea was taken from Blackpool yet ended up running for her life on Walney, and Des is missing, probably injured, or if he isn't someone is. Milly Blake is missing, and we ended up with a DS from Barrow that is from the same town as Walney to give us a hand.'

Ben was staring at her. 'It's too early for cryptic clues, help a guy out.'

'All roads I think are leading us to Walney Island.'

He nodded. 'Why there?'

'Figure that out and you've probably cracked the case.'

'I think that this is getting way too complicated for my poor brain, which is why you should be sitting your Sergeant's exam. It's a complete waste of your time and energy if you don't. You're special, Morgan, you are made for more. Then you could take some of the pressure off me.'

He winked at her, but she knew he was being serious about it, and she would in the future, just not yet.

'I will when the time is right. I like how things are at the moment. I want to work with you and not get shipped off to Maryport or somewhere else. Unless you're trying to get rid of me.' She arched an eyebrow at him, and he shook his head.

'Absolutely not, Brookes, I think we're a great team. I just don't want to hold you back.'

She watched his eyes cloud over with sadness. Walking over to him she sat herself down on his knee, managing to step on his bare foot with her Docs that she'd slipped on whilst talking to Declan.

'Ouch, my poor toes. Don't you ever fancy wearing a pair of Converse?'

He was laughing.

'Nah, they're not much good for kicking bad guys.'

Wrapping her arms around him, he buried his head in her neck and they stayed that way for a few moments until Ben's phone began to vibrate on the table in front of them. She let out a sigh.

'It's never-ending, good job we love it.'

Standing up she let him grab his phone and left him to it whilst she went to upload a map of Walney Island on the desktop computer in the office upstairs.

She stared at the screen; it was a much bigger area than she'd thought. The page in front of her told her that it was eleven miles of beautiful, unspoilt coastline beaches, a mile wide and linked to the town of Barrow-in-Furness by a bridge. Was this where Des had gone? Where on earth should they start looking? Then she remembered the blood in his car; if that was his, could he even have made it there? She smelled Ben's aftershave behind her and turned to look at him. He looked a little better now, freshly shaved, his white shirt was tight in the right places, his suit jacket thrown over his arm. He had lost weight since she'd first started to work with him and realised it was probably all the stress she'd caused him.

'Blimey I haven't been to Walney for years, not since Cindy decided to pack up a picnic for us to go have a day at the beach.' He smiled, and she wondered if he realised he'd just talked about her without the usual look of pain that seem to embed itself across his face whenever he talked about his dead wife.

'What was it like?'

'The beach was wonderful, the picnic not so great; we left it on a blanket on the sand to go and paddle in the Irish Sea and when we got back it was covered in these tiny red mite things. She was so mad about the wasted food, but it was a great day apart from that.'

'That's good, maybe we could have a paddle in the sea.'

Ben laughed. 'Not in this weather. I'm much older and a complete wimp now, but you can knock yourself out if you can be bothered to unlace those boots.'

Morgan shrugged. 'You might have a point. I'll pass on getting my feet wet for now, but I think we need to go pay the island a visit and see if we can locate where Shea was kept and killed once we've caught up with what's happening at work.'

TWENTY-NINE

Will was already in the office; Amy arrived a little behind Morgan and Ben. All of them had a look of apprehension on their faces, combined with the wide-eyed fear of what today was going to bring them. Ben smiled at her.

'Did you get any sleep?'

'Not really, you?'

'Some.'

As they trailed in, Will stood up. 'Morning, nothing to report I'm afraid.'

'Neither of them has turned up?' Amy's voice was indignant.

Will shrugged. 'As you know something of this magnitude requires a little help from above. DI Claire Williams is on her way down to muck in and give a hand.'

'That's good, we'll take all the help we can get. I have some news about the forensic samples retrieved from Shea Wilkinson.'

'Great, that's sure to be a big help. I think your DI is calling a briefing at 8:30; he said about meeting in the blue room.'

Ben gave him a thumbs up and slipped into his office, where

he sat down behind the desk and logged on to his computer. Morgan, feeling awkward, sat down at hers; Amy collected the cups from last night and disappeared to the kitchen, leaving her and Will alone.

'I take it there's nothing. No sightings, no bodies?'

'No, I told you I'd let you know if anything came in. I wouldn't keep something like that from any of you. Des is your colleague and friend. I may have to run the investigation, but I'm open and honest; there's no sneaking around behind anyone's back.'

'Sorry, I know, I guess we're all a little freaked out about this. It's just so weird.'

'Where do you think he is?'

She glanced at Ben's office. He was now on the phone and pacing up and down his office; Amy was still making coffee.

'I don't think Milly and Des disappearing within such a short space of time is a coincidence. It must be connected; I just don't know how. He's not the violent type; in fact he gets scared if he has to work with me because he thinks I'm bad luck and will get him killed.'

Will arched an eyebrow at her. 'Ahh, yes. You have been in some difficult situations. You really need to meet Annie, you could trade horror stories with each other.'

'Where is she now?'

'Out of harm's way or at least I pray she is, and running a quirky little shop near to Bowness pier that sells crystals and all that kind of stuff, home-made bath salts, candles. I don't think she particularly enjoys it as much as she did being a police officer but something had to give, especially when she found out she was pregnant with our son, Alfie.'

'She sounds cool, I think I know that shop. I've been in it a few times. I bet she'd like my aunt Ettie, she makes these amazing home-made teas for different ailments.'

'Jesus, what is this, world share your family history day?'

Amy was shaking her head at the pair of them. 'We need to find Des and stop messing around. No offence, guys, but come on, who gives a shit about herbal tea and all that voodoo stuff?'

Will nodded. 'You're right and I'll tell you what we've done overnight to try and locate him at the briefing. There's no point boring you stupid twice.'

She tutted and sat at her desk; Morgan felt bad for Will, but she knew this was Amy's way of coping with the stress of what was going on. He didn't look in the least bit offended, so that was a big bonus for him. The door pushed open and in walked Claire with her laptop bag slung over her shoulder and a backpack full to the seams.

'Morning all, have I missed anything?' They all shook heads in unison. 'Great, that's a relief.'

Morgan looked around the room, it wasn't the same without Des and his miserable face. Ben came out of his office with a clipboard and crossed to the printer that was spewing out sheet upon sheet of paper. He collected them, turning around. 'I'll meet you in the blue room.' Then walked out with Claire following behind.

Amy shrugged. 'Not sure I can sit around twiddling my thumbs all day.'

Will smiled. 'I don't think you'll need to. Let's go see what the rest of the station is doing, and we'll take it from there. I'm pretty sure there's lots for you to be getting on with.'

He followed Ben out of the door leaving them both behind.

'He's trying, Amy, don't be so hard on him.'

'Is he though? Are we? If this was you, Ben would be charging through Rydal Falls with blue lights on to come to your rescue. How come no one gives a shit about Des?'

She walked out leaving Morgan staring at the door. Morgan thought they were all trying; it was hard enough but it wasn't just Des who was missing. Where the hell was Milly Blake?

THIRTY

The blue room was standing room only it was so full of officers, detectives, task force, CSI. Morgan and Amy squeezed in next to Al and Cain, who shuffled up for them both. Marc was on his phone, not paying the slightest attention, which irked Morgan more than it should. It was probably work-related to be fair, but still she found his disregard for the investigation irritating.

Ben stood up. 'Cheers for coming, we are in a right mess, there's no other way to say it. I can't gloss over it and make it seem any better than it is. I'm sure you're all aware that seventeen-year-old Shea Wilkinson's body was found forty-eight hours ago. Yesterday teatime, around the same time Milly Blake was reported missing, we realised that Des Black was also nowhere to be found. Milly's and Des's investigations have been passed over to DS Will Ashworth; however I'm still running the Shea Wilkinson investigation.'

Cain put his hand in the air. 'Are they connected? I mean, it's all a bit of a coincidence that there's a dead seventeen-year-old, a missing seventeen-year-old and a missing thirty-nine-year-old detective.'

There was a low murmur around the room, heads were nodding, and people were whispering to each other.

Amy stood up. 'Before you go thinking that Des has flipped his lid and started killing teenagers, you should know that his phone was found in the ditch where Shea's body was dumped, and his car was outside the station covered in blood.' All eyes were on her. 'So, don't go thinking he's some murderous pervert, okay.'

Cain reached out for Amy's arm, tapping it lightly, so she turned to look at him instead of glaring at the entire room. Morgan wondered if he was going to give her one of his famous hugs but realised that even Cain wasn't that brave.

Ben continued, 'Thank you, Amy, we're not accusing Des of anything. We're gathering facts and trying to find him. I'm as worried as you are about him, this isn't a witch hunt.'

Ben glanced at Will.

'I'm afraid we don't have much more than that. All address checks for Des and Milly were negative. Hospitals, train stations, bus stops across the Lake District have been searched. Ben, did you say you had something back from forensics?'

'A report from the forensic botanist has shown that soil collected from the ball of Shea Wilkinson's foot came back with the following composition of a high percentage of sand, shells and a specific pollen from a species of geranium which is only found on Walney Island; this is pertinent to the case because there were several pink petals found on top of Shea's body which are from the same plant. I've just had a very interesting conversation with Forensic Palynologist and soil analysis expert Doctor Isabelle Burrows and she's on her way here. She believes she has narrowed down an area where Shea Wilkinson was kept captive or at least where she tried to escape from her abductor. So myself, Morgan and Cain will be heading down there with the doctor as soon as she gets here.'

'Where's she travelling from?' Marc was finally paying attention.

'Cardiff?'

'That's hours away, how many four, five?'

'Depending on traffic four maybe, but luckily for us she was already on her way out of the door when I phoned her back.'

'Did we agree the costs?'

Ben looked aghast. 'I'll pay them myself if it's a problem. We're going to need her to take samples from the area to submit for analysis and court when we make an arrest, and she's offered her services. I think we'd be foolish to turn them down when we need all the help we can get.'

'It's not a problem.' Marc was holding up his hands; he must have realised that now wasn't the place to have a budget meeting.

Cain whispered in Morgan's ear, 'He's pissed he didn't think of it first, get in there, Benno.'

Al, who overheard him, grinned at the pair of them and lowered his head before Marc could see.

Will nodded. 'That's great, if you take a team down there and then let me know what you need, I'll get a search team from Barrow ready to assist.'

Morgan couldn't help herself. 'This is all a bit nuts. Will is from Barrow, shouldn't he be the one working the investigation from down there? He knows the area more than we do, so it seems backwards that he's stuck up here and we're off to his patch.'

Will smiled at her. 'Morgan, you're right, it is completely nuts, but it's how it is. I'm sure you and Ben will manage to find your way and make use of the staff down there to assist you, just as I'm going to be utilising the staff here.'

Marc stared over at her. 'Force policy, Morgan. Yes, it seems pointless, but everything has to stand up to scrutiny. Should we get investigated, they can't say there was any misconduct or improper protocols in place.'

She sighed; it wasn't that she minded going to Barrow, she didn't. What she minded was feeling helpless when it came to Des, and out of her depth. The thought of having to meet lots of new people was not a comfortable one; she liked to keep herself to herself, which was why being a part of such a small team worked so well for her.

Will continued, 'As for potential witnesses we have Father Theodore Edwards who discovered Shea's body and was seen talking to both Des and Milly yesterday afternoon at the church fair. I'm going to bring him in for an interview, nothing too intense but he seems to be the only thing connecting all of them together at the moment. Any objections to that? Did intelligence checks bring up anything about him we need to focus on? There's no sordid history or unexplained dead parishioners from his previous parishes?'

Amy nodded approvingly. Morgan stole a glance at Ben who shrugged.

'He seems to have a clean sheet, Will. We ran the background checks and nothing came back that shouldn't have, for a vicar anyway.'

She'd like to be a fly on the wall for that interview. She was glad it wasn't her who was having to do it. There was something about Theo that made her feel uncomfortable, not that it meant he was a killer, but she'd mentioned this all to the others. If he wasn't a killer something was going on with him, like the way he was always around and the fact that he wasn't when they wanted to ask him if he'd seen Des.

'What about the blood in Des's car, anything from that?'

'Not yet, but we should have something soon. These things take more time than we'd like, especially when that's something we don't have to spare.'

Amy nodded. 'So, what are we thinking then? Truthfully, about the whole situation?' She was glaring at Will.

'I don't want to speculate but, in my opinion, all three are connected and I wouldn't be surprised if the blood results come back as Milly Blake's.'

The room was so still, no one dared move or speak and Morgan wondered how Amy was going to react. Her shoulders drooped; her head lowered as all the fight left her.

'Anything to add, Ben?'

Ben shook his head.

'Then I think if you and your team focus on finding the place Shea tried to escape from, we'll begin with CCTV enquiries, bring in Theodore Edwards for a statement and continue with the search of the area. Al, I take it you're happy to crack on with coordinating the searches?'

'Absolutely.'

'Bottom line is we need to find both Milly Blake and Des Black; Shea was kept captive a few days before she was killed. We have the narrowest time gap in which to do this and bring her home safe.'

'Unless,' Cain spoke.

'Unless what?'

'What if Des *has* run away with Milly? It is a possibility.'

Ben turned to him. 'How do we explain the large amount of blood in his car?'

Cain raised his hands. 'No idea, boss, just thinking out loud.'

'Will, I think we should get the morning shift PCSOs to go around the hotels and B&Bs just to rule it out.'

'Good call, we'll do that.'

Morgan raised her hand, and every pair of eyes fell onto her and she wished she could for once stop making herself the centre of attention, but she couldn't ignore the feeling.

'Morgan.' Will was smiling at her.

'There was a robbery in Grasmere before the body was discovered, and I think it might be connected.'

'I saw that, but I'm not sure what makes you think that?'

'We don't get many crimes of that nature. For what he stole it just wasn't worth it, so I think it may have been a distraction. The killer did it on the way to dump the body, knowing that patrols would be sent there and tied up, leaving him free to dump Shea's body in the church without the chance of being caught.'

Will's brow creased as he thought about it; there were some deep lines on his forehead that almost matched Ben's. He began to nod at her. 'You may have something there. Have all the enquiries been carried out, CCTV seized, statements?'

'Yes, it's a bit of a dead end.'

'We'll keep it in mind though. Should another burglary of that type happen it could mean that it's a smokescreen so the killer is able to carry out his actions. Thanks, Morgan, for bringing that up, it's a good call.' He smiled at her then turned and began to issue directions to the staff who were waiting to be told what to do, whilst Ben, Morgan and Cain left the room. Amy was watching them.

'Do you want to come to Barrow or stay here and look for Des?'

'Stay here please, Ben.'

He lowered his voice. 'Keep me updated and don't be too hard on Will. He's doing his best, none of this is anyone's fault.'

'I know, I just feel so useless.'

Ben reached out, patting her arm, then he was out of the door. Morgan was relieved to be out of there it was too stuffy and far too intense for this early on a Monday morning. They headed back to the office, grabbing laptops, notebooks and anything else they may need. Cain was hovering in the doorway.

'Are you sure you need me?'

'Yes, you're my muscle power, but if you'd rather stay here that's fine, we'll manage.'

He looked down at both Morgan and Ben, who he towered over, and shook his head. 'Nah, I'll come. I'm not sure you two should be let out unsupervised if you get my drift.'

Morgan laughed. 'Cheeky.'

'True though, isn't it? Tell me it's not.'

She couldn't, because he was right in so many ways.

'I'll go get my stuff.'

He left them alone, and Ben looked at his watch.

'I don't really want to waste hours waiting for Isabelle Burrows to get here. It might take a couple of hours yet. Time is precious and we can't mess around.'

'She'll be able to continue driving to Walney, so ring her and tell her where we're going and that we'll meet her when she arrives.'

'Why didn't I think of that?' He winked at her.

'I'm just saying it out loud, I'm sure you did.'

She glanced at Ben; she didn't like the deep crease in his forehead that seemed to have arrived overnight, his shoulders were tight and as he turned, she saw a glint of silver on his head where his once shaved hair was growing in. She didn't want him to get any more stressed because of this case, she wanted to wrap him up in a protective bubble, wrap them both up and cast some kind of spell to stop them from getting older, she wanted to spend the rest of her life with him. She wondered if her aunt Ettie had some tea for that, eternal youth, stay young tea, never age a day tea. Ettie was in her sixties, with a head of platinum hair that was stunning; she didn't look any older than the day Morgan had first met her. She imagined Ettie had always looked this way; she was a beautiful woman who gave off an ethereal glow that was simply magical.

'Morgan.'

She realised she'd been daydreaming. 'Yeah'

'Just checking you were still with me, you drifted away.'

'I'm here, wishing that we weren't though.'

'I know, me too. What I'd give to be lying on a sunbed on a Caribbean beach somewhere.'

'Then why don't we? When we find Des and Milly let's take a holiday. I don't remember the last holiday I had.'

'You know what, I think you're right, we should.'

'Definitely.'

'Only one slight problem, won't you combust under intense heat with your copper hair?'

She pushed him out of the door. 'That's offensive you know, not all gingers evaporate in the sun, there is such a thing as Factor Fifty. You're buying lunch for that remark.'

'Sorry, you're right and I will.'

They made their way downstairs to wait for Cain, who came out of the locker room carrying a huge kitbag.

'You can't be too prepared, especially not with you two.'

They smiled at him, and an overwhelming sadness washed over Morgan for the distress she'd caused everyone the last couple of years. She wanted to find Des and Milly safe, reunite them with their loved ones and whisk Ben away to some tropical destination, where the two of them could do two weeks doing nothing more taxing than sipping cocktails by a pool and she could catch up on the reading pile by her side of the bed that seemed to grow every time she left the house.

THIRTY-ONE

Milly's eyelids fluttered open; she had been having the scariest nightmare of her life. Flashes of the man's face who had been waiting for her at the riverside were flickering inside of her mind and her heart was racing. It had been so real. She lay there in the dark and tried to stretch her arms but they wouldn't move. Her hands were stuck together. She heard screaming in the distance, but it wasn't a person. She breathed out a long sigh through pursed lips, seagulls screeching is what that was. God, they were loud, why were they squawking like that outside her window? They never did usually, in fact she didn't really see them anywhere around by her house. There was a cool breeze blowing and she shivered. Had she gone to bed with her window open? *Deep breaths, Milly, in through your nose and out through your mouth then open your eyes and everything will be okay. Your hands will unglue themselves; those birds will disappear into the darkness, and you can grab your duvet off the floor and snuggle up. You might even be able to grab another thirty minutes before your alarm goes off.*

The thought of this made her smile, and she tried to turn onto her left side but a sudden, shooting pain of fire burned through her head and she felt a wave of nausea come rushing up. Trying to open her mouth she realised that she couldn't. She couldn't be sick because there was something in her mouth. She realised that she was lying on a rough surface and not curled up on her luxury divan at the same time she realised that she couldn't move her hands because they were tied together. The whoosh of panic that filled her chest, taking away what little oxygen there was inside of her lungs, was like a door opening into a burning room. She hadn't been having a nightmare. She wasn't at home – she was in a cold, damp place with the salty tang of the sea lingering in the air along with a much darker smell that she couldn't put her finger on, but she thought it smelled as if something had died in here. Panicking now she strained to break the rope that was binding her wrists, but it only cut into her skin even more. She couldn't breathe, she was suffocating and the more she moved her head the more she felt sick and dizzy. Milly forced herself to lie still on the cold, pebbly ground beneath her, inhaling the terrible air, trying to calm herself down before she passed out. As she lay there in the dark, her breath laboured, she realised she had two choices: she could let whoever had done this to her kill her or she could fight back and try her best to escape. The fear inside of her chest was all-consuming, making it tight and hard to breathe, but she made up her mind. She had a party to attend in a few days, and she didn't know how but she was going to make it. She would rather die trying than let the sick arsehole who had done this to her win.

THIRTY-TWO

Ben drove past the factories and industrial units on Park Road leading into the busy town of Barrow-in-Furness. He bypassed the police station, instead heading straight for Jubilee Bridge, which would take them across the channel to Walney Island. Morgan was staring at the boats below the bridge. Cain, who was sitting in the passenger seat, turned to look at her.

'Have you ever been sailing?'

'No, I like the thought of it but I'm not sure me and a boat would be a good match.'

Ben laughed. 'I agree, unless it's a cruise ship I don't think that I would want you anywhere near a tiny boat like those especially if the tide was in.'

She shook her head at him, but silently agreed. 'What about you, Cain?'

'A bit, my dad was a fisherman, and we used to sail quite a lot when we lived down here.'

'You lived on Walney?' Ben asked, surprise in his voice.

'Yeah, years ago. I was only around eight or nine when we moved up to Ambleside. You want to turn right at the lights if we're going to north Walney. It's a bit of a trek, isn't it?'

'Why bring Shea all the way here? Why not kill her in Blackpool? If he's got a thing about beaches there's plenty of them there,' Morgan asked.

Ben looked over his shoulder at her. 'Blackpool is more densely populated, but this doesn't look like it is.'

Cain continued, 'There are busy spots, Biggar Bank, West Shore, Sandy Gap, they get really jam-packed in the warmer weather. But there are also plenty of deserted beaches. He's going to have needed a hut, shed or some kind of place to have kept Shea in, if he had her for days. Somewhere secluded where no one would hear her or him. What did the report say?'

Morgan, who was holding it, looked down. 'The Walney geranium is endemic to certain parts of the island; it's a tiny pink, purple viola that only grows in the dunes of north Walney and nowhere else. That's pretty cool, don't you think?' Morgan looked up from her Google search on her phone. 'It also states you have to walk two miles along the beach to reach the north end where the flowers grow.'

Ben glanced at her in the rear-view mirror. 'Two miles? Do you think he managed to walk a scared teenager two miles along a beach or path to get to that area? Impossible, most teenagers won't walk to school these days.'

He carried on driving until he could go no further, reaching an airfield that said, 'No Entry to the Public'.

He stopped the car. 'Now what? Do you think they'll give us access because we're the police?'

'Keep on driving and find out.' Morgan smiled at him. 'I heard they have their own police force now, with big guns to protect BAE Systems, that's the local shipbuilding company. The airport is owned by BAE.'

'Jesus, why does everything have to be so complicated?'

'He wants it that way, he's thought this out. There is a specific reason why he brought Shea Wilkinson all this way. He must have connections to the area, maybe he lived here like

Cain and has fond memories and wants to bring his sick fantasies to life in the place he loves the most.'

Cain turned to look at her. 'Morgan that's seriously freaky, you know that right? How do you even know this stuff?'

Ben smiled. 'Have you ever seen her bookshelves, Cain?'

Cain shook his head.

'She's a hardcore true crime fan. She knows more than the FBI.'

She rolled her eyes at them both. 'I have an interest in serial killers; I find them fascinating.'

'You couldn't have a hobby like gardening or swimming?' Cain was laughing. 'You're one of a kind, Brookes.'

'Actually, for your information you will find that a lot of the female population has an interest in true crime, especially serial killers.'

'Whoa for real, why is that? Does it do stuff for you, excite you?'

She looked at his face to see if he was being sarcastic and realised he was being serious, he was trying to understand it.

'No, although some people do, they call it Hybrystophilia when people are sexually attracted to serial killers. As for most of the true crime fans it's just fascinating reading about the cases and how the police solved them. True crime podcasts are my favourite, they're totally addictive. You should give them a listen. It's terrifying to think that these kinds of predators exist and are walking amongst us. Take whoever abducted and killed Shea Wilkinson. Do you think they look like a red-eyed monster with horns on their head, or do you think it's some average-looking guy who probably never stands out and his neighbours would say "but he's so nice or he's so quiet"?'

Cain turned back, leaning his head against the seat.

'Well, I doubt he'll be wearing a mask and walking around the neighbourhood in a pair of grey overalls carrying a bloody knife.'

Ben smiled. 'If he's Michael Myers, we're screwed because you can't stop that dude. Right, as interesting as your conversation is what are we going to do?'

'You started it, boss.' Morgan emphasised the boss. 'This is exactly why Will should be down here leading this and we should be back home. He will know who to contact.'

Ben took out his phone and rang the office, leaving Cain and Morgan looking at each other. She got out of the car and began walking back the way they came; she had spied a public footpath through a field full of sheep. It should head down to the beach. She would rather set off walking and see how far she got than sit around for ages twiddling her thumbs in the car. She heard a car door slam and Cain shouted, 'Wait up, I'll come with you.' Grinning to herself she didn't turn around but slowed her pace until he'd caught up with her.

'Nice afternoon for a walk on the beach anyway.'

He was right, it was warm enough not to need a coat but not too hot that the sun burned her skin. They walked along the path towards the wooden stile at the end. The sheep weren't interested in them, going about their business without giving them a second glance. Climbing over the stile which straddled the drystone wall, allowing people to get over to the other side, Morgan went first. On the other side was a sandy, pebbly path and the beach. Her Docs crunching on the gravel, she walked down to the shore and looked around, then shouted back to Cain, 'I can't see anything but beach. There's no way he marched her this way, impossible.'

The salty tang of sea air filled her nostrils and she inhaled – it smelled so good, so fresh. Clean in a different way to the air in Rydal Falls, up on the mountains and fells.

'How lucky are we to live in an area where we have the most beautiful scenery and only a short drive to fabulous beaches? I don't think we appreciate what we have on our doorstep.'

'That's because you spend all your time chasing killers or reading about them.' He winked at her.

'You're an arsehole at times, Cain.'

'But you love me, right?'

She nodded. 'Someone has to. I'm going to walk a little further and see if there's anything.'

'I'll observe you from a safe distance, I can't see you getting into trouble here.'

She walked away thinking, I wonder if that's what Shea Wilkinson thought before she was running for her life trying to escape her abductor? The path soon disappeared, and it was hard work keeping her footing on the pebbles even in her trusty boots.

'Mor—' The wind took the rest of her name, but she turned around to see Ben waving his arms at her frantically. He was beckoning her to come back. She couldn't see anything of value, no shed, shacks or structures and wondered if there were any caves around here. Turning back, she headed towards Ben and Cain.

'Jesus, Morgan, we don't know when the tide's due in; it's dangerous, you could get cut off by the sea.'

She looked to the shore, to see that the tide was quite some way out and the tideline was a few feet away from where she'd been walking.

'I didn't think.'

'I've spoken to Will, he's going to speak to security for the airfield and get someone to meet us at the gate, and they'll drive us through to the far end.'

'Great.' She didn't say it, but she doubted very much that their killer had contacts in the security department at the airfield. Unless he worked there himself. They headed back to the car where a large white Ford pickup was waiting for them. There was a guy leaning against it, his arms folded across his broad chest, baseball cap covering his shaved head.

'Detectives Ben Matthews, Morgan Brookes and Officer Cain.'

'Roy Brown, what do you need?'

'Access to the beach at the north end of Walney; do you know where the Walney geraniums grow?'

Roy shook his head. 'No idea, mate, best I can do is escort you as far as the northern perimeter. But it's all fenced off, there isn't any access to the beach from there.'

'Oh, none at all?' Ben looked defeated.

'No, why don't you jump in the cab, and I'll drive you around? That's easier than having to sign you all in as well as the vehicle.'

They clambered into the pickup, then they were reversing and through the gates. The area wasn't huge; the triangular runway didn't look big enough to take off and land planes on, but Morgan reminded herself these were small planes, not jumbo jets.

'Have you worked at the airport long?'

He looked back at Morgan. 'Few years, we swap around, there's a lot of buildings to patrol on Barrow Island and here, although it's a lot easier now we have the MOD police as well.'

'How many staff work here, do you know?'

'Honestly, I have no idea, it can get quite busy. Not Manchester Airport busy, but you know, busy enough.'

It didn't take long for Roy to drive them around, and he was right, there was no direct beach access from the airfield. It was all fenced off and some walk across the fields surrounding it. Before long they were back at the white Ford Focus and saying goodbye. Roy drove away, leaving them looking at each other.

'Now what?' asked Cain.

'We ask a search team of Barrow officers to scour the beach or any possible ways to the northern tip of the island.'

Ben's phone began to ring, and he answered it walking away from them.

'I guess we're screwed. We need someone who knows this area a lot better than I do. I lived on the south end not near this part. Someone who knows it like the back of their hand to give us some direction as to where he took Shea.'

Ben turned to face them, his tanned face ashen.

'They've found Des.'

'Is he okay? What's wrong?'

Ben swallowed a lump in his throat. 'They've found his body, or the caretaker has.'

Morgan took a moment to let it sink in; Cain was shaking his head.

'What, how?'

'We need to get back to Rydal Falls.'

Ben passed the keys to Cain who was the only one of them wearing a uniform. He could get away with driving faster than either of them, just.

THIRTY-THREE

Morgan was numb from the top of her head to the bottom of her feet; the words were swirling around inside her mind *they found Des's body, his body, he was dead.* Ben was deep in conversation with whoever it was that had broken the news to him, and she was desperate to know more. Cain glanced at her and she shrugged. It was too hard to speak because there were no words. She'd expected him to turn up sooner or later. Even with the blood in his car and the dark possibility that he could have taken Milly, deep down she hadn't *really* thought he was dead, or a murderer. It seemed she'd been wrong about the first part. None of it made sense. A coldness had settled along the full length of her spine. Amy was going to be devastated, those two were close despite their arguments.

'There's nothing on the radio, it's deadly silent. Control must have switched onto another channel so everyone can't listen in,' Cain whispered.

She didn't know what to say, coherent words didn't want to form. So she said nothing and sat staring out of the window, wishing that they'd never left Rydal Falls, that she hadn't taken her eyes off Des yesterday afternoon and that Milly Blake would turn up safe and well.

Ben put his phone down. 'I don't understand how this has happened.'

'Where is Des?'

'St Martha's graveyard.'

Morgan gasped so loud that Cain jumped.

'No way, how? We were there, we can't have missed him.'

'I don't know, Morgan; I can't think straight. I don't understand how he has ended up dead.'

Cain said what Morgan had been thinking. 'Is it a suicide? Did he do something stupid that he couldn't come back from and thought this was the only way out?'

'Al said that he's on scene and no, it's not a suicide unless Des is the kind of person that would be brave enough to cut his own throat. It's bad, not a lot of blood but there's plenty in his car so that could explain the reason why. How did he get from the station to St Martha's with a gaping cut across his throat? That's just not possible.'

'Unless it's not his blood in his car.'

Morgan could feel the pressure inside her mind just thinking about it all. How on earth would Des's family feel when they were told the horrific news? She hoped to God that it wouldn't be her that had to break it to them. Some things were simply too hard to bear.

No one spoke the rest of the way. Cain drove as fast as he could and when he turned onto the main street, they all sighed at the sight of the numerous police vans, cars, CSI vehicles and officers that were milling around. It looked as if every officer from Rydal Falls, Kendal and Keswick was in attendance. Morgan glanced at Ben who she knew was going to go absolutely crazy with them when he got out of the car. Cain stopped the car and whispered, 'Are you ready for the shitshow?'

Ben was out of the car and jogging down to the church gates before Cain had turned the engine off.

Cain looked at her. 'He's going to go running in there and compromise the whole scene.'

Morgan threw herself out of the car after Ben. She had to pump her legs hard to catch up to him. Al was standing at the entrance to the church his arms outstretched, stopping Ben from going any further.

'You know the score, Ben, suited and booted before I can let you in, my friend.' He lowered his voice. 'It's the least we can do for Des now. We need to focus and not make any mistakes, right?'

He had his arm on Ben's, who was straining to look over his shoulder. Morgan caught up and gently put her hand on Ben's other arm. She felt the fight leaving his body as his shoulders relaxed.

'Will is in there right now with Wendy, and Marc arrived not long after I did. He's also inside.'

'Inside?'

'Yes, inside the church.'

Ben looked at Morgan, and she knew that he'd assumed Des's body was outside just like Shea's had been, because she had assumed he would be there too.

'I'm not going to stop either of you from going in – you have a right to see this and know exactly what has happened.'

Marc walked out of the church doors. His eyes were glazed, and his face looked as if it had aged ten years since this morning. He lifted a hand to wave at them, then shuffled over in the white paper protective suit he was wearing, where he removed it, not looking at anyone. Once he'd bagged up his protective clothing, he got inside his car and drove off. Ben stared after him for a moment, shrugging his shoulders, then crossed to the CSI van. Opening the sliding door to grab a paper suit, he passed a packet to Morgan who paused before accepting it. She wasn't sure if she really wanted to see Des like this, at his most vulnerable. She wasn't sure that he would want them to see him like this either, but she tried to put herself in his place, and she realised that she wouldn't want anyone to see her that way. But that everyone *had* seen her injured, at death's door and fighting for her life. What made her so different to Des? Why had she survived, and he hadn't? Movement broke her spell, and she realised that Ben was already dressed and walking back in Al's direction. She tore open the packet and tugged on the suit. She owed it to Des to give it her best, whether it made her feel uncomfortable or not. This wasn't about her; it was about giving him their full attention and finding out what the hell had happened to leave him bleeding to death inside a church.

THIRTY-FOUR

Churches for Morgan were always places of quiet solitude, a safe place to go when she needed time to think about life and the crap it sometimes threw at her. She had spent quite a lot of time in church after Sylvia had died. While Stan, her adopted dad's church had been the local pub and his religion had been alcohol, Morgan's had been sitting in silence at the back of the church praying for the nightmare to end. Then when Brad had been buried here, she'd done the same, trying to be as close to him as she could. A deep void filled with regret she'd not been there when he needed her. As she forced one foot in front of the other to move herself forwards, she could feel her heart racing. The palms of her hands were hot and sticky inside the double pair of gloves she was wearing. Ben was so focused on getting to Des he didn't speak. Her mind was spinning, she had tunnel vision and she didn't know if she could do this right now. Where was Amy? Surely, she was here. She hadn't left the police station when they'd set off on their quest to try and find the primary crime scene where Shea Wilkinson had been held captive and likely murdered. Her question was answered as they stepped through the arched oak doorway into the church itself. Amy was tucked into the corner, standing still staring into the main part of the church, her eyes wide, her complexion pale, and Morgan realised that she was probably numb with shock. She didn't even acknowledge the pair of them as they walked past, her eyes so fixed on Des. Will was standing inside, blocking the view of the body of Des. No, she couldn't call him a body, it wasn't right. He was their colleague, their annoying work friend. Morgan felt a wave of sadness about how they'd been with each other the last few months. Regret that she'd let him wind her up at times when she should have let it wash over her.

Will turned to look at them both. 'I'm so sorry for your loss.' Then he stepped to one side.

The gasp that echoed around the church hadn't come from her mouth; she realised it had been Ben. It took her a moment to understand what she was looking at and then her eyes focused in, and she let out her own high-pitched gasp.

Des was draped across the steps to the altar, a grotesque life-sized puppet who had been posed in the church, a bloody red cloth beneath his body. He was fully clothed; the white shirt he'd worn yesterday, that had been ironed with the precision of an army drill sergeant's, was now drenched in a brownish fluid that she knew was dried blood. His arms and legs were spread out as if he was being crucified. She tried not to look at his face or the fact that his hair had been so crudely chopped off close to his scalp, or the gaping wound across his neck. But she knew she was going to have to – she couldn't leave Ben to face this alone; when the nightmares came for them both she needed to see the same terror he did. Her eyes moved up from the heavily stained shirt, past the bloodied flesh of the gaping open wound on his neck and on to his face. She'd expected his eyes to be closed, had said a silent prayer that they would be, but as her gaze fell on his she realised that they were partly open, a look of pure surprise and pain captured in them. The lids were permanently stuck in a half-open position, and he was looking directly at her. She closed her eyes, swaying a little and heard Des whisper in her ear. *'This is all your fault, Brookes, you brought this pain and suffering to us and now look what's happened. Look at me, I'm dead.'*

'Morgan, Morgan.' A voice whispered in her ear. It wasn't Ben's. She opened her eyes at the same time a hand took hold of her elbow, and she saw Will standing next to her. 'You've got this, okay? Come on, let's wait outside.'

She let him lead her away from the church steps where the brides and grooms knelt before God to say their prayers for a lifetime of happiness. Where the babies were held when they got christened, promised a future of eternal love, where the old people came to take their communion to absolve their sins, which were now tainted with blood and evil, where all faith and hope had been ripped apart and was now fighting a battle between light and dark. She didn't fight it, she let Will help her outside where she sucked in huge gulps of fresh air. Her knees threatening to buckle underneath her, she leaned back against the rough stone wall of the church. Grateful that it was there to support her when she couldn't support herself. Looking around at everyone, she wondered if this was somehow her fault. Had she brought this on them? Was she cursed? Would everyone she knew die an awful death and, if so, where did that leave Ben? He was the most important man in her life. She loved him so completely – what was she going to do if something terrible happened to him because of her?

'How are you keeping up, feel a bit better out here?'

Will's blue eyes were full of kindness and compassion. She nodded.

'I'm good.'

'You sure? Do you want to go sit in a van with Amy, take a bit of time?'

She shook her head. She didn't want to face Amy in case

she said what she was thinking out loud: that this was all brought on since she'd arrived on the team.

'I need to go and speak to Ben. There's nothing here that you can do, either of you. I'm hoping that you'll be able to get that through to him because he's going to struggle with this. I know what it's like, I've been in a similar situation before twice and it's harder than you could ever imagine.'

Morgan looked at Will, his eyes full of sadness, and she didn't know if she could take this any more. It was too hard to keep living this life and losing people that you knew in the most horrific of ways.

THIRTY-FIVE

They left the scene in a silent convoy, not one of them speaking to each other. If this was any other kind of job, they'd have been sent home, given time to absorb what happened and try to come to terms with it. But this wasn't like any other job: they still had to find Milly Blake before something terrible happened to her. Des was out of bounds; his murder wasn't theirs to investigate, even though the impact of it would affect them forever. Morgan was driving, Ben was next to her, Amy sitting behind them both. Morgan wished she would say something, be her usual sarcastic self, but she didn't: she stared out of the window watching the world go by as the car slowly crawled back to the station.

When they stopped in the car park she spoke, 'I want to go with whoever is telling his mum.'

Ben nodded. 'Of course, should we go do this now?'

'Yes.'

Morgan left the engine running and got out of the car. Ben got out and was walking around to her side. She looked at his washed-out face, his eyes filled with unshed tears.

'Are you sure you want to do this?'

He nodded. 'I have to, Morgan, it's the least I can do. We already despatched a family liaison officer first thing this morning when we hadn't found him last night. At least they will be there to help her with whatever she needs.'

'I'll continue to look into Shea's case then, unless I'm allowed to join in with looking for Milly Blake now that we know Des hasn't run away with her.'

He shrugged. 'Ask Marc what he wants you to do. Are you okay?'

'Yep.' Her voice was strained though. She wanted to hold him, pull him close to her and never let go. Instead, she turned away and walked to the back door to let herself inside, hearing the car door close and the engine as he began driving back towards the exit.

Inside, the station was empty, there wasn't a single person around. Everyone had been despatched to St Martha's to scene guard or help out in some way. She hadn't realised just how creepy it was in here when there was no one around, no laughter, no banter, no gossip. The atmosphere inside here was one of complete stillness. She walked up the spiral staircase to the second floor, expecting to see Marc in his office, but he wasn't, he must be in theirs. She reached the door to the CID office, feeling more than a little uneasy. Pushing it open she walked inside and saw him there, sitting at Des's desk looking through his drawers.

'What are you doing?'

He looked at her, and he had the decency to look a little embarrassed. He stood up, pushing the drawer shut.

'I was, erm, I was looking to see if there was anything that may be of evidential use. How are you, Morgan, and Ben and Amy? We've all had an awful shock.'

'They've gone to speak to Des's mum, break the news to her,

and I don't know how I am, shocked and numb are probably the best I can come up with.'

He was standing in front of her, a look of concern on his face that made her feel uncomfortable. She wasn't good at sharing her feelings with anyone, especially Marc.

'It's okay to cry, I'm here, you can cry on my shoulder anytime.'

He reached out for her, pulling her towards him to hug her but she pushed herself away, horror chilling her insides. She didn't know him well enough for him to be hugging her. If she needed that she had Ben, not this guy who was supposed to be her boss and who she just couldn't get a handle on.

'I'm good, thanks, I have Ben to comfort me.'

A look of anger crossed his face that she didn't miss, and she realised that he wasn't used to being rejected by anyone. What had he expected? That she'd melt into his arms, begging for him to comfort her? She barely knew the guy and he'd just gone from being bearable to a creep in less than sixty seconds.

'Ah, yes you do. Of course, sorry, I was just being friendly, no harm meant. I hope I didn't offend you?'

'No, you didn't. I appreciate your concern.'

'I've been meaning to have a chat with you about the relationship between you and Ben and the dynamics within the team.'

Alarm bells began to ring inside her mind. She didn't want to be having a discussion with Marc about her and Ben, it was none of his damn business. Especially not now when she couldn't think straight.

'What about it?'

'Well technically it's not really acceptable, especially with this being such a small team. It's not professional and where I'm from we weren't allowed to work in the same office or department as our partners. I think it might be better if we split the pair of you up, send you to work somewhere else so there's no case of anyone speculating that Ben favours you over the rest of the team, or that you're behaving in a manner that brings the department into the spotlight.'

She glared at him, not believing the audacity of the guy to even consider having this conversation now, when she was already distraught over Des. Now he was telling her she was going to have to move departments.

'I know this isn't a good time to bring this up, but I guess there never will be. How do you feel about going to work in Kendal or Barrow? At least you've met Will who is an excellent boss, or so I've been told.'

He was looking directly into her eyes, probing her with his gaze in a way that wasn't comfortable at all, but she would not give him the satisfaction of looking away first.

'I'll speak to Ben about it.'

'No need to do that, he's going to be so busy, and guilt stricken over Des that he doesn't need to be worrying about you transferring, don't you think? If you care about him, you should just do it quietly without a fuss. I'll organise everything for you; it will be seamless. I'm sure it will help you both anyway if you're not living, breathing and working out of each other's pockets twenty-four hours a day. Let me know tomorrow and I can sort it out. You don't need to put this on his shoulders, or at least you won't if you care about him.'

The rage inside Morgan's chest was so black and burning that she feared for Marc's life if he didn't get the fuck out of her sight. She could feel her knees trembling and her hands were shaking. She didn't trust her voice to speak in case she screamed at him and flew at him. He was smiling at her with the smuggest look across his face that she'd ever seen. She sat down at her desk and wondered if she hadn't just caught him snooping through Des's stuff and had let him hug her would they be having this conversation at all? She asked herself had she been wrong to think that they'd begun to understand him, when all along he'd had an ulterior motive to move in and rip them all apart? He was worse now than when he'd first joined them.

'What about Milly Blake?'

'What about her?'

'I was going to help out with her investigation.'

'She'll turn up, one way or the other.'

She couldn't believe what she was hearing and wished she'd had the foresight to record it. 'She'll turn up one way or the other? Meaning dead or alive and you don't care. You're not wasting your time and resources to look for her.'

'I never meant that, we have a lot on. Des, Shea, Milly missing, we don't need to concentrate all of our efforts on finding her when there's two murder investigations to run. Response are capable of carrying out missing person enquiries. It's a matter of prioritising them. This is what happens all the time in a major force. It's harsh but that's reality. We're still looking for her but she's not the top priority at the moment.'

'Well, it's not how it happens here, sir.'

'We already have Claire Williams assisting Ben, who is being very helpful and has a lot more experience than you. We don't want you to go charging off and getting yourself into some mess that you need rescuing from, do we? Like you have many times before.' His phone began to ring. 'Excuse me, Morgan, I have to take this. Don't forget to have a think about where you'd like to go.'

He left her sitting there with her mouth open and her fingers clenched into tight fists. He was moving her; she had no say in the matter. Ben would be furious with him for this. She didn't want to go anywhere, she loved working here but if she had to, she'd go to Barrow. Will seemed like a good boss. She could work with him if she had to, or if she had no choice. She'd rather choose and be in control of the situation than be forced by Marc – there was no way she would give him the satisfaction.

THIRTY-SIX

Amy found her voice when they visited Des's mum and poured out everything to her. Ben had been thankful for the FLO who had sat the whole time with her arm around Natasha Black's shoulders. He'd made the tea, unable to think of any other way he could be of any use. He felt so damn tired, as if his energy had been drained from the top of his head through the bottom of his feet. He had a sharp pain in his chest and wasn't sure if he was about to have a heart attack, or if he had awful indigestion. Natasha was composed, she was well spoken with a soft voice that he had to strain to listen to at times. They hadn't told her how he'd died and she didn't ask either; she didn't need to know that just yet. Give her time to accept that her son had been murdered before taking away the last shreds of her sanity from her. If she had asked, he would have told her in the least graphic way possible, although was there a way to tell someone their son had their throat slit from ear to ear and had bled to death on the church altar steps? It occurred to him that whoever had done this had taken their time, watching and waiting for Des to take his last breaths before they began to pose his body. Who had access to the church and was so confident they wouldn't be disturbed that they'd hung around long enough to do this? Theodore Edwards was the obvious suspect; Will had said he was bringing him in, so where was he?

Eventually Amy nodded to him that they could leave, and he couldn't get out of the house fast enough. It was the cosiest cottage he'd ever been inside – the complete opposite to Des's own house which had been sparsely furnished. As they got outside, he whispered, 'Did they bring the vicar in earlier?'

'Not sure, do you think he did this?' There was a cold, hard glint of anger in her eyes.

'I don't know, but he has access to the church, he would know when it was likely to be undisturbed. Let's get back to the station. I know we can't work it, but we can advise, or would you rather go home?'

'I can't, I can't go home and know that I've done nothing to help find the bastard who has done this.'

Ben knew exactly how she felt; he felt the same way.

They walked into the office to see Morgan sitting there in the dark, a cardboard box on her desk. Ben flicked the lights on but didn't say anything. Maybe she needed a bit of time to get her head together.

'His mum knows, she was so nice, my heart is broken for her.'

Amy addressed Morgan who nodded. 'Awful.'

'What's in the box?'

'I'm helping out at Barrow.'

Ben lifted his head to look at her. 'What?'

'I've been asked to help with Will's team for a bit. I couldn't say no.'

'The hell you are, and yes you can say no. I need you here, Morgan, you can't just bugger off to Barrow the minute things are a bit rough here.' He felt as if he'd just been slapped across the face with a block of ice. What was going on? He didn't understand.

'We've lost Des, I'm a man down, two men down if you swan off to bloody Barrow. What the hell are you thinking?'

He saw her neck move up and down as if she was swallowing a hard lump. Marc walked in, and he saw him glance at the box on her desk, a small nod of his head as if he approved.

'Tell her, boss, she can't walk out and leave us like this. I don't care if Barrow are short staffed, they haven't just had one of their team murdered in cold blood, she has to stay here.'

'I'm afraid neither of us have a choice, Ben, someone has to go, and Morgan very kindly offered to relieve the burden. There isn't going to be a lot of investigating going on here; you're both getting sent home on compassionate leave.'

Amy laughed. 'Are you for fucking real? You're splitting this team up, why? Because you're scared we'll solve this or because you don't care that Des has been murdered?'

'I'm doing no such thing, Amy, I'm following orders. Will is running the investigation into Des's murder and the murder of Shea Wilkinson. He has a bigger team; Morgan can advise him – it makes sense.'

'I'll go, you can't send Morgan off on her own like that.'

'Now that's very kind of you, but yes, she can go, she's a grown woman, a fully capable detective who is going to give her expertise to Will's team for a short while. Amy, as of now you're on compassionate leave, go home.'

Ben was glaring at him, not believing what he was hearing but the pain in his chest from earlier was nothing compared to the stabbing pain he felt now. Morgan hadn't even put up a fight. She'd packed her stuff ready to go, so what did that mean for the pair of them? He had never felt devastation like it. His entire world was crumbling around him, and he couldn't do a damn thing to stop it.

THIRTY-SEVEN

Amy stormed out of the office, slamming the door behind her. Ben was still staring at Morgan, and she knew he knew something wasn't right, but what could she do? At this moment she hated Marc more than she'd ever hated anyone, except for maybe Gary Marks who was always going to be top of that list no matter how long he'd been dead. Her heart was broken. Ben looked as if she'd just peeled his fingers from the edge of a cliff and was watching him fall in slow motion. All the while Marc had this smug look on his face. One day, she was going to wipe it off with her fist, or her Doc Marten boot, either would do. She would speak to Will once she was in Barrow, see a Federation Rep and ask them where she stood, although she knew that Marc would be covering his back from all angles. Hopefully it would only be a couple of days and she'd be back here where she belonged with the people she loved and cared about. She picked up the box and headed out to the car, leaving Ben staring after her. She had never felt so angry and upset at the same time. She had this ripping pain inside her chest that was unbearable. She expected Ben to run after her, grab the box off her and at least beg her not to go. He didn't, and she had the feeling that she had just finished him off for the day. His emotions were all over the place and instead of rushing to her he was probably about to lose his temper and the last of his sanity.

Driving to his house she left the box in her car and went inside, disabling the security system so she could go pack a suitcase of what she might need for a few days. She looked around, she didn't want to go, didn't want to leave the safety of this house that Ben had purposely turned into a safe haven for her. Who was going to have her back in Barrow? She guessed she was about to find out if she could still look after herself or whether she had got too reliant on Ben's kind nature to be her hero and protector all rolled into one. Why was Marc doing this to her now, to them? He was splitting up the team and not for any reason other than separating her and Ben. She picked up the notebook she kept for writing any thoughts inside, a bit like her diary but not so obvious, and a photograph fluttered to the ground; she picked it up. It was the wedding photo of Ben and Cindy, the one she'd kept to one side. They looked so young, probably her age now, only Morgan didn't think she'd ever looked as young and innocent as Cindy had then. Her whole life had been tainted with grief and a sadness so deep that it was sometimes hard for her to push it down into the void. Tears began to fall down her cheeks. She pushed the photograph back inside the book as she cried for Des, for Ben, for Cindy and herself. She sat on Ben's side of the bed which smelled faintly of Eau Sauvage and the peppermint shower gel he always used. She shouldn't be doing this. Why hadn't she told Marc to go fuck himself? Where was the feisty, take no crap Morgan that would have said that to him? He was playing on her being so upset over Des that she wasn't thinking straight, and she had done exactly what he asked. She also wondered if she'd taken the chance to run away for a while because it was easier than facing and dealing with everything that was happening here. At least this way she could focus on finding Shea's killer or at least the crime scene. Even if she was hurting Ben and herself, at the end of the day she had a job that she knew required her to work wherever it sent her. Had she got too cosy thinking she was untouchable, that they wouldn't dare move her because of her reputation?

Standing up she finished packing the small suitcase with everything she might need for a couple of days. She could come back whenever she wanted, she didn't even have to stay over in Barrow – it wasn't that long a drive, but as she walked out of Ben's house, she realised deep down that she was running away and taking the easy option because staying here was too hard.

THIRTY-EIGHT

Ben was left alone in the office. He was raging inside that Marc had made the decision to send Morgan to Barrow without consulting him first. He knew that this wasn't a big deal usually, but it was Morgan. Someone had killed Des. What did that mean for the rest of his team? He wanted her close by so he could keep an eye on her and make sure she was safe. He couldn't do this from Rydal Falls could he? Then he realised that he could: if he was being sent home on compassionate leave, he could go with her. He was angry with Morgan for actually doing as she was told, which didn't happen very often. Angry with Marc for being the sneakiest arsehole in the world, and furious with whoever had done this to Des. Who had the gall to think they could murder a copper, dump his car outside his place of work and then leave his body inside a church posed like a crude statue for the world to see? Ben didn't know but he was going to find out and soon. He looked around the office which had been disbanded in the space of a couple of hours. Not for the first time did he wish that Tom hadn't retired, that he hadn't left them. He was going to get his own back on Detective Inspector Marcell Howard; he was going to regret thinking he could come in here, tear apart his team and get away with it.

He grabbed his jacket off the back of the coat hook then went into his office, where he scooped up the file he'd put together earlier of everything they had up to now on Shea Wilkinson, Milly Blake and Des's misper report. He wasn't officially working any of them now, but that didn't mean he couldn't from wherever Morgan was. He didn't think Will would object; he was a decent guy, and he knew that he'd been through similar situations with his wife, Annie. He would speak to him once things had calmed down a little, confident that Will would do his best to find the bastard that had killed Des; but he could help out from behind the scenes and Marc wouldn't have to know.

Cain was leaning against the brew station, waiting for the kettle to boil, and he looked up at Ben.

'Boss, how are you, how's everyone? I can't believe it; I mean who would want to kill Des?'

Ben looked around to see if Marc was anywhere near. Satisfied he wasn't he lowered his voice and replied, 'Not good, he's sending Morgan to Barrow, and me and Amy have to take compassionate leave.'

Cain straightened up. 'What?'

'It's bollocks, I don't know what he's up to but it's like he's been waiting for a chance to split us up.'

'He can't do that; he can't send Morgan off on her own to a place where a girl was killed, and we still don't know where. It's a disaster waiting to happen, why's he's doing this?'

Ben shook his head. 'No idea, but he can do it. It's just not right, especially not if there's a chance he's putting Morgan in danger.'

Cain leaned towards Ben. 'Does he have an alibi for the time Shea Wilkinson went missing, or Des?'

'I don't know.'

'Des wouldn't have got in a car with someone he didn't know, maybe you should be thinking about that. What if he wanted you all out of the way? This is the perfect way to do it. He knows that you and Morgan would figure this out, so he's splitting you up, so you don't figure it out.'

Ben thought about it. 'He's a dick, but I don't think he's a killer.'

Cain shrugged. 'Something to think about though. Do you want me to put some annual leave in, go make sure Morgan's okay? I've got plenty of holidays left, no one to go anywhere with at the moment.'

'That's kind of you, but I think it might be better if you're here and keep an eye on him and what he's up to. I'm going to go with Morgan but don't let him know that.'

'Yes, boss.'

Ben walked away, then turned back. 'Cain, thank you for looking out for her.'

Cain shrugged. 'Someone has to, she's like an annoying little sister that keeps getting you in trouble, but I care about her, and you.'

Ben smiled at him, touched and grateful that they both had Cain watching out for them.

When he arrived home Morgan's car wasn't outside. He'd been hoping she'd wait for him but then again, he'd been furious with her for agreeing to do it in the first place. He hadn't spoken to her when she'd left and he regretted that now. He tried ringing her phone, but it went to voicemail. Her car was a knackered old VW Golf, and it didn't have hands-free. Going inside he realised she must have left in a hurry because she hadn't reset the alarms, was this because she didn't care any more or because she didn't think Ben was in danger? The house felt empty, and just knowing that she wasn't coming back tonight made him sink into a dark pit of sadness. A part of him thought he should let her go without any fuss, let her go it alone, stand on her own two feet and prove she was a very capable detective. She didn't need his approval to live her life. He would never be that way with her; hadn't he been the one telling her she should move on whilst she could?

As he walked into the kitchen, the bottle of Jack Daniel's he kept in the cupboard for emergencies was calling his name. He needed a drink. Needed to blot out today, the last couple of days. He'd give Morgan a chance to get to Barrow safely, then he'd travel down first thing in the morning and book into the Holiday Inn Express that had recently opened down there. He didn't want her to think she couldn't make her own decisions; he would never stop her from doing anything or try and control her. Taking out the bottle and a glass, he took the bag of ice from the freezer and dropped a couple of cubes in the glass, pouring over the amber liquid. It had been a while since he'd been acquainted with this particular vice. After Cindy had died this had been his only friend, his liquid gold that had sent him down into the depths of oblivion and made him forget the sadness and pain she'd left him with.

Throwing his suit jacket over the back of the chair, he tugged off his tie and undid the buttons of his shirt, then unzipping his trousers he kicked off his shoes, stepping out of his trousers so he wouldn't crease his suit when he fell into a drunken stupor on the sofa. In just his boxers and shirt he carried his glass and bottle into the lounge where the TV was; the ice clinking against the side of the glass was the only sound in the entire house. He sat in silence, thinking about Des, wondering where he had messed up to end up with his colleague dead and what he could have done to prevent it. As the bottle was almost empty, he sat back, leaning his head against the soft leather chair, closing his eyes. The room was swaying; he knew he shouldn't be drinking on an empty stomach, he had to do something, but he couldn't remember what and his last thought before he sank into oblivion was of Des's cat and who was going to look after it. The glass still in his hand, he let out a loud snore as the last few drops of JD spilled onto his thighs and the glass slipped out of his fingers.

THIRTY-NINE

Ben's phone was vibrating somewhere, but he couldn't open his eyes and the slightest movement set off a wave of vertigo. He also stank of stale bourbon. He let out a groan as he felt around for his phone. Finding it, he'd missed the call but there was a message. Opening one eye he looked at the clock and forced himself to sit upright. It was almost nine a.m., he'd been unconscious the entire night. His first thought was Morgan. He dialled her number, relieved when she picked up straight away.

'Are you okay?'

'Yes, are you?' Her voice seemed strained, not like her at all.

'Sorry for being an arse. I know it wasn't your fault.'

She paused. *'I'm in a briefing, it's about to start, I'll ring you soon.'*

The line went dead, and he stared at the phone in his hand. Life went on, she was busy working, doing what she did best, and he was here doing what he did best; he'd reverted to being a hung-over mess. His phone rang again.

'Change your mind?'

'Pardon? I'm sorry, is this Detective Ben Matthews?'

'Yes, it is. Sorry, I thought you were someone else. Can I help you?'

'I hope so, seeing as how I travelled down from Wales to speak to you.'

He sat up straight. 'Doctor Burrows, I'm sorry about yesterday, things happened that were out of my control.'

The soft Welsh lilt in her voice made it sound comforting.

'No need to apologise, I'm sorry for your loss. I spoke to a lovely lady, Brenda I think it was, on the front desk, who told me there had been a sudden death of your colleague. I'm staying at the Premier Inn in Kendal, as there were no places in Rydal Falls to stay, all booked up.'

He squeezed his eyes shut. What was he supposed to do now he'd been sent home?

'What I'm intending to do is travel to Walney this morning. I must be back at the university for tomorrow afternoon. I want to take a look at the area and get some samples, if that's okay. Would someone be able to accompany me or at least give me the directions of where I need to go?'

'I'm free this morning. If you could give me an hour to get everything together, I can meet you.'

'Yes, that's fine. If it's easier for you I can pick you up.'

Ben had the phone tucked under his chin, and he placed his hands in the prayer position. 'That would be amazing.' He gave her his address, and she hung up. He looked down at the empty glass on the floor, the empty bottle on the coffee table and groaned for the second time. He had an hour to get himself together; at least he didn't have to drive. If he took an overnight bag with him, he could get Doctor Burrows to drop him off at the hotel after they'd been to Walney. Then when Morgan finished, they could spend some time together; it would be nice to be out of Rydal Falls even if it was only an hour away in Barrow.

He pulled himself up. First things first: he hunted the emer-

gency paracetamol he knew Morgan kept for headaches out of
the kitchen drawer, swallowed them down with a glass of milk.
He made some toast and ate it to line his stomach. Back in the
days when he had no one to care about but himself he'd often go
to The Coffee Pot for a full English breakfast. He realised he
was hungry for a greasy fry-up and missed Morgan even more
because she loved them as much as he did. He loved that she
didn't care about what she ate and just enjoyed food without all
the usual worries that Cindy used to go through. She had been
obsessed with calorie counting, and it had slowly ruined both of
their lives the way she would be in such a foul mood when she
weighed herself and put a pound on. She'd been perfect in his
eyes. He'd tell her time and time again that she was beautiful,
but for Cindy it had never been enough, and this had broken his
heart. Finally she had ripped it into tiny shards the day he
found her body in the bath, and he'd honestly never thought he
could love anyone else. Then along came fiery, determined
Morgan Brookes, with hair the same colour as her temper and
the greenest of eyes. He'd fallen in love with her the more time
he got to spend with her, and she was good for his soul.

He stepped into the shower. Look at him, one night without
her and he'd gone to pieces. He smiled to himself. He didn't
think he would ever find love again after losing his wife, but he'd
been given a second chance and he wasn't going to screw it up
this time around. Marc could do his best to split them up, it
didn't matter, they wouldn't let him. As the icy cold spray hit his
body he yelped, but he didn't move, he needed the equivalent of
an ice bath to rejuvenate his body and his mind. He was never
drinking again unless he was in the company of the woman he
loved. It was time to get his act together. And then an image of
Des lying spreadeagled on the altar steps in St Martha's flashed
across his eyes and he remembered why he'd had such a crappy
day yesterday. The pain was so intense in his chest he squeezed
his eyes closed, hoping he wasn't about to die of a heart attack,

not whilst he was naked in his shower. That would be all he needed right now, especially after Cindy died in this same bathroom. He had a thought; would she be there waiting for him if he did or had she moved on somewhere much better? He hoped wherever she was that Des was there too; maybe they could be friends in the afterlife, wouldn't that be something?

Ben was dressed, shaved, had sprayed himself in his usual cologne and was waiting in the front room watching out of the window for Doctor Isabelle Burrows to pick him up. As he stared out of the bay window, he realised that he had no idea what she looked like or what car she drove; hopefully she'd either ring or knock on his door when she arrived. His headache was easing off thankfully, but there was so much to do he didn't know where to begin. His phone rang and he looked outside to see a battered old Land Rover outside his house. There was a woman in the driver's seat with pastel pink hair, and for a moment he wondered if it was Susie from the mortuary. She waved at him, and he waved back realising that she didn't look anything like Susie, they just shared the same taste in exotic hair colours. He set the security alarm behind him and, dragging the overnight case down the path, he got into the passenger seat.

'Ben Matthews, thanks for picking me up and for being so understanding about yesterday.'

'Isabelle Burrows and it's no problem at all, I'm just sorry that you're going through such awful circumstances. Was it sudden, or had it been expected?'

He realised that she didn't know it was murder and wondered if he should discuss it with her, then he realised that if Des had been killed by Shea Wilkinson's murderer, there may also be forensic evidence transferred to him too that would be looked at by Isabelle.

'He was murdered.'

She gasped, turning her head to look at him as if she didn't believe he was telling the truth.

'Murdered, oh my God that's horrific. Do you know who did it?'

'I'm assuming it's the same person who killed Shea Wilkinson, as both of their hair was crudely chopped off. This is all a bit of a mess now, because we have another missing girl too and I think she has been abducted by the same person. I have no idea how long we have to find her, but time isn't on our side. What I need your help with is finding the location of the primary crime scene where Shea was killed, or where she was kept captive. Your email to Declan helped narrow it down to somewhere along the north shore of Walney Island where these flowers grow, but apart from that it's a huge area of untouched beauty. It could be where the missing girl is being held now.'

'I'm glad I could help. I was thinking on my drive up actually, that I'd like to have another look at the petals in particular. I haven't checked yet, but once I get back I'll examine them to see if they come from a wild-collected plant or one that has been grown from seed, for example in a greenhouse. As for the soil on the bottom of Shea's feet, I hope that some of the samples we collect today will be a firm match, and even more helpful in pinpointing the location where she was kept. I'm sure we'll find this place, and hopefully also the other girl who has been taken. I do wonder though, why is your killer dumping bodies in Rydal Falls? Why not on Walney?'

'Something about Rydal Falls is appealing to him. I'm assuming it's a him because it can't be easy moving dead bodies around, although I wouldn't rule out a female.'

Ben was staring out of the window, what *did* make a killer want to dump bodies in Rydal Falls? What was the attraction, was it the church, was he some religious nut who liked St Martha's? Was it the vicar? But he was originally from Birmingham, wasn't he? Taking out his phone, Ben rang Will.

'Theodore Edwards, do we know where he was originally from?'

'I'm not sure, he's currently waiting to be interviewed. Claire and I are going to be having a long chat with him. I'll get someone to give his Intel records another once-over and check to see if he has anything we may have missed.'

'Whoever this killer is, Doctor Burrows has pointed out that they must have close links with the north side of Walney. We need to know what's making them take a huge risk by driving all the way to Rydal Falls with a body in the back of their car. If he was from that area, it would make sense that he'd know the most deserted places.'

'I'll certainly ask him where he's from. He's been a bit cagy and I'm sure he's panicking about being brought in. Where are you, Ben, how are you holding up?'

Ben wondered if he should tell Will what he was doing. He didn't really know the guy well enough to trust him implicitly, but he did like him a lot more than he liked Marc.

'I'm on my way to Walney with Doctor Burrows to take a look around.'

'That's great, I've had a search team out at first light to see if they can find anywhere remote where he could have kept Shea. I'll let them know you're on your way down. If Marc asks, I haven't spoken to you, it'll be easier that way.'

Ben smiled, those last few words told him everything he needed to know about Will Ashworth; he could trust him implicitly.

'I appreciate it.'

'Oh, one last thing. Morgan is working alongside my team down in Barrow, and they have strict orders to help her and to keep her out of any possible trouble. I just wanted you to know that she's okay. We're not a bad bunch.'

He turned away from Isabelle as tears filled the corner of his eyes.

'Thank you.' Ben struggled to get the words out, he was so choked up. Will hung up, and he took a deep breath.

'You know, please stop calling me Doctor Burrows or Isabelle, I prefer Bella. It's much easier to listen to than Doctor Burrows. Half of the time I forget who people are addressing.'

She was grinning at him, and he laughed. 'Bella is a lovely name.'

'I think so too. Right, so what's happening, where are we going? Let's get the samples, we need to nail this dude to the cross and quick.'

Ben smiled back at her; Des had been spread out as if he was about to be crucified but she couldn't know this – he had never mentioned that part. Would the killer have nailed Des to the cross if he'd had time? His mind, despite the painful headache, was beginning to kick into action. They were going to find Shea's primary crime scene, he was confident of it. Morgan was going to be happy to see him, and they were going to spend the rest of their life together. He'd made up his mind: he didn't want to be apart from her – Marc had torn them apart yesterday, well he hadn't won anything, in fact all it had done was prove to Ben that he loved her more than he'd ever realised, and regardless of whether they were allowed to work in the same office, they could still be together. He would go back on Response if he had to; it didn't matter what job he did as long as he had Morgan to share his life with him.

FORTY

Morgan had spent a pleasant enough morning scouring the beaches of north Walney before returning to the office. She was wearing a hoody, leggings and trainers for a change, after Ben's teasing, instead of her trusty Docs. Looking for those bloody geraniums and not finding any, she had been in the company of a detective called Adele Dean and they'd gotten along well, but she missed her team. She missed Ben; they had parted so awkwardly and it had been a long night without him. Picking up her phone she looked around to see who was in the huge open-plan office. This station was only a couple of years old, and the entire thing was one big floor on each level, only a few separate offices for different departments. She was the only one here; she hadn't even realised the others had left.

'Hey.'

'Hey, you. Are you okay?'

His deep voice sounded so comforting; she closed her eyes. 'This is a disaster; I'm not staying here tonight. I'd rather travel each day, I miss you.'

'I missed you too. I'm on my way to Barrow with Bella. We could meet you if you're not busy.'

'Bella?'

'Doctor Burrows.'

She smiled. 'I don't know if I can. There's another briefing when everyone comes back, maybe you could join in.'

'I doubt it, I'm here unofficially. I'm supposed to be on compassionate leave.'

'Damn, I forgot. How are you holding up, any news on Des or Milly?'

'No, Will is attending the post-mortem, which I'm relieved about to be honest. He knows I'm on my way here, but I'm trying to keep under the radar in case Marc finds out and tries to make things difficult.'

'I don't get it, why has he suddenly got a bee in his bonnet about us? It's not as if our relationship gets in the way of our work because it doesn't, not one bit.'

'I don't know, Morgan, something shady is going on, but I'll sort him out when we have Des's killer in custody and Milly home with her parents.'

She let out a sigh. 'We've been searching all morning and haven't found anywhere suitable where he could have kept Shea, and there's no sign of those bloody flowers either.'

He laughed, and she felt her heart warm at the sound of it.

'I'm beginning to think this is some kind of wild goose chase, maybe he knows where the flowers grow and purposely planted that pollen on Shea to make us waste precious hours searching the wrong place.'

'Damn it.'

'What?'

'What if you're right? We might be looking at this the wrong way. He can't have taken Des far, he would be a lot harder to drive to a deserted beach, murder him in his car then drive his body back and risk getting all the way to Rydal with it in his car. We're missing something and I can't bloody think what it is.'

'We're missing everything, none of it makes any sense.

What if Des's killer isn't the same as Shea's killer? What if Shea and Milly have been taken by the same guy, but Des's killer is someone completely different? He doesn't fit at all with the pattern of the other victims – young attractive women.'

'Why chop off his hair if it was a different killer though? That detail hasn't been released to the press. Maybe he could have seen or found something in the church, though, that meant the killer had to act?'

She stood up; she couldn't sit still any longer. Walking towards the stairs she began to make her way down them; she needed fresh air to make her brain think. She walked out of the double security doors, into the spacious, busy front office and out of the sliding glass doors into the car park. She could smell the salty sea air, even though she couldn't see it. She stopped looking around trying to figure out how she could smell the sea.

Ben let out a long groan.

'I don't even know where to go with this. I feel like a fish out of water not being able to work from the office. It's ridiculous.'

'Should I meet you for lunch when you've finished?'

'Yes, I'll ring you when we've had a look around. Bye, Morgan.'

He ended the call, and she knew he was going to be driven to distraction trying to figure out what was going on. The area surrounding the station was on a business park, surrounded by a steep grassy hill. As she turned to go back inside, she recognised the white pickup from the airport security; it was slowly driving around. She lifted a hand and waved not knowing if the guy driving it would have a clue who she was or remember her, but he smiled and waved back.

Adele came out of the station with a file tucked under her arm. 'You, okay?'

She looked at her; too tired and stressed out to lie she shook her head.

'Not really, I don't know why I'm here. I feel as if I'm some

naughty schoolkid who has been sent away and blamed for
something I didn't do.'

'Yeah, it's not right if you ask me. Why don't you go find a
Fed rep and ask them where you stand? Ours is called Smithy,
he's usually in the canteen.'

'Thanks, I will. Hey, why are the airport security guards
patrolling this area?'

'They cover all of the BAE area and this one too; it's a huge
area to keep secure.'

'Oh right, where's the beach from here? I can smell the salt
in the air, but can't see or hear the sea.'

Adele pointed to the grassy banking. 'On the other side of
that, well it's more like the channel on this side and not an
actual beach you can sit on. But the sea comes in, that's why you
can smell it. Walney is directly opposite.'

'Do you need me to do anything?'

'To be honest, not really. I've told Will that we've come up
blank searching for a hiding place for Shea and Milly. We need
something more than what we have.'

'Yeah, I know. I was just thinking that.'

Adele got into her car, and Morgan went back inside the
station to go in search of Smithy, not that she needed anyone's
permission to return to Rydal Falls. She could go back when she
wanted; if she wasn't needed here and there was nothing for her
to do, there was no point in her being stuck in Barrow.

FORTY-ONE

He came out of his bedroom to the smell of liver and onions, and he cringed; he hated it with a passion, but Julia loved it and he couldn't for the life of him tell her, so that was that. She really was a Saint; and she'd married a Sinner. He wished not for the first time that she'd leave. He wouldn't even be a little bit bothered because then he wouldn't have to keep the door to this room padlocked. Not that she really seemed to have any interest after he'd told her not to disturb him, that he was working on his project. She probably thought he was writing a book. He often threw that one at her, told her that she mustn't go in his special office because he'd never be able to finish his memoir if she did. She was such a good person she never doubted him. If it had been the other way around, the minute she left the house he'd have busted the lock and been snooping around. Taking the key from his pocket he opened the door, careful to bolt it behind him. He didn't want her to see what was pinned to these walls, the photographs he took. He turned to the desk where he sat down on the leather chair bought for a tenner from the charity shop. It creaked and groaned but held his weight. It was old, but it was comfortable. He stared at the photographs on his wall, his eyes hungrily moving from one to the other, his smile one of complete satisfaction. If only he could get closer to her without giving it away, but he didn't want to risk that just yet.

He'd almost had the chance on Sunday, so near yet so far. He hadn't expected her to be there walking around like that. So carefree and untroubled. He knew she'd been working, but still it was almost too much to bear seeing her within touching distance and him being unable to touch her. He'd wanted to reach out and feel her skin with the tips of his fingers, brush them along her arm. Even better, run them along the back of her neck through her silky hair. He stopped what he was doing, ashamed of the thoughts he had about her when he could hear Julia downstairs.

Reaching out he plucked the enlarged photograph of her from the wall, pricking his finger on the pin. 'Ouch.' He lifted it to his mouth, sucking the end of it. He was hot, and it wasn't his fault – it was hers, she made him feel this way and he couldn't control it. He was going to have to do something with the other girl soon; he could only keep her for so long, it was too risky. He wanted to move her tonight, take her to her final resting place. He'd need to check he could though. It was a shame he couldn't use the church again, but even he wasn't that stupid. The police would have it under surveillance, but he could take her home or as near to home as he could get without getting caught.

He could hear Julia moving around below. Maybe it was time to get rid of her for good too. That way he wouldn't have to risk breaking his neck to get his girls to their hiding place. If he made one of the rooms soundproof and brought them in through the garage in the dead of the night, they could be kept here. He liked the sound of that. It was a lot more appealing than the place he was using now. A plan began to form in his mind; he had so much to do and so little time to do it.

FORTY-TWO

The briefing wasn't too busy, not what Morgan had expected. Will had dialled in on Teams. Smithy had told her that she could go back as long as Will said he didn't need her to keep up the staffing levels. He also agreed that Marc was being an arse-hole, but advised her to do things properly so she didn't make things awkward for herself. Will looked stressed, no wonder, he'd been plucked from his place of work, given a dead detective and a missing girl to find and here she was feeling sorry for herself. This made her realise how selfish she was being. She sat up straighter. Adele was talking Will through the searches they'd made this morning for Shea Wilkinson's primary crime scene.

'I have a theory.'

Will's face paused on the huge smart TV in front of them, and all eyes turned to look at her.

'I'm listening, Morgan.'

'What if this is all some big game to him and he never brought Shea or Milly here, he didn't keep them on Walney? Lots of the lakes have shingle and narrow beaches, look at Buttermere and Windermere.'

'*But the forensic botanist pinpointed a specific area on Walney where the samples are from.*'

'I know, but how do we not know that he deliberately planted the samples to mislead us? For all we know he could have a bucket of the sandy soil from the beach on the floor where he keeps them captive. He could also have planted the pollen too; I watched a YouTube video last night and it's possible to get the pollen out of a geranium plant. We might be searching in the wrong place.'

Will buried his face into his hands, and she felt bad, but she couldn't ignore it. The warning signals were there, like a red flag to a bull. They had combed this island and not found anything, so they had to consider that Milly wasn't here at all. Morgan had suspected something didn't add up, and now she had to figure out where Des came into all of this. She was thinking about Theo again: he lived alone, he had the keys to the church, he had access to the church grounds and would know when it was a good time to be sneaking around in the dark. He also knew who Des was, had been talking to the pair of them on Sunday, as well as Milly.

'Sir, did you speak to Theo Edwards? Also, who found Des?'

'*Yes, we've interviewed him, and he didn't have anything that raised any red flags. He was very sincere and understanding about being brought in. He said he had nothing to hide and would like to get his hands on whoever had hurt Shea. Then apologised and said he wasn't a violent man, but he still had feelings and seeing her body would send anyone over the edge. He's charming, there's no doubt about that, apart from that I think it's a case of the wrong place at the wrong time. Whoever this killer is probably chose the church as a dump site long before Theo turned up, well that's my theory. As for Des, it was a call from the caretaker of the church. He'd gone to open up, and well you know the rest.*'

'How old is he, the caretaker?'

'I'd be lying if I said he wasn't a day over eighty.'

'I wanted to be there; I wanted to question him with you, Theo I mean. I could have been the friendly face he thinks he can trust; you could have been the bad cop.'

'I know, Morgan, and I'm sorry but he's been released, and Marc was insistent that none of the Rydal team go near him, so he can't say he's been victimised.'

It was her turn to close her eyes, momentarily. When she looked at Will she nodded, not trusting herself to speak because as she kept reminding herself none of this was his doing.

'Let me speak with Claire, see what she thinks. I'll ring you, okay, if she thinks we need to bring him back?'

'Thanks.'

At least he hadn't said he was going to ask Marc; Claire was okay and knew her stuff. There were no mind games going on with her.

Morgan left the briefing with the pressing feeling that they were missing something completely. Booking herself a police car, she went outside to the huge car park – it was at least ten times the size of the one back home. She found the car and got inside it. Ben was looking around with Bella, so she would go and meet them, see what they thought. She used her radio this time to call him. He gave her the directions, and she headed that way. All the time her mind was working overtime trying to figure this mess out. She saw an unfamiliar Land Rover parked on a grass verge where Ben said they would be. She parked behind it and got out; the white pickup Roy had been driving on their last visit to the airfield pulled alongside her, but a different guard was driving.

'Afternoon, can I ask what you're doing?'

She looked at him, he was younger than her and had a

cocky, self-assured attitude. Pulling out the lanyard she kept
tucked underneath her shirt, she flashed her warrant card at
him. 'Detective Constable Morgan Brookes, we're investigating
a missing person.'

'What, around here? They must be desperate to come here.
If they've chosen to go missing, then they don't want to be
found if you ask me, probably walked into the sea.'

She stared at him; he was grinning at her as if he was funny.

'No, we don't think they've gone into the sea. We're looking
for places they could hide out in.'

He sucked his bottom lip inside the top one, closing his eyes
momentarily, and she thought that he was possibly the most
annoying person she'd ever met.

'Around here?'

She nodded.

'There's a few of the farmer's barns and stuff over the far
end of the airfield. Have you checked those?'

'No, we didn't know about them. Roy drove us around the
airfield then escorted us back out.'

He let out a snort, followed by a loud laugh. 'Bloody Roy.
He's a lazy bastard; he won't have told you in case you asked
him to take you to them. Do you want me to show you where
they are? Hop in, it won't take long.'

She wondered if she should, but as she looked around there
was no sign of Ben or Bella, and she decided they must be down
on the beach.

'Go on then, if you don't mind.'

He shrugged. 'Nothing better to do, it's no problem. I'm
Andy.'

She hopped in, a little uneasy that she was going off with
this guy when no one knew where she was, but also desperate to
know if these barns could be the place they were looking for.
He began to do a ten-point turn to reverse the truck and turn
around.

'Thanks, Andy, are we not going through the airport?'

'Can't get to them from there. You can see them just, but if you want to take a look inside, we'll have to go through the farmer's land. Old Bill won't mind, he's used to us coming and going when we do a full-on perimeter check.'

He drove back down the narrow lane until he reached a gate, jumped out and opened it. She texted Ben, just so he knew where she was. The track through the side of the field was bumpy and she had to hold on to the door handle to stop herself banging her head.

'Sorry, it's a bit rough. You'd think he'd have put a proper road in, but I guess it didn't bother him and he's too old now. He only keeps a few sheep, got rid of his cattle a few years ago.'

'I guess farming is tough enough for people our age, must be difficult when you're older. It's not the kind of job I could do.'

He glanced at her. 'Really, yet you can be a detective? That must be really hard. I'd love to be one; I always wanted to be a copper, but I never passed the paper sift. I had to settle for being a security guard, only got that because my uncle is one and he got me the job, you know, he put a good word in for me. It's how it works around here – it's not what you know it's who you know. If you ever get fed up chasing the bad guys, you could come work here.'

She laughed. 'Thanks, I'll bear that in mind.'

He turned a corner and there to the side of him was a run-down farmhouse. There were no cars outside. Behind it, set back, were a few ramshackle barns. Morgan felt the skin on her arms prickle. This would be the perfect place to hide someone, especially if the farmer didn't use them and was too old to be bothered checking on them. Andy carried on driving as far as he could then stopped the pickup. Morgan opened the door and got out.

'Hey, should I come with you just in case you need a hand or something?'

'No, it's okay. I'll shout you if I do – if you wait here that would be great.'

He nodded, and she smiled at him. She would feel better if he stayed in the cab of the truck, as she didn't know who he was or his background.

She walked towards the first barn, where the door was ajar. Taking out her phone she pressed the torch button and illuminated the darkness she could see through the gap. Squeezing inside she shone the light around. It smelled of hay inside here, nothing else. It was full of the stuff too. No hay had been found on Shea Wilkinson, so it wasn't this one. Turning around she walked straight into Andy and shrieked.

'Sorry, I felt bad letting you go inside on your own. Not much of a hero, waiting in the pickup for you. No wonder they never wanted me on the force.'

'Christ, you scared the shit out of me.'

He was holding the palms of his hands up. 'Not as much as you scared me screaming like that.'

She laughed and he joined in. Composing herself she said, 'It's not this one.'

He nodded and turned around, and she followed him across the field to the next one. This one had a thick chain around the handles, secured with a padlock.

'He must keep whatever farming equipment he has left inside here.'

'How old is he?'

'At least eighty I'd say.'

'Does he have a son, younger brother?'

'Not that I know of. His wife isn't too well, it's just the pair of them. They're really nice, and if you ask me, they should be living out their retirement in one of the chalets over on West Shore Park instead of worrying about this place, but he won't leave, told me they'll be carrying him out in his coffin.'

'Aw, bless him, that's sweet and yet so sad.'

She couldn't imagine an eighty-year-old man being their killer, although she couldn't rule it out completely. She remembered that the church caretaker was in his eighties too. They walked around the perimeter of the barn. Morgan pressed her ear to a gap in the wall to listen for any signs of life inside there. It was silent. She shouted, 'Milly, it's the police, are you in there?'

There was no reply, no shuffling sounds or signs of anyone trying to get her attention.

'You could come back later when Bill's home. He'll open up for you and show you around.'

The disappointment must have shown on her face, and she nodded. 'Thanks, I will.'

'I'm sure you'll find her. Milly. I'll keep an eye out and get the others too, and if we see her, we'll let you know.'

'That's very kind of you. Could you take me back to my car now, please?'

They climbed back into the pickup, Morgan feeling deflated because she'd really hoped that she would find Milly here. It was the perfect hideaway, so off the beaten track no one would ever know.

FORTY-THREE

Andy stopped the pickup back at Morgan's car, where she could see Ben and a woman who had the prettiest, pale pink hair she'd ever seen, which was in a topknot, strolling alongside of him.

'Busy here today, there were lots of officers here yesterday too.'

'I know, we're running out of time. Thank you for being so helpful, Andy, I really appreciate it.'

'No problem, glad to help. If you need anything come stand at the gates to the airport, someone should come see what's happening, well, unless it's Roy and he can be bothered to haul his backside off the chair.'

She laughed. 'I will, take care.'

She got out of the cab, and he waved as he drove off. She waved at Ben who broke into a jog leaving the woman behind. He pulled her into his arms, and she sighed; he smelled so good. She hugged him back, then they both pulled away remembering the woman, who was grinning at them both.

'Aw, that was sweet, it was like something out of a movie. How long have you two not seen each other?'

Ben blushed. 'Erm, around eighteen hours. Morgan, this is Doctor Isabelle Burrows.'

'Bella, please, and hi, Morgan, it's lovely to meet you.'

'You too, Bella, your hair is amazing. It's so pretty.'

'Why thank you, but so is yours. Is that copper colour your natural colour?'

Morgan nodded.

'You lucky thing, no need to be bleaching your hair to death when you have such gorgeous colour. I'm so envious, I love red hair.'

'Where have you been and who was that?' There was a genuine look of concern on Ben's face, even though he sounded like there may be a hint of something more.

'I've been here all morning, went back to the station then came looking for you and was stopped by Andy, one of the security guards, who asked who I was and what I was up to.'

Ben arched an eyebrow at her.

'Turns out he was pretty good; he took me to a farmhouse way off the beaten track with outbuildings to search for Milly. No sign of her, although one of the barns was tightly locked up, but there were no sounds coming from inside when I called out her name and told her the police were here.'

'You went off with a guy to some remote location without telling anyone?'

'Actually, I texted you to let you know. It was a spur of the moment thing. It got me thinking though, that what if there are other disused buildings that we have missed? And what if this is the wrong end of the island? Who says those flowers can't grow on the other side of it? Or what if he's cleverer than we're giving him credit for and has managed to get the pollen from those flowers to mislead us? I watched a YouTube video last night and it doesn't look that difficult to get pollen from a flower, I think even I could do it.'

Bella was nodding her head. 'I see what you mean. And I

can help with this, as I was explaining to Ben on the way here, there are certain differences between an artificially propagated plant, and one which has grown in the wild. As soon as I get back to my lab I'm going to have a detailed look at the petals that were found with Shea's body, that should show whether they came from a wild-collected flower or not.'

Ben spoke up. 'Okay, well getting that information should help, thanks, Bella. There's also the samples you've collected just now, hopefully we'll be able to get a solid match from them to the soil on Shea's feet and then we'll know the location she was kept for certain.'

Bella patted the side bag she was wearing and smiled.

Ben continued, 'I'll reserve judgement until we've got the results, but personally I think the killer is operating from somewhere far closer to home, because I just don't see the point of him coming all this way and back again. It's far too risky.'

Morgan made a frustrated noise. 'Unless you're cocky and full of yourself, have a job in the police that makes you seem trustworthy and if you got stopped, they would apologise and wave you on.'

'What are you saying?'

'I don't know, I guess Marc seems to fit the profile of each maniac we're looking for.'

She laughed, but Ben didn't. 'The man's an arsehole, full of himself and up to no good within the department, but a killer? What would he get out of killing Des?'

'I don't know, he got to split the team up, didn't he? Maybe that's his ultimate goal, to tear apart our team then move on to the next. Look, we don't have these results yet, and Milly is missing *now.*'

'You think we should go check out his house, see if he has any sheds or a greenhouse full of Walney geraniums?'

Bella nodded thoughtfully. 'If the flowers are propagated

rather than wild, that would certainly be something to look out for.'

'Worth a shot.'

The look Ben gave her when he realised that she was being serious was nothing short of bewildered. Morgan sighed, maybe she was overreacting and being super sensitive because he'd sent her here without a moment's hesitation when he hadn't got what he wanted.

'We need to go back home.'

'I know, but how?'

Bella smiled at them. 'Well, I need to talk to whoever is running the investigation and, seeing as how I'm here because you requested me, Sergeant Matthews, it looks like the perfect excuse to go back, and you can introduce me. Then I could keep your boss busy, whilst you go have a snoop around his house, if only to put your mind at rest and rule him out.'

Morgan grinned at Bella. She liked her a lot – she was down to earth and on her wavelength.

'You're as bad as she is. Please don't encourage her, at this rate we're all going to be jobless.'

'If it's playing on your mind, it needs looking in to, right? I won't be able to confirm whether the petals are from wild or artificially grown flowers, or test the soil samples, until I get back to Wales, and the girl will be in danger all that time. It seems logical to me to get this over and done with. Morgan is right, anyone with a little knowledge or help from a quick internet search can get pollen from a flower – it's not that difficult.'

'Why do I get the feeling I'm being set up?'

'You two go back to the station. I have to take this car back to Barrow station, and I could tell Adele I'm finishing early then drive home and go straight to his house. If you two keep him busy I'll do the snooping. He can't punish me any more than he already has. I literally have nothing to lose and don't care anyway.'

'That's what I'm afraid of, Morgan. I don't for one minute think that any of this is what's going on by the way.'

'But you'll do it just so we have peace of mind.'

'I don't want you going anywhere near his house on your own.'

'I'll ask Amy to come with me.'

'That doesn't make me feel any better.'

'Take it or leave it. If we find a shed full of sand and Milly Blake you won't be so unhappy about it then.'

'Be careful and if I phone you to tell you not to go because we haven't found him, keep away, promise?'

She smiled at him, but they both knew that she wouldn't because she was far too stubborn for her own good.

She waited for them to get into Bella's monstrous Land Rover, and when she had expertly reversed until she could turn the 4x4 around, Morgan got into the car and did a much simpler three-point turn. She still needed to check out the other barn at the farm to put her mind at rest; maybe Bill might know of somewhere else around here that could be used if Marc's house was a dead end. Not sure if she wanted to drive to Rydal Falls, then back here again, she decided that she would if she had to because it wasn't about her: it was about finding Milly Blake and bringing Shea Wilkinson's and Des's killer to justice.

FORTY-FOUR

Morgan dropped the hire car off and nipped inside to see if she could find Adele, but there was no sign of her, or of anyone. She sent a quick email to say that she'd had to go back to collect something from Rydal Falls and would see her tomorrow. Then she left Barrow station and headed along the A590 back home. Her mind was trying to piece everything together so that it made sense, but all it kept coming up with was a complete jumbled mess. She phoned Amy just before she set off, but there was no answer and she figured that this was really between her and Marc. For some reason he had decided to make her life a misery, not Amy's, there was little point dragging her into this mess. She wasn't scared of Marc; he could turn on the charm with the best of them and was able to disarm most people with his warm smile and handsome face. She didn't know if she was bitter because of the way he'd treated her or if she believed he could genuinely be responsible for the murders. What would he get out of that? She reached the outskirts of Rydal Falls, and though she knew that Marc lived along here she realised she didn't know where. Pulling over to the side she rang Ben.

'Where are you?'

'Just about to introduce Bella to Marc.'

'Where does he live, I'm not sure.'

'You're not going to believe this.'

'Try me.'

'I just checked with personnel; he's renting your old apartment.'

Morgan felt the wind knocked out of her; she blew out her cheeks as she sank back against the headrest of her car.

'He's never.'

'Sure enough, don't you think that's weird?'

'I don't know, it's a nice apartment and I moved out just before he appeared on the scene. It's a small town, maybe that was the only one available.'

She was coming up with valid excuses and none of them felt right to her. She had this sticky, uneasy feeling across her chest.

'I think it's weird. You didn't have a shed or outhouse there, did you? You could ask Emily about him if she's still living there. She'll have a better idea than we do. He keeps his personal life very close to his chest. He told us he'd had an affair and his family left him; maybe he has moved his lover in with him.'

'No, no shed, nothing of the sort. I'll have a drive past just to make sure.'

She didn't tell Ben about the huge cellars that ran underneath the old Georgian house. The door to the steps down there was always kept padlocked shut, and the guy who rented it to her in the first place told her it was where the owner stored the maintenance stuff, tools, paints, that kind of thing. There was a small window that led into the cellar around the back of the building, though she had never in her life thought about going down there. For one thing she didn't particularly like attics or cellars, because what she did like was horror movies and almost everything bad happened in them.

She drove through the gates and felt a moment of sadness for the apartment that used to be her home. She had barely been able to afford it, yet had loved it. It had been the complete opposite of the two up, two down house that she'd grown up in with Sylvia and Stan. If she hadn't had such a run of bad luck here, she'd probably still be renting it, or would she? Ben was everything she could ever dream about, she loved him completely, but she'd also loved being independent and able to do her own thing whenever she wanted. She parked her car in the empty drive; she could always tell Marc she was visiting Emily if he turned up. She hadn't seen her for a while, and they were friends. Maybe not close friends, but friends and neighbours all the same.

Hurrying around the back to where the small window was, Morgan knelt down on the gravel and tried to peer inside. The pane of glass was filthy, the inside murky; even when she tried to clean a spot with the sleeve of her hoody, she couldn't see anything inside. Trying to get it open, it wouldn't budge at all, it was shut tight from inside. If she wanted to get in, she was going to have to break it. That was a last resort. Standing up she decided to try the obvious first and go inside, try the cellar door just in case it had been left open.

But the front door was closed, so she buzzed Emily's apartment. There was no answer. The top floor apartment hadn't been let when she left, but she tried it anyway. Surprised when a male voice grunted, *'Yeah.'*

'Police, can you buzz me in, please?'

'Yeah, you're not coming to see me, are you?'

She had no idea who he was. 'No, middle apartment.'

The door clicked and she pushed it open, wondering why the guy in the top flat had asked that. She didn't have long – being caught snooping around might not be so easy to explain if Marc turned up. She glanced at the oak stairs and banister where she had been hung from and almost choked to death by a deranged killer, a cold shiver running down her spine at the thought of it. The cellar door was tucked away underneath the staircase. She stepped behind it, out of sight, and was about to twist the doorknob when the sound of a key being inserted into the front door froze her to the spot. She pushed herself back, trying to blend in with the walls she froze, her car if this was Marc he was bound to realise who it belonged to. She didn't really have time to chat with Emily, and if Marc found her here, he'd think she'd lost it. Footsteps crossed the polished marble tiles; whoever it was didn't run up the stairs. Emily always ran up and down them, so it wasn't her. Then she heard another key go into the lock of her apartment – she corrected herself, her old apartment. Scared to breathe out she waited until the door closed, thankful that the entrance hall was huge and not enclosed, otherwise he'd be able to smell her new perfume that she'd liberally spritzed herself with this morning. So Scandal was pink and pretty, so nice she'd followed a woman around Boots in Kendal after she'd walked past her and had to ask her what she was wearing.

The door closed and she felt her breath release. Twisting the round brass knob it didn't budge – she should have known it wouldn't be so easy. Peering around the corner she made a dash for it, hoping the landlord hadn't installed cameras, and then she could have kicked herself. Her Landlord had put a Ring doorbell on her front door as a precaution due to all the criminal damage that had happened when she was there. Doing the only thing that would explain her presence here, she walked up the stairs towards Emily's front door, her fingers crossed that she wasn't home because this would be awkward: not only had they been neighbours, but they had also shared the same taste in men. Emily had all but thrown herself at Ben and they'd gone out a few times. Morgan had told herself it didn't matter, but deep down she'd been devastated. When there was no reply, she went back downstairs and strolled out, purposely not looking across at the camera on her old front door. Outside there was still only her car, so who had gone into Marc's apartment?

Leaving the front of the converted Georgian house, Morgan went back to the cellar window, looking around for a rock. She pulled her hoody off. Picking up a rockery stone she wrapped it inside of her top, swung back her arm and hit the pane of glass with a satisfying crack that was muffled enough not to cause any alarm. The glass was so old the crack right across the middle began to creak as a multitude of tiny fissures began to appear on it, running away from the central crack. Morgan watched transfixed at how pretty it looked, a bit like a spider web of glass. And then it fell in on itself with a louder crash than she would have liked. Holding her breath, she felt like a criminal and then it struck her: she was one – she had just caused criminal damage to a window that wasn't hers. Using her rolled up hoody to make sure there were no sharp shards of glass sticking out, she held up her phone torch and shone it around. It was very dark inside and very dusty.

'Milly, are you down here? It's the police.'

She was met with a silence so all-consuming that she knew this had been a big mistake. There was no turning back now, though. She'd gone this far she may as well make sure *dead girls don't make a sound*. She froze wondering who had said that and then realised it had been her own whispering voice. Lowering herself into the gaping dark hole before she changed her mind, she found a footing on a rickety chest of drawers and had to use every inch of her balancing skills to stop it from falling over with her weight on top of it. She managed. Scrambling to jump off it she pulled her phone out of her bra where she'd tucked it and shone the light around, hoping to God there was no one crouched in the corner watching her. There wasn't, but there was no sign of Milly either. Walking around through the boxes and old, broken pieces of furniture, she concentrated on the floor to see if there were any buckets of sand that had been tipped over. There was nothing and the more she looked the harder it was to see because the tears of frustration pooling in the corners were making her blind. She was angry and tired, it wasn't fair. Shea hadn't deserved what happened to her, neither had Des and if they didn't find her soon Milly was sure to suffer the same fate, and Morgan didn't think she could take it. She made her way back to the broken window, the smallest pool of light shining through it showing her the way. The cellar was huge, damp and she was desperate to get out of it. Pulling herself up on to the chest of drawers the light suddenly disappeared, and a dark shadow filled the empty space. Morgan felt her heart skip several beats and, opening her mouth to scream, a familiar voice asked:

'What the hell are you doing down there?'

FORTY-FIVE

Cain was blocking all of the light with his huge frame. He bent down and offered her his hand, which she took, letting him pull her out of the broken window.

'What are you doing here?'

'Report of a break-in in progress by a Mrs Howard, who is visiting from Manchester. She said there was a strange woman sneaking around in the apartment block then heard breaking glass.'

Morgan was standing up now, her mouth open in surprise.

'Let's get you out of here, should we? I want you to drive to The Coffee Pot, if it's still open, and wait for me there. I'll handle Mrs Howard; you need to leave before her husband turns up, if he's who I think he is.'

She did as she was told, no arguing. She was well and truly going to have to stay working in Barrow now; Marc wouldn't let her anywhere near him or the office.

Her hands were shaking. She'd been so scared that it was the same person who had Milly, she'd been about to pick up a piece of the broken glass and slice whoever it was if she had to.

Survival was her main objective, she was no good to Milly Blake if she was dead. Her knees shaking and hands trembling, Morgan got back into her car and drove away on auto pilot. She knew where the café was with her eyes closed.

Taking a seat she waited for Cain, not sure what he'd want but ordering him a latte when the waitress took her order. The café was empty: it was almost closing time. After what felt like hours he walked in. He'd removed his body armour and was wearing a lightweight, black jacket on top of his uniform. Sitting opposite her he picked up the latte.

'What the hell was that about, Morgan?'

'I got a little carried away.'

'You got a lot carried away, not a little. You'll be pleased to know that Mrs Howard had been unable to get hold of her husband, who is a very important policeman. I'm assuming she's talking about Marc and if she is, bless her, she's delusional. Wherever he is he's blissfully unaware of what just happened.'

She shook her head. 'They have a Ring doorbell; he will be able to watch the footage of me in the hallway then going upstairs.'

'Doorbell is broken; she said it's never worked properly since they moved in. She saw you going past the window outside.'

'What did you tell her?'

'That you used to live there and needed to get hold of some important documents that had been mistakenly put in the cellar for storage. That you're very sorry and are good friends with the landlord, who told you it was okay to break the window because he couldn't get there to help you.'

'She believed that?'

He shrugged. 'I have a way with words.'

Morgan laughed, feeling all the tension and pressure lift from her shoulders.

'Shit, that was close.'

'Too close. I don't know what she's going to tell him and if he'll put two and two together that it was you or not, though. So, tell me, Brookes, what the hell were you doing down in the dark, creepy cellar?'

'I thought he might have Milly Blake down there and that it was where he'd taken Shea and Des.'

Cain held up his hands. 'Whoa, that's a big leap from him being a dickhead to a serial killer.'

'Yeah, well I was willing to try anything. I can't give up on finding Milly. Marc has been acting shifty. He fits the profile of male and strong, plus we thought he'd killed Shirley Kelley when he first arrived.'

He laughed. 'It's a pretty vague profile. You really don't like him, do you?'

She grinned. 'It was worth checking out, sorry you got dragged into it. Let me buy you lunch.'

He nodded, picking up the menu. 'You know the way to forgiveness is through a man's stomach, don't you? Seriously though, Morgan, you need to be careful. He's already got it in for you and you're not helping matters.'

'I know. Did you see Ben at the station?'

'I did and who was that hot piece of pink-haired stuff with him? Now, she had a smile that made my heart do a back flip.'

'Cain, that's Doctor Burrows, the forensic botanist from Wales.'

'Bloody hell, couldn't he have found one in Manchester? Wales is a bit far to travel to declare my undying love for her.'

'I'll put in a good word for you if you like.'

'Nah, I'm good I was only joking. I'll have a ham and cheese toastie on white bread, please.'

She stood up, going to the counter to order his sandwich. It was the least she could do.

Cain ate his toastie, shoving the last piece into his mouth when a call came in for an RTC. He jumped up. 'Can you maybe try and stay out of trouble for a little while?'

'I'll try, thanks again.'

He leaned over and ruffled her hair. 'You really are like an annoying little sister.' Winked at her and was out of the door, jogging back to the van he'd parked a little further up the street.

The waitress was hovering around, and Morgan realised she wanted her to leave; she'd already turned the 'closed' sign over in the door. She stood up, she was bone weary, the weight of not knowing where the hell Milly Blake was weighing her down. She took a five pound note out of the cash she had on her from her pocket and tucked it under her coffee cup.

'Sorry, you should have told us to leave.'

She smiled at her. 'Don't be daft. Are you both looking for Milly?'

'Yes, we are. Do you know her?'

She nodded. 'Yes, she's my friend. It's her birthday party in a few days. Well it should be.'

'I know, we're trying our best to find her so she's home in time for it.'

The teenage girl's eyes filled with tears. 'Good because she's so lovely. I don't want anything bad to happen to her. It's not fair, she is so kind and always helps everyone. I hate this place, there's always something awful happening to someone.'

Morgan had an overwhelming urge to reach out and hug her, even though she only ever hugged Cain or Ben. Instead, she reached out and patted her arm.

'Don't give up hope.'

The girl dabbed at her eyes with the sleeve of her shirt, nodding.

'Thanks, I won't if you don't.'

'That's a deal.'

She walked out of the café, closing the door behind her and heard the sound of the girl locking it. She thought about going to the station and decided to go home instead; she was in enough trouble without adding anything to it. She would wait for Ben to come to her, hopefully with some good news.

FORTY-SIX

Marc was talking to Bella, and Ben was watching his every movement and expression, though he didn't seriously think he had anything to do with the murders and abduction, and he hoped Morgan was okay. His radio was in the car, so he was oblivious to the call that had come in for the break-in in progress, otherwise he might have passed out on the spot. Will walked in, his face ashen, and Ben realised he'd just come out of Des's post-mortem, and suddenly it hit him just how messed up this whole thing was. He felt the room tip on its side as everything started spinning.

'Hey, Ben, are you okay?'

He could hear Will's voice talking to him, but it sounded as if he was talking through cotton wool. Ben nodded slowly. He needed to get out of here, get some fresh air, take a break – do something. He turned around and leaning against the wall made his way out into the corridor. Not trusting his legs to carry him down the stairs he took the lift and walked out into the car park. The sun was setting across the fells of Rydal Falls, the air had a definite nip to it and he didn't have a clue where Milly Blake was or who had killed Des or Shea Wilkinson. There was a memorial bench for the officers and staff who had died whilst in service in front of a small patch of grass, where someone had planted some rosebushes. He sat down on the wooden bench, running his fingers along the carved names; how strange to think that Des's name would need to be added to them. There was a bunch of white roses placed at one end – someone had left them for Des. He leaned forward, burying his head in his hands. He didn't know whether he was going to be sick, pass out or cry; probably all three. He wanted to rewind time, stop Des and Morgan going to the church fair. If they hadn't gone would Des still be alive? Would Milly Blake have made it home? It all seemed to hinge around the church, and the fete: how did they manage to take Des and Milly within such a small timescale? His phone began to ring.

'Matthews.'

'I'm so sorry, Ben, I had no idea when I came into work that Desmond Black was your Des.'

'Thanks, Declan, of course you didn't.'

'That dishy William told me that you and Morgan had been removed from the investigation, what the hell? If anyone can figure out why your colleague is lying in one of my fridges then it's you two. What's up with your boss? He needs a boot up his arse and a wake-up call.'

Ben smiled, he would indeed like to stick his boot up his arse or even better one of Morgan's Docs would do a superior job.

'It's a mess, I don't know what the hell is going on, Declan. I feel absolutely useless and I'm so angry with the world right now.'

'Where's Morgan?'

'He shipped her off to work in Barrow, said we couldn't work together and sent me home on compassionate leave.'

'Holy Mother of God, that man must have a death wish himself. What is he thinking?'

Ben let out the longest sigh. 'I have no idea, to top it all off I have double vision and feel as if I'm about to pass out.'

'Should I call an ambulance? Where are you?'

He closed his eyes, the pain behind them too intense. 'No, I'll be okay.'

'Where are you?'

'On a bench in the station car park.'

'Stay there, don't move a muscle.'

Ben doubled over as a sharp pain pulsated through his brain. He felt the phone slip from his grasp as his fingers went numb and then everything went black as he slumped to one side.

Cain was driving the van past the front of the station when he saw Ben collapse and slammed on the brakes. The car behind nearly rear-ended him and blared their horn as he jumped out and ran across to Ben.

'Control we have an officer down in the front car park, ambulance required now.'

He didn't listen to their reply before lifting Ben's limp body down onto the floor and checking to see that he was still breathing. His complexion was grey, his eyes were unfocused, but he was breathing. He rolled him into the recovery position. The pink-haired woman came running over to them.

'Oh my God, what's happened?'

She began to loosen the top buttons on his shirt and undo his tie; a few officers that had been in the report writing room came running out. He needed to call Morgan, but how was he going to break this to her without her collapsing too? Sirens and the flashing blue lights of an ambulance as it came racing around the corner made him feel better. The paramedics ran across to take over. One of them looked at Cain.

'You're lucky, we were on our way to Keswick, there's no other ambulances available.'

'I'd have carried him to the hospital if you hadn't been here. Is he okay?'

Cain knew this was a stupid question, they had only just arrived, but they couldn't lose Des and Ben in the space of twenty-four hours. Morgan would be devastated beyond belief, they all would be. Ben was the good guy, the great boss, the one you wanted on your side when the shit hit the fan, which it so often did. Ben let out a groan, and Cain looked up to the sky and whispered *thank you, God.*

'What's his name?'

'Ben.'

'Ben, can you hear me, Ben? Hello, Ben.'

Ben's eyes fluttered open; he looked dazed. 'Yes, I can. I'm okay, let me get up.'

Cain shook his head. 'You look like shit, stay where you are and do as you're told. I'll go find Morgan, we'll come to the hospital.'

The paramedic looked up. 'Westmorland General.'

Cain gave him a thumbs up and jumped back in his van, reversing and driving off at speed to go and find Morgan. He'd only left her ten minutes ago but she wouldn't still be at the café, it should have closed by now.

He drove to Ben's house, where Morgan was pale faced and running back towards her car. He stopped and she jumped in.

'He's okay, he's talking.'

'What happened? My heart is going to burst out of my chest. Declan phoned to say Ben was telling him he felt ill then the line went dead. Is he okay, please tell me he's okay?'

'Morgan, calm down, he's talking. He also looks like death warmed up, but corpses can't talk so he's not too bad.'

She slumped back against the seat. 'Sorry.'

'I know, we're going to the hospital now. The paramedics

are with him, he's in the best hands. Deep breaths, I don't want you collapsing too. I can't cope with you lot at the best of times.'

She glanced at him, but he was smiling at her and she smiled back.

'Thank you.'

'You are very welcome, now hopefully it's nothing too serious and he just needs a check-up. Maybe a few weeks off to let his stress levels calm down or something like that.'

'I hope so.'

'Let's not tell him about the incident at your old house, eh? He doesn't need to know about it and, if Marc asks, tell him what I told his wife.'

She didn't argue with him. The last thing she needed was Marc suspending her for her crazy behaviour. Her heart was so heavy in her chest. They were no closer to finding Milly and now Ben had collapsed. Neither of them deserved this when they were doing their best to help.

FORTY-SEVEN

Milly stumbled as she was dragged along the path, gritty sand filling her white work shoes. They weren't suitable for walking along a beach path. She was blindfolded, but she could smell the salty tang of the sea air as it filled her nostrils. The path was bumpy, her feet kept slipping, and she realised she was walking on pebbles. Panic filled her lungs with a burning sensation. There were no beaches anywhere near Rydal Falls, the nearest were on the west coast or in Barrow. It was completely dark, so she knew that there was no daylight left, even though the blindfold enveloped her completely. When she'd woken briefly earlier, she had been able to see tiny shards of light that penetrated the thick material. She tripped and fell to her knees, letting out a grunt of pain as the small pebbles pressed into them. She was still wearing her uniform, no jeans or leggings to protect her legs.

'For Christ's sake be careful, you nearly pulled me over.'

The voice was soft, and there was a bit of an accent that she couldn't place. Clamping her teeth down on the thick band of material in her mouth, she tried to scream out in anger, but all that came out was a muffled 'humph' that was never going to be heard over the screeching of the gulls and the wind that was picking up by the second. She wanted to stay where she was, she didn't want to go any further because she knew it was pointless and dangerous. This man was a madman.

'Get up.'

She didn't move: he could go and fuck himself.

'I said get up.'

The words were growled in anger, and the boot that kicked her hard in her ribcage made her cry out against the gag as sharp splinters of burning hot pain radiated up her ribs. She felt a hand grip her hair in a tight fist as it curled itself around her ponytail and dragged her to her feet. She was winded and thought that he'd maybe cracked a rib because it hurt when she tried to breathe air in through her nose. Then he was dragging her along, tears filling her eyes, screams of pain filling her mouth and she couldn't do anything to let either of them free.

He dragged her in a standing position, and she wanted to hurt him so bad. She'd never hurt anyone in her life, but she realised that she would if she got the chance. She couldn't see, couldn't scream, couldn't use her hands to hit him, but she realised that she did have feet that weren't tied together. So if she could somehow pull down the blindfold, she could make a run for it. His grip was tight on her elbow, though, and she knew he was to the right of her and if she slowed down enough, he would be slightly in front. Without pausing to think she stopped dead, lifted her hands and pulled the blindfold down enough so she could see him. Then she lifted her foot, and swinging it back, she booted him from behind with as much power as she could. He stumbled forwards so she kicked him again even harder, despite her flimsy shoes and the pain in her toes. She felt a satisfying feeling as her foot landed square beneath his crotch and he fell forwards to his knees. Not waiting another second, Milly turned and ran. She had no idea where she was, but she could hear the waves in the distance. The pebbles underfoot were slippery and difficult to run on but she didn't care. She managed to pull the material from her mouth and began to scream as loud as she could. She didn't dare look back, just kept on running, her feet burning. Eventually she saw a field and didn't care that there was a metal fence with barbed wire. Climbing up it she threw herself over it, scraping and slicing the flesh on the palms of her hands. Despite the ripping, searing pains she kept on moving. There was a light in the distance, and she heard footsteps limping heavily behind her, but he was still on the stones, and she was on the grass.

'Help me, help me he's going to kill me.'

A voice in the direction of the light that was wavering around shouted, 'This way, I'm phoning the police. What the hell is going on?' Then much louder. 'I'm phoning the police.'

It was a man's voice; he sounded older a bit like her grandad.

'Come on, love, keep coming towards me.'

Her feet were in agony, the skin on the palms of her hands was in shreds but she kept on, until finally a tall figure loomed in front of her. Behind him was a tractor – it was the best thing she'd ever seen in her life. Milly felt her knees give way underneath her and she fell onto the hard grass behind her, where sheep were bleating.

The guy shone his torch onto her. 'You're safe now, don't worry, I won't let anything happen to you.' He was on his phone, which was clamped under one ear, and he put his arms under hers, lifting her gently.

'Can you climb up into the cab, love? We'll go to the house, you'll be safe there... Yes, I'm on north Walney near the airport. There's a young girl needs help, someone is chasing her. I'm taking her to my house now. I've let my dog off to go find him. That's right, Sandy Farm, yep, okay.'

She used the last of her energy to clamber up into the cab of the tractor, where she curled up in a ball on the floor. No idea who this man was, but grateful that he'd been there when she had needed him.

FORTY-EIGHT

Morgan was led through to the cubicles, horrified to see Ben wired up to so many different machines. His eyes were closed but he must have sensed that she was watching because he opened them and smiled at her.

'Hi.'

She rushed to sit next to him, grabbing hold of the hand that didn't have a pulse oximeter on it and the cannula.

'You scared me. How are you feeling?'

'Like shit, but I'm okay.'

She leaned over and pressed her lips to his cold forehead. It felt clammy.

'We haven't got time for this. Milly.'

'You have all the time in the world, the rest of us will figure it out. You need to rest, Ben, and take it easy.'

She watched as tears pooled in the corners of his eyes, but she knew he wouldn't cry in front of her. He blinked several times, then closed his eyes. She didn't want to leave him here, but she also knew they were running out of time to find Milly Blake alive.

The curtain opened and she was relieved to see Declan

standing there, still in his work scrubs, although he'd lost the white rubber boots. He stepped through, closing the curtain behind him.

'Christ, Ben, I don't know about you, but you almost gave me a coronary.' He looked over at the chart on the table next to Morgan and gave it the once-over. 'Well good news is you didn't have a heart attack, but it looks as if you've had some kind of atrial fibrillation according to these.'

Morgan looked at him.

'Serious, but not deadly. He may need surgery, but they can also stabilise him with a chemical cocktail of drugs and restore the heart's natural rhythm. Also, for the record, my current bit of stuff is a heart surgeon, so aren't you the lucky one? He's on his way here to make sure you're being well looked after. You can thank me later when you feel better. Until then I'm staying here to make sure you get the best care, so Morgan, I love you and Ben loves you, but don't you have work to do? I can't bear to see you sitting here looking so maudlin. What do you say, Ben?'

'I say yes, go do what you have to do but not on your own. I have my own personal doctor to keep an eye on me.'

'He does and do you know why? Because today was dreadful having to work on Des. There is no way on this earth I'm having you drop dead and end up on my table too, I can't take it. So, for now I'm keeping an eye on him and making sure he's going to be fit for duty as soon as he possibly can. I only have one request, Morgan.'

She couldn't help smiling at Declan; she loved him almost as much as she loved Ben. 'What would that be?'

'Don't do anything stupid that is going to endanger your life, because I can't be in two places at once and you don't want to finish your good man off completely, do you? Safety at all times. If that little radar in your head begins to bleep telling you to get the hell out of wherever you are, do it and call the cops.' He laughed. 'For the love of God, I sound like your granny, but I'm serious.'

Ben was smiling. Morgan laughed but stood up. She was torn between staying with Ben or going back to work, but she knew he was in the best possible hands, especially with Declan watching out for him. She kissed Ben's cheek, then she turned and kissed Declan's.

'I love you both very much, thank you. I'll go and do my best.'

She walked out of the accident and emergency department with her hands clasped saying a silent prayer to whoever may be listening to take care of Ben and help her find Milly.

Bella had arrived and was sitting on a chair waiting with Cain. Morgan almost didn't want to interrupt their deep conversation, but she waved them over. 'He's okay, thank you. Our friend who is a pathologist is looking after him.'

Bella's mouth dropped wide open in horror, and Morgan corrected herself.

'Oh God, no he's sitting with him until the heart surgeon can get here to assess him.'

Cain smiled. 'You have a way with words, Morgan, abrupt and to the point.'

'Thank goodness, I guess I can head back to Wales now. I'm sorry I haven't been much help, but it's been lovely to meet you all. What an amazing team. I will analyse the samples I took today in my lab, to see if they match the samples recovered from Shea's feet, and I'll be in touch. I'll also let you know about the petals as soon as I can. Please can you pass my well wishes on to Ben and let me know how you're all doing? I don't think my mundane life is ever going to be the same after spending twenty-four hours with your team.'

'Thank you, yes, of course I will. We do work well together, which is why I don't understand why our boss wants to split us up.'

Bella shrugged, fishing a business card that was crumpled from her pocket. 'Envy, maybe he used to be part of a team and then it all went wrong. Now he's all bitter and twisted, doesn't like seeing how close you all are. Or maybe he wants to be part of the team but is still feeling like an outsider.'

Morgan nodded, maybe she had something. She took the card from her, and looking up she realised that Cain and Bella were standing close to each other, and this made her heart happy. She smiled at them.

'Cain could you drive me back to grab a car from the station? I need to go back to Walney, to speak to a farmer who may have some disused farm buildings we haven't checked out yet.'

'Should I come with you? I don't want you going on your own.'

'It's okay, you finished work hours ago. Why don't you go grab a bite to eat with Bella before she leaves? If Will's still at the station I'll ask him to come with me.'

Cain's cheeks turned deep red and he dead-eyed Morgan.

Bella smiled at her. 'I'd like that, if it's okay with you, Cain, and you don't have any other plans.'

'No, no plans at all.'

'Good, I brought Will with me though, he's waiting outside in the Land Rover.'

They strode out to where Will was staring at the three of them. He opened the door.

'How is he?'

'He's in the best hands and okay,' Morgan answered. 'He's had some kind of fibrillation thing that can be sorted. Cain is going to drive me back to grab a car. I have some more enquiries to carry out on Walney.'

'Great, I'll come with you if you want.'

She gave him a thumbs up then turned to Cain. 'Give me your keys. Bella can drive you back to get your stuff then me and Will can get down to Walney.' She knew Cain was going to be annoyed with her for so blatantly setting him up with Bella, but if anything came out of all this tragedy it was that he deserved a little happiness, and who was she to stand in the way of a blossoming love affair?

She still felt sick and unsure about leaving Ben, but at least she knew he was safe, and with Declan watching over him like his guardian angel nothing was going to happen to him. What she'd desperately wanted to do was to climb on the hospital bed next to him and lie with him, but at this moment in time it was Milly Blake who really needed her help. She couldn't do much for Shea or Des now, but she could put her everything into bringing Milly home, which she was determined to do. Why had Marc put her investigation to the bottom of the list? She should be the highest priority. She thought about Milly's parents who had already suffered the most terrible of tragedies in losing their toddler. She wasn't going to be the one who stood by whilst they lost their teenage daughter, too.

FORTY-NINE

The man helped Milly out of the tractor, gently holding her arm, leading her to the door of the huge farmhouse.

'Come on, girl, let's get you inside where you're safe.'

She didn't argue, she had no idea where the guy who had hurt her was, she just wanted to go home to see her mum and dad. She wanted to eat a greasy cheese smothered pizza and drink an ice cold can of cherry cola. She'd also be grateful for some of her mum's hardcore painkillers to ease the throbbing in her head. Soon enough the police would be here, and she'd be safe, home. She didn't think she would ever set foot on the river-bank again. The house was cold inside, no central heating. The air felt frigid. The tall man, who looked older than her grandad, led the way. He locked the front door behind him, and she felt a little scared; her face must have betrayed her feelings.

'We don't want whoever hurt you getting in, do we? Once we know the police are out there searching for him, I'll open it and let them in.'

Milly couldn't speak; her voice had gone dry after the screaming and lack of water. She nodded her head instead and whispered, 'What about your dog?'

He smiled at her. 'Don't you worry about Scar, he'll have hopefully bitten him and scared the life out of him.'

He led the way to the kitchen, past the doorway to a darkened living room. She glanced in and saw a woman in the chair and felt her heart miss a beat as she jumped.

'Don't you worry about her either; she's been asleep for an hour and dead to the world. She never wakes up for anything. I'd have an easier time summoning the devil than waking her up to get her to go to bed.'

Milly glanced back at her. She was dead to the world indeed, breathing so deeply. She smiled at her saviour, thankful for his help.

'Now do you want me to clean up those wounds on your hands or would you rather wait for an ambulance? I'm a dab hand at the old first aid, been a first aider for years and you never know on a farm when some silly bugger is going to chop their finger off on the combine harvester.'

He was talking, trying to make her feel at ease, and she thought he was probably the sweetest old person she'd ever met.

'Yes, please.'

He sat her at the old pine table and began to run the hot water then opened the cupboard under the sink to get out the green first aid box. Milly could feel herself trembling, and her teeth were chattering with cold and probably shock. He tenderly wrapped a woollen throw around her shoulders and patted her gently.

'It's okay.'

'Can I ring my parents; do you have your phone, please?'

He nodded, pulling it out of his pocket and passing it to her. Neither of them noticed the dark shadow passing the window.

'You can try but the signal is terrible in this house. It's the thick walls and being in such a remote area. I don't think it penetrates through them but try all the same. When we've sorted out your hands we'll go outside, but if I'm honest with you, love, I don't want to until the police get here.'

'Where are they?'

'On their way no doubt. This house is well and truly off the beaten track and unless it's someone who has been here before they're going to struggle to find it. I'd go out and flag them down, but I'm scared to leave you alone in here. If they don't arrive soon then we'll lock you in and I'll make my way to the main gate.'

Milly realised that she didn't want him to leave her alone either, but she might have no choice in the matter. She just wanted to go home.

FIFTY

Morgan didn't talk much on the journey to Walney. She had too much going on in her mind to even think about mindless chatter. Will kept quiet, respecting her need for a little peace, until they reached the outskirts of Dalton.

'Do you have a plan?'

She smiled at him. 'Not as such, earlier today one of the security guards from the airport took me to a farmhouse at the very tip of north Walney, where there were quite a few barns and buildings. One of them was locked up tight. I think we need to go check it out and also ask the farmer if he knows of anywhere that Milly and Shea could be hidden.'

'Did we not check it already?'

'I don't think so, it's way off the beaten track down a dirt road that's bumpy as hell. I have this feeling that we need to go back there. Don't ask me why, it's just one of those things.'

He nodded. 'Are you sure you're not related to Annie? She says stuff like this all the time, or she used to.'

'I don't think so, my family are all dead, except my aunt, and she never had kids.' She didn't have the energy to explain her family tree to him; even though Taylor wasn't technically dead he may as well be for what he meant to her.

'Do we need to ask for backup or a search team?'

'I don't know, I suppose we should have someone on backup, but it could be a complete wild goose chase because this literally is just a hunch.'

Will sighed, and she felt bad for him; what a nightmare couple of days he'd had trying to get to grips with all the crap they had going on and not working from his usual station. He picked up his radio and asked for the Force Incident Manager to ring him. Moments later his phone rang, and he answered it using the vehicle hands-free set.

'It's Will, I'm with DC Brookes and we're on our way to the far end of north Walney to check out some possible locations for a misper, Milly Blake. Can you have some officers make their way across the bridge in case we need a hand?'

'*I'll do my best, there's been a serious domestic down Vulcan Road. As soon as I can free some up I will. Do you need the dog handler?*'

He looked at Morgan who shrugged.

'If there's one on duty it might be good if they could be on standby too, thanks, ma'am.'

'*No problem, Will, I'll get as many patrols as we have spare heading in that direction once they're available.*'

Morgan nodded, she felt better already although she'd be feeling a lot more confident if it was Cain who was backing them up. But she'd left him behind so that was her burden to bear if anything went wrong. She stared at the industrial units as they whizzed by. What was going to go wrong that hadn't already? Des was dead, Ben was in hospital; at least Milly Blake hadn't turned up yet so that could mean that whoever had her hadn't had the time to hurt her yet, at least that was the result she was praying for. Will drove across the deserted bridge heading to north Walney, the lights twinkling from both sides of the channel reflecting in the dark water. Shadowy boats bobbed around on the incoming tide and even though she loved the sea she didn't find anything about it comforting or beautiful like she usually would. There it was, that heavy feeling of dread wedged into the base of her stomach like she'd swallowed a basketball.

'Head towards the airport, please, and I'll tell you which gate it is we need to go through.'

He headed through streets lined with the pretty barns and houses along North Scale, following the road. Before she knew it they were at the entrance to the airport.

'Oh crap, we must have passed it. Sorry it looks completely different in the dark – the fields all look the same.'

'I'll reverse and we can go back slowly.'

A white pickup stopped behind Will, and he muttered, 'Well, I can when that moves out of the way.'

Morgan jumped out of the car hoping it was Andy, who could lead them there. She couldn't make out the person in the driver's seat and walked close enough to see Roy.

'Hey, do you remember me, Roy?'

He nodded slowly.

'Good, do you know where the farm is? I can't remember the name; I think the farmer is called Bill?'

'I do, want to jump in and I'll take you there?'

'Yes, please, that would be great, Could you hang on a minute?'

Rushing back to Will's car she opened the door. She didn't want them to not have access to a police vehicle, if they needed one, so she said, 'Follow us. Roy is going to drive me there, and if you come behind us that's probably easier.'

Will gave her a little salute, and she grinned at him then went back and got inside the cab of Roy's pickup.

'Thanks, you're a life saver, Roy. We missed the turnoff already and I don't want to waste hours driving in fields and getting lost.'

'You in a rush?'

'Yeah, I guess we are.'

'I can help you then, buckle up it's a bumpy road. Have you been down it before?'

'Yes, Andy took me earlier.'

'That's good, you know what to expect then.'

He began reversing, and she prayed that this time they were going to find Milly Blake before anything awful happened to her. He drove until he reached the metal gate that looked like all the other metal gates, then he jumped out and pushed it wide open. Driving through, he waited for the car behind to catch him up.

'Do you want to leave that car behind and get your mate to get in here?'

She did, but she also didn't want the pair of them reliant on Roy's good nature to drive them around, and also, if he needed to leave they were going to be stranded, so it was better for Will to follow behind.

'Thanks, but it's okay.'

He shrugged, side-eyeing her as if she was crazy, and continued driving through it onto the rocky, uneven path.

FIFTY-ONE

The old man was pacing the kitchen, and Milly began to feel uncomfortable. She was in so much pain. Surely the police knew she was missing? Her mum and dad would have phoned them. What was taking them so long? She looked at his ancient iPhone on the table. There were still no signal bars in the corner and no WiFi either. She didn't want to go outside again in case the guy who was chasing her was still out there, but she also didn't want to spend hours sitting here waiting for the police to arrive if they didn't know where they were going. She stood up, clutching his phone.

'I'm going to open the front door and see if there's a signal outside, this is taking too long.'

His mouth dropped. 'You can't do that, girl, it's not safe. We don't know where that bloke is.'

'I need help, I need to get to the hospital.'

As she spoke a dull throb began in her head and the stinging pain in her hands was almost unbearable. She limped towards the front door, down the dark passage past the room with the sleeping woman in and glanced through the door. She was in the exact same position with not a single sound coming from her; it was then that Milly noticed the house phone on the table next to her and the overturned glass, and the hairs on the back of Milly's neck began to prickle. Something wasn't right. She continued towards the front door. Why hadn't he used the house phone to call the police or offered it to her to use? She sensed the man standing in the doorway to the kitchen watching her. Was he as old as she'd first thought? He seemed suddenly younger somehow. Scared to let him know that she'd seen the house phone, she said nothing. The front door was within reaching distance, and she wanted to be outside; she would take her chance on her own. A floorboard creaked behind her then she heard his footsteps. Her heart was racing fast, and then he was behind her.

'I can't let you go out there, love, it's not safe. Give me the phone and I'll go outside and phone the cops again.'

He was holding out his hand, which wasn't as wrinkly as she'd have expected for an older guy. Nodding slowly, she passed him the phone and he clasped it in his hands. Unbolting the door he stepped outside into the blackness, and she slammed the door shut behind him. With fingers that were shaking she slid the bolt across. She didn't know what was going on with him, but she wasn't taking any chances. She would ring the police herself. He began hammering on the door with his fist, but she ignored him and limped back to the room with the sleeping woman, where the house phone was. She picked up the receiver and cried out in frustration that there was no dial tone. Pressing her finger on the little button she jabbed it again and again. The woman hadn't moved an inch, and when she glanced at her in the glow of the fire her eyes were wide open staring at the wall. Milly jumped: she recognised that look – she had seen it a few times at work when residents had died suddenly. The old woman was clearly dead. A bubble of panic filled her lungs and she wanted to scream but the fear had gripped her throat so tight that nothing came out.

FIFTY-TWO

Roy was driving pretty fast, and she was clinging on to the arm rest to stop herself from banging her head. She could see Will's lights some distance behind, but they were moving much slower. Obviously his car was never going to be able to cover the terrain in the same way this could. After what felt like forever the ramshackle farmhouse and buildings came into view, and Roy stopped the truck.

'What now?'

'I beg your pardon?'

'What are you going to do now?'

She thought it was pretty obvious that she was going to go and search for Milly, but he wasn't a copper – he wouldn't know. She opened the door, the lights illuminating the cab, and looking over at him saw that Roy's trousers were all torn and damp and covered in sand. His cheeks were red, and he looked as if he was having a rough night. Fear filled her chest along with the strongest survival instinct she had ever felt. He was staring at her, his eyes looking right through her.

'What happened to your trousers, Roy? Did you fall over?'

She knew she had to stall for time to give Will a chance to get here before either of them made a move. Roy glanced down at his ripped trousers, then back at her.

'I fell over at the airfield, slipped on some oil. Hurt my bloody knees and had to jump up fast before anyone saw me. I'll never live it down.'

The words were hard to form in her mouth. Where the hell was Will? He should be here but there were no car headlights or engine noise.

'You wait here, I'll be okay.'

She didn't want Roy anywhere near her; she didn't trust him.

'I can't let you go on your own.' His tone was whiny, like a spoiled child. 'I'd never live that down either if I sat in the cab whilst you were out searching for a missing girl.'

'No one has to know, Roy, it's between me and you. Do you know where Milly Blake is?'

He shook his head, a look of pure misery etched across his face. 'You don't know what it's like. They make fun of me all the time. I'm not lazy, I do my best.'

She nodded. 'Of course, you're not. Look, I must go look for Milly, but you wait here, okay, and if I don't come back phone 999, and you can tell Will where I am when he gets here. I don't know why it's taking him so long.'

She expected Roy to chase her, reach out and grab her, but he didn't; he sat in the pickup looking like a rabbit caught in headlights. She ran towards the house, not seeing the tall figure standing still in the shadows. He was solid and didn't move. Morgan screeched as she ploughed straight into him, her head only chest height against him.

'Jesus.'

'What are you doing?' The man wearing a plaid checked shirt just visible through the light from the window asked her.

'I'm looking for Bill. Are you Bill?'

'Yep, that's me. Who are you?'

'Police, I'm looking for a missing girl and wanted to check your barn. Is that possible? Could you show them to me?'

His head moved slowly, up and down. 'What makes you think she's out there?'

'A hunch, we can't rule anything out, it's a matter of life and death.'

She couldn't see his expression very well in the darkness, but if she could every hair on the back of her neck would have stood on edge.

He was looking around, over his shoulder but he nodded. 'Who's in the pickup?'

'Security guard, he's waiting for me.'

'Come on then, lass, let's show you the barn and then you can get yourself back home and stop wasting your time.'

He walked much faster than she thought a man in his eighties could; in fact she struggled to keep up with him. Old Bill was fitter than she was. She waved at Roy who was still in the driver's seat watching them. Something was very wrong. The farmer clearly wasn't as old as Andy had told Morgan he was. He led the way towards the barns, his stride purposeful, his stance not what she'd have expected. If Morgan hadn't been so focused on seeing the inside of the barn for herself, she might have noticed the shadowy figure near to the pickup, but she didn't.

———

Roy didn't like this; he was scared for both himself and the copper. He began to climb out of the cab, about to follow her, when he heard banging and muffled shouts coming from inside the house. Before he could close the door to go and see what the noise was, a fist shot out of the dark and punched him hard on the temple. He never saw it coming, but an explosion of stars signalled that it had done its job as he swayed forwards. He tried to turn to see what had happened, completely stunned, as another one took him down and out cold. He felt himself falling forwards and landed heavily onto his knees, then face first on the sandy path.

He knew he had little time. He didn't think Bill would chance hurting the copper, his copper, but it wouldn't take Bill long to show her the barns. He dragged the unconscious man by his feet as best as he could towards the long grass and overgrown field. He had to finish the girl now. He couldn't wait any longer because she was making such a fuss from inside the house. If the copper with Bill heard her it would be game over. What he needed was for Bill to keep his cool and get rid of her before she got too suspicious of him.

The front door was locked and bolted, so he made his way around to the back of the house, where the kitchen door was always open. He had to shut her up for good, this had gone entirely wrong. He shouldn't have let Bill in on it, but Bill had caught him with the pretty young girl when he'd taken her to the disused bomb shelter that was only accessible through Bill's fields. Expecting Bill to be horrified when he came across them that he had her blindfolded, tied up and gagged, it had been quite the opposite. Bill had got openly excited and asked if he could help. What a turn up for the books that had been. But when it came down to it, he knew he should have cut his losses and carried on working alone. The kitchen door was locked, and he threw himself against it in frustration. This old sandstone farmhouse wasn't the easiest of places to penetrate. When the pensioners said 'they don't build them like they used to' they were right. It was like a fortress; his only hope was that the window Bill's wife always kept open was ajar. Never in a million years had he anticipated this girl being so feisty and she had taken him by surprise, taken both of them by surprise. He pressed himself against the wall and made his way to the small window that led into the downstairs toilet. Closed. Suddenly he felt fierce, uncontrollable anger rushing through him.

FIFTY-THREE

Morgan walked slightly behind Bill. The more she watched him striding towards the buildings, the more convinced she was that he was clearly not in his eighties. He had no stooping, hunched shoulders that came from a lifetime of manual labour on a farm, his gait was purposeful and determined. She had her phone torch on to light the path in front of her that he was navigating in total blackness, the heaviness in the pit of her stomach uncomfortable. She'd begun to think that Roy was their killer, because he looked so shifty with his ripped trousers and red face. Now she wasn't so sure. Bill had the perfect place to hide girls. Though he wasn't as old as eighty, his maturity was perhaps more trustworthy to a young girl than a younger man would be. But would he have driven to Blackpool to abduct Shea Wilkinson? Something didn't add up. She was torn between believing he was innocent or up to his neck in it.

'How did you know about this place? It's a bit out of the way.'

'Andy, the security guard, brought me here to show me the barns earlier today.'

He turned to face her, his lips parted slightly, a look of surprise etched across his eyes.

'Really, that was kind of him but I'm afraid he's wasted your time. There's nothing in them except rusted old junk, not even sure why I bother to keep it padlocked. If anyone stole the contents, they'd be doing me a favour.'

He chuckled but it sounded strange and set Morgan even more on edge than she had been a second ago. A voice inside her head was screaming at her to get out of there, go find Will and wait for backup. She had promised Declan she'd listen to that voice, but she knew that she couldn't turn around now. If she left and Milly was inside it could be fatal for her.

'I understand what you're saying, Bill, but I might as well put my mind at rest and then that's another property ticked off the list of jobs I have to do.'

He nodded in that slow way, and she realised that he was humouring her. Looking down at her phone she hoped that the signal would be restored soon. In her trouser pocket was her airwave radio; the bulk of it felt good pushing against her thigh. She was praying that there was still a flashing green light on the top, signalling that she was in range of a transmitter and she could get hold of patrols if she needed help. For some reason she didn't want Bill to know that she had it; it was her emergency backup plan. The huge run-down buildings came into view and she felt a small sigh of relief escape her lips. It was almost over, she was sure of it.

Taking a bunch of keys from his pocket, Bill took forever to rifle through them until he found the right one. He removed the padlocked chain, slipping it through one handle of the door, leaving it dangling loose, and then he pushed the massive door inwards. Morgan hovered outside. Nothing smelled putrid or decaying; in fact the air from inside it was musty and filled with the faint smell of petrol fumes.

'Take a look around, help yourself.'

He stood leaning against one of the doors, arms folded across his chest, and she partly expected him to say *I told you so.* He didn't. He let her go inside on her own whilst he stood watching her from the door. The smell of oil or petrol, maybe both, was much stronger inside, it filled her nostrils, and she shone the torch light around.

'Milly, are you here? It's the police.'

Silence greeted her, that thick air of nothingness except for the echo of her own desperation. Morgan had pinned all her hopes on finding her here and putting an end to Milly's ordeal. She walked around, looking between the ancient farming equipment that she had no idea about except that Bill was right. It was old, rusty and thieves would be doing him a favour if they took the lot. She turned around; all her hopes dashed.

'Come on, I'm sorry you haven't found what you were looking for.'

Morgan left the building; he pushed the doors closed but didn't bother padlocking them again. He was already walking away, and his voice echoed in her mind: *I'm sorry you haven't found what you were looking for.* He was cold, that was for sure. Milly was a young girl, a person and he was talking about her as if she was a lost purse.

FIFTY-FOUR

Returning, Morgan felt a huge weight had been lifted when she saw the pickup and the farmhouse. But where was Roy? He'd been sitting there waiting for her to come back when she'd walked off with Bill. That creeping feeling of uneasiness ran the full length of her spine again, and where the hell was Will? He was supposed to be her backup and he was nowhere in sight. She heard the sound of fists pummelling against glass and turned to look at the farmhouse, letting out a gasp as she saw a woman with her face pressed against the glass screaming at her. It was Milly. Morgan began to run towards the house, but Bill was faster. He threw himself at her, and she felt a dead weight on her back as she began falling towards the ground, unable to stop herself. Milly was alive, but now Morgan was being taken out by an elderly farmer. She hit the rough ground with a large bang, the wind knocked out of her, but she swiftly moved to one side so that Bill wasn't on top of her pinning her to the ground.

'Will, Will.' She screamed at the top of her voice. Bill was lying on the ground groaning, his arm twisted at a strange angle. Rolling onto all fours she breathed deeply, trying to catch her breath.

'What the fuck, Bill?'

He lay there staring at her, his eyes crinkled, and he began to laugh in-between grimacing at the pain in his arm and shoulder. Standing up she stared down at him. 'You, it was you who took Milly. Did you kill Shea and Des?' She felt a black rage begin to fill her frozen insides. Reaching back she went to kick him, but his good arm shot out. His grip was like a vice, his fingers so strong as he squeezed her ankle, pressing his thumb deep into her calf and making her yell out as her eyes watered. Taking her radio out of her pocket Morgan pressed the red button on the top and the whole unit began to vibrate. It meant that her entire conversation *was* being broadcast to every patrol and the control room on this channel.

'Urgent assistance now, the farm near Walney airfield.'

The radio was knocked from her before she could say anything more, but Bill was still on the ground. An arm from behind grabbed her around her neck and she felt herself being dragged backwards; her windpipe was so constricted she struggled to catch her breath. She used both of her elbows to jab her assailant in the ribs as hard as she could, and the grip on her hair released. Morgan turned around, furious. Roy and Bill had been working together the sick bastards. And then it was her turn to let out a yell of surprise to see Andy standing there clutching his side but still smiling at her. In one hand he was clutching a bloody hammer and she felt her heart sink, *oh Roy*. Bill had managed to drag himself to his feet, his arm hanging low, and she realised he must have dislocated his shoulder.

'Are you okay, Bill?'

Bill slowly moved his head up and down. Morgan wanted to take him out and wipe that smug, knowing smile off his face.

'She's locked us out; I can't get in anywhere.'

'Break a window, we don't know what the girl's doing in there.'

Andy stepped forward, and reaching out he took a handful

of Morgan's hair, running his fingers through it. She pulled
away. Knowing that Milly was safe inside the house for now she
drew back her fist and punched Andy as hard as she could. He
let out a yell that filled the night air as blood spurted from his
broken nose. Underneath the yell she heard the sound of sirens
– they sounded a long way off but at least they were on their
way. With Andy and Bill momentarily thrown off guard the
front door of the house opened, and Morgan ran towards it,
noticing a patch of untidy ground off to the left where tiny pink
flowers grew in clusters among the unkempt grass, Walney geraniums. Pushing herself through the small gap, Milly slammed it
shut and they both leaned against it whilst she locked it.
Morgan stared at the girl. She had dried blood matted in her
long blonde hair and her hands bandaged, her face pale – she
looked awful, but she was alive.

'There's a dead woman in the lounge; he killed his wife.'

'The police are on their way.'

'He said he'd phoned them when I got away from the man. I
thought he was my saviour, a friendly guy who would keep me
safe.' Her voice broke and she let out a loud sob. Morgan
grabbed the girl, pulling her tight, and she hugged her briefly
then let go.

'We can't stay here; they're going to break a window. We
need something to protect ourselves with.'

Milly pulled a huge knife out of the waistband of her
leggings; Morgan took it from her shaking hand. 'That's good,
but we could do with something else for you to use.'

The sound of breaking glass shattered the hushed silence.
Morgan grabbed Milly's hand and dragged her up the dark
stairs. They had to find somewhere to hide until the police
arrived. She pushed open all the doors except for the one
furthest away down the long hallway, then she dragged Milly
back to the second room along. It smelled faintly of aftershave
and sweaty socks, and there was a double bed and some drawers

that she could make out in the gloom. The only place they could
hide was under the metal bed frame, so Morgan pushed Milly
towards the bed and whispered, 'Get underneath and don't
move.'

Milly didn't need to be told twice, aware that this was all
that stood between her life and death, and she scrambled underneath the bed frame. Morgan couldn't see her in the dark and
felt confident that she would be okay there. Another loud
breaking sound filled the air. She stepped behind the door,
pressing her back against the wall but leaving it wide open like
the others. If they stepped into the room, she would use the
knife to incapacitate them. Gripping the handle tight she closed
her eyes to listen where they were. The fact that there were two
of them working together filled her heart with more fear than
she'd ever felt. She could hear her pulse beating a dull rhythm
inside her head as her heart beat wildly, waiting for one or both
of them to come and find them. Instead though, what she got
was the acrid smell of smoke. Thick, black fumes began to fill
the room and Morgan slammed the door shut. Milly emerged
from underneath the bed. 'They're going to burn us alive and
get rid of the evidence.'

'No, they're not, we'll get out of here.' The inky sky outside
of the window filled with blue and white lights. Morgan had
never been so relieved to see the police. She hammered against
the window trying to catch their attention, but the fire had them
all distracted, no one paying them the slightest bit of notice. She
could see the dark shadows around the house getting brighter,
and she realised it was the flames from downstairs lighting up
the whole area around it. The fire had taken a hold of the old,
worn building full of wooden furniture. They didn't have long.
Grabbing the duvet off the bed Morgan rolled it up, putting it
against the gap at the bottom of the door where the smoke was
billowing through. Milly was already coughing and soon the
smoke was making Morgan hack too. She ran across to the

window, seeing they were some height off the ground and there was no fire engine in sight. There was no way one could reach them in time. The pickup had gone, and no doubt Bill and Andy along with it. Morgan didn't know an awful lot about fire, but she knew that if she put the window through there was a good chance the night air would cause a backdraught. What choice did they have, though? Die of smoke inhalation and be burned to a crisp or take their chances and maybe pay with a few broken bones? She felt along the wall for the light switch, pressing it down and illuminating the room. For a moment both Morgan and Milly had to shield their eyes against the brightness. When Morgan looked around, she found herself staring at a wall full of pictures of a woman who she knew very well.

Milly gasped. 'Oh my God, it's you.'

There were pictures of Morgan working crime scenes, coming out of the police station, pictures taken of her in Ben's car and on Ben's front street; there were even photos of her and Des taken at the church fete. Grabbing a handful of them she stuffed them into her pocket as evidence. Then grabbed a rickety wooden chair and launched it through the window with a loud clatter. Something exploded downstairs, but so far so good, although the smoke was billowing through the gaps around the edge of the door now, making their eyes water and both of them cough their guts up until they were retching. Shouts came from below – they finally had the attention of the officers – and Morgan began to hope that they were going to get out.

'Help us.'

She was at the bed, tugging the covers off until they had a hold of the heavy mattress. The two of them struggled to carry it, both of them barely able to breathe, but then it was at the window. Bending it as best as they could, with an almighty shove it fell out until it splatted against the ground.

'Jump.'

'I can't, I'm scared of heights.'

'If you don't, you're going to burn to death. Close your eyes, I'll guide you. Do you trust me?' She held out her hand. Milly's tear-stained, blood-streaked face looked at her and nodded. The women held hands and Morgan squeezed Milly's hard. 'Now close your eyes and I'll help you, okay?'

Milly did as she was told and Morgan helped her up onto the windowsill. Before she could change her mind, Morgan shoved her with both hands in the back with all of her might and watched as she toppled out of the window into the cold night air. The fear that she may have just killed the girl she was trying to save was almost crippling, and she heard a chorus of shouts, scared to look down. She forced herself to open her eyes and felt the wetness on her cheeks as tears of relief ran down them. Milly had landed somehow miraculously onto the mattress and was lying there dazed. Morgan took one last look around the room. A large gust of wind caused the flames that had been licking at the bedroom door to break through and then the room was burning behind her. Clambering onto the windowsill she wished there was someone to push her and then she closed her eyes and jumped.

FIFTY-FIVE

Two pairs of strong arms lifted her off the mattress. She hadn't fallen as gracefully as Milly, and she yelped in pain as the ankle she'd twisted a while ago bent backwards. An ambulance finally arrived and she saw Milly, who was sitting on the broken chair, flinch. She hobbled over to her wincing in pain.

'What's up, they're here to help us?'

'He brought me here in an ambulance; it was a really old one.'

So that was how he'd managed to lure Shea away; he probably offered her a lift home and what were kids told at school? If you need help ask a safe stranger, someone in uniform, a shop worker, a family friend. 'Who was driving the ambulance, Milly?'

'The other one, not the old man.'

A loud groan from the side of the track made her turn and hobble towards it. She saw Roy lying there his eyes wide, his mouth taped shut, his arms and feet wrapped in layers of tape. Not too far away was Will who was sitting up rubbing his bleeding head. Morgan felt a rush of relief flood her veins that everyone was here and accounted for, injured yes and had plenty of war wounds, but they were all alive.

'Thank God you're alive.'

Will, who looked dazed, smiled at her. 'You too, I'm so sorry I didn't get here sooner. I hit a pothole on that track and the tyre exploded. Morgan, what did you do to the house?'

She smiled. 'I only broke a window; they did it, Andy and Bill. They just left in Roy's pickup, and they won't get stopped because it's a security truck.'

A fire engine finally pulled up, and one of the officers ran towards two coppers who were looking helpless. Morgan dragged herself across to them.

'What's wrong?'

'There's a security van down the lane, head-on collision with a broken-down car. I've had to leave a couple of men down there dealing with the casualties.'

She turned to the officers. 'Get down there now, those men are the cause of all of this and dangerous.'

The fire officer shook his head. 'It's a mess, one dead and one unconscious. They must have been going at some speed to have hit it at such force, and neither of them were wearing seat belts. Flew straight out of the windscreen. They were lying there like a couple of crash test dummies. Arnie there almost ran straight over them, it's a right mess.'

Morgan, who had always believed that what goes around comes around, felt a small hint of satisfaction that Bill and Andy had been dealt their karmic consequences a lot faster than normal.

'Mate, that car is a complete write off if it belongs to any of you.'

Will, who had joined them, shrugged. 'Company car, not mine.'

The fire officer ran to join his crew who were busy trying to control the fire that was now raging out of control. The building was beginning to collapse in on itself, and the only thing left now was damage control and stopping the fire from spreading along the dried grassy fields that surrounded the farmhouse.

'There's a dead woman inside.'

Will looked at Morgan. 'Why does that not surprise me in the least? God rest her soul, what a shame for her, this is a complete mess. We're going to be sorting it out for years.'

She felt awful, had she brought him her bad luck, or had it been unavoidable? Then she remembered the photos in her pocket and took them out, handing them over.

'I'm not sure, I think it was Andy's room, but one of them had a wall of these.'

Will took them from her and looked down at them. 'Oh God, they're all of you.'

She nodded. 'I guess I was next on their list. Maybe they couldn't get to me so took Des instead. Milly said she woke up in an old ambulance. I remember seeing a first aider at the church fete that day parked up in an ambulance. I didn't take too much notice of him he wasn't old, but he spent a bit of time talking to Des. What if Andy took Des and killed him, then Bill helped him with Milly?'

'I don't understand any of this.' He looked defeated, and she felt terrible.

'Me either, but at least Milly is okay. Battered, bruised and mentally scarred for life but she's alive. Roy's okay, you're okay and I am too, so technically we got out of it relatively unscathed.'

She put her sprained ankle down too hard on the floor, sending shockwaves of white-hot pain shooting up her leg.

'I suppose so, come on you need to get off that foot. I'd offer to drive you to the hospital but my car's a wreck.'

They both grinned at each other. Dark humour, the stuff that kept you sane when the whole world was crashing in on you, was a useful coping mechanism.

A long line of headlights began to make their way up the beaten track to reach the house, another two fire engines, two ambulances and as many available police officers as were spare until it literally looked like a Hollywood disaster movie. Milly was being treated in the back of one ambulance and Will walked Morgan over to it, helping her inside.

'See you on the other side, Morgan.'

'What about you? Your head needs looking at.'

'I haven't got the time and it's just a bump, I'll be okay.'

She smiled, nodding and wondering if Cumbria Constabulary realised just how amazing some of their officers were. The doors were slammed shut, and she lay her head back against the headrest, closing her eyes. All she wanted was a hot bath and to see Ben.

FIFTY-SIX

After Morgan had been taken to the minor injuries clinic to get her ankle strapped up she phoned Ben. He didn't answer but Declan did.

'Tell me you're alive, you caught the bad guys and there are no more bodies for me tomorrow.'

She laughed. 'How's Ben?'

'He's drifting in and out, but he's listening. I'll put you on speaker phone. Good news is, if he behaves then he's allowed home tomorrow. He's had all his meds to sort him out and he's to come back in three weeks for a chemical cardioversion.'

'Morgan, are you okay, is Milly okay?'

She felt her eyes brim with tears at the sound of Ben's groggy voice and blamed the painkillers she'd been given on arrival at A&E.

'Milly is alive, battered and bruised but she survived me pushing her out of a window. I didn't land as good as her and badly sprained my ankle but we're both good.'

'What?'

Ben sounded more alert.

'I'm okay, it's okay, don't worry, Ben. It's a long story; can I tell you tomorrow when I see you in person? There's a huge mess that needs sorting out over on Walney, and I'm sorry, Declan, you have one fatality from a head-on collision. The other one lived and is being transferred to intensive care, but yes, we caught the bad guys. Oh, there's also a poor woman who was murdered in her home that was then set on fire, so you'll have her coming to the mortuary too.'

'For the love of God, Morgan, what the hell happened? It sounds like even more carnage than usual.'

'It's horrific and for once nothing to do with me.' She lowered her voice. 'Will was knocked out and has a huge bump on his head, plus the mother of all crime scenes and it was his car that was in the head-on collision, so it's safe to say he's had enough of me for tonight. I guess poor Theo is off the hook now. We can let him get on with being a vicar.'

'Morgan, I love you, but I don't know if my heart can take it.'

She heard him and Declan laughing, and she smiled.

'One last thing, I wouldn't have hurt my ankle if I'd had my Docs on, just saying, so you can make fun of me for wearing them but in future I will not be wearing anything else. You can stick your trainers where the sun doesn't shine. I love you both dearly, good night.'

She ended the call to more laughter which made her feel much better. She could see Milly in the cubicle across from her. Her parents had been rushed through and they were hugging her as tight as they could without hurting her. Milly looked over her mum's shoulder and mouthed, 'Thank you,' at her.

Morgan nodded, smiled and blew her a kiss. Then she lay her head back and closed her eyes, grateful that it had turned out Milly was safe, despite the horror of Des and Shea's murders. Tomorrow was a new day. Her eyes flew open – they forgot all about the cat. She would tell Ben the good news they were going to have to adopt Des's cat. It was the least they could do for Des now. She knew Ben would agree even though he told her he didn't like them. She would bet before long he'd be letting it curl up on his lap. At least it could keep him company until she was back working on his team. Until then the cat would have to do.

TWO DAYS LATER

Morgan could have gone on the sick with her ankle but she hadn't. She'd worn the boot the hospital gave her and used the crutches to hobble into Barrow station. Will was now working from here and he'd asked her if she wanted to help tie up all the loose ends and complete her reports that this case had left them with. A part of her had immediately said no, but she knew if she wanted to be able to ever sleep again, she would have to do this. Too much was going on inside her mind to ever let her push it away. She owed it to Des. At least Ben was home, along with Des's cat, Kevin, who Amy had collected and left with Ben. Des's mum hadn't taken it because she had a dog that hated cats. None of them had even known what it was called until Amy found a box of flea treatment with 'Kevin' on it. Morgan had laughed, only Des would call a cat Kevin.

She missed Ben, missed the comfort of his house but this wouldn't be for long or at least she hoped. Waiting for the lift to take her up to the second floor the doors pinged open, and she smiled to see Will standing inside.

'Morgan, are you sure you want to do this?'

Her head moved up and down. 'Absolutely.'

They made an odd pair, Will dressed in a three-piece suit with expensive loafers on his feet, Morgan on crutches, dressed head to toe in black with one Doc Marten on her foot that wasn't injured. Andy had been moved out of intensive care and into a side room on ward four. As they reached the entrance to the ward she hadn't expected her stomach to start churning the way it was. Will turned to her and smiled, and she nodded and followed him along the corridor. It wasn't hard to spot which room their prisoner was inside because there was an armed police officer sitting on a chair outside of it. The officer stood up when they saw Will.

'Is there anyone inside?' He pointed to the closed door.

'No, boss, just him.'

Will leaned forward and knocked, then walked straight in. Morgan wasn't sure what she expected but she hadn't expected him to look so young and scared. Andy was staring at her, his purple and black bruised eyes wide.

'You came, I can't believe that you came to see me.'

A slither of ice ran down her spine, but she forced herself to step closer to his bed. Will hung back by the door letting her do the talking.

'Of course, I came, we have a lot to discuss.'

He patted the side of his bed, and she shuddered; instead, grabbing a hard plastic chair she placed it near to his bed, but not near enough he could reach out and touch her. She did not want his hands on her skin knowing what he'd done to Shea Wilkinson.

'How are you?'

He laughed. 'I've been better, my family are all dead and my home has burned to the ground. I also have a really bad headache that no one seems to give a shit about and a broken nose.'

Morgan kept eye contact with him, biting her tongue. She

didn't remind him that they were dead because of what he and Bill had done.

'Are you ready to talk to me, Andy? I need to know what happened.'

'I need a solicitor, unless you let me talk to you alone. I'll only tell you what happened if it's just the two of us.'

Will shook his head. 'No can do, you're a dangerous man who is under arrest for kidnap and murder.'

Morgan didn't want to be on her own with him, but they needed something to work with. None of it made sense. She needed to know how it had all started. She turned to Will and smiled.

'I'm good, do you want to wait outside for me?'

Will looked at her as if she'd gone mad but turned and stepped outside. When the door was closed, she looked back at Andy.

'I want to know everything.'

His face was chalky white, the only colour was his blackened eyes and he had a deep cut running down the side of his face from his temple to his jaw that had been stapled together. His eyes were partially closed and kept flitting to the door nervously.

'I'm scared, I didn't want to tell him that, but I'm terrified of what's going to happen to me, Morgan. None of it was my fault really. Bill was my hero, he was my grandad; the only male role model I ever had. My parents died when I was too young to remember them.'

'Your grandad, so you lived at the farm too?' Morgan thought fast, everything was clicking into place. She wanted his confession though. 'Look, Andy, I can't help you unless you talk to me. You don't have to of course, we've got enough evidence to put you away. We've had confirmation from a forensic botanist that the petals left with Shea's body came from the wildflowers growing around the farm, and we'll have the results from the soil samples any moment now. Bill won't be talking, I want to hear your story.'

He paused, his head bowed, and she noticed that he'd clasped his hands together as if he was praying. After a few moments he squeezed his eyes shut, then opened them and stared straight at her.

'It wasn't me, I mean I helped him. I drove the beat-up old ambulance and lured them in, but I had nothing to do with the killings – that was all Bill.'

'Why take Shea from Blackpool, did you know her?'

'I had never set eyes on her before that night. He said no one would miss her. It was far enough from here that they wouldn't come looking for her.'

'How long did he keep her for?'

The knots in her stomach were tightening and she was scared she was going to throw up.

'Four days.'

'Why? Why did you cut off her hair? Why did you take her and do that to her?' Her voice was strained with emotion.

Andy lowered his gaze, and he shrugged. 'Why do people steal? Why do they graffiti, take drugs? For the thrill, I suppose. Bill's lifelong ambition was to do this. Some people want to be artists, others have the desire to kill.'

'Why did you kill Des?'

'He noticed me following him and pulled over to talk to me, so I had no choice but to stop the van. He asked if he could take a look inside. It was so pointless, why he wanted to do that. I tried to laugh and joke with him, telling him that I was converting it. He didn't get it, he asked if I was an actual first aider and if I wasn't what was I doing pretending to be one. What could I say? No, I wasn't, I had only come so I could be near to the action. I mean, come on, there was a murder scene opposite and there was a church fair going on across the road, who wouldn't take advantage of that? Not to mention, Bill was hiding in the back.'

'What happened?'

'It was all so fast; Bill was inside the van. I opened the doors, and your friend knew something was wrong. He told us not to move, took out his phone – to ring you I presume – but Bill was always a lot faster than he looked. He lunged for him and dragged him inside, and then he picked up a knife and slit his throat just like he was slaughtering one of the animals on his farm. It was over in a matter of minutes. We dragged him back into his car and pushed his body into the footwell of the passenger side. I was furious with Bill, but he didn't care. He was out of control, Morgan, and I was scared to stop him. Imagine being so scared of your own grandad that you do whatever he tells you to? Milly walked past, she kept turning to stare at the ambulance and your friend's car. Bill was in a vile mood. He said she would be our next girl because she was too nosey for her own good.'

Morgan felt numb. He was talking about these horrific crimes as if they meant nothing to him.

'How did you know where she lived?'

'Wasn't too hard to figure out. We followed her, then when she walked along the riverbank, I sped up enough that I could get ahead of her.'

'Did you hurt her?'

He nodded. 'Yes, I'm sorry, I did. I got scared and hit her over the head, but I didn't kill the other one. It was all Bill. She was a bit out of it that's all.'

'What did you do with Des?'

She already knew some of it but wanted to understand more.

'Waited until it was dark and that vicar who is a pain in the arse stopped faffing around in the church. He was too busy talking on his phone to notice he hadn't locked up. Bill said to dump the body in the church and throw the phone into the ditch to confuse you all and send you into meltdown. Then I drove his car to the station, and Bill waited for me around the corner. We knew you were going to be looking for him; we were just trying to buy ourselves some time.'

The sickness that had been swirling around inside her stomach was threatening to force its way up her throat. She tried her best to push it back down. She needed the answers before he realised what he was doing and lawyered up. Des had known something wasn't right. After all these years of ignoring his copper's instinct he'd finally followed it through and ended up dead. Andy had his head bowed; she didn't want to look at him but forced herself to.

'I don't understand, whose room had the photographs of me pinned to the wall?'

Andy glared at her, a calculating look came into his eyes then he blinked, and it was gone.

'That's Bill's office, he did. He really liked you, Morgan. He said you brought him back to life when he'd thought it was all over and he had nothing left to do but die. He followed your cases and talked about you nonstop.'

'Why me? Why was I so fascinating that he had to abduct and murder teenagers to get my attention? Could he not have just introduced himself to me, emailed me? He could have rung the office and spoken to me if he was that bothered.'

She didn't get it, something didn't add up. She glanced up and saw the hint of a smile play across Andy's lips, then it was gone. She'd had enough. Pushing back the hard chair she stood up.

'There is no excuse for what you and your grandad have done. You took two beautiful girls from their families when you had no right to and you killed a serving police officer, who was loved and well respected by his family. You make me sick.'

Turning to walk out of the door, Andy called out, 'Morgan,

he did it all for you.' His voice was high-pitched; he almost sang the words and then he let out a giggle.

She didn't look back at him. If she had she'd have seen the grin on his face. She didn't believe him for one minute that he'd had nothing to do with the murders. It was easy to blame a dead man because everyone knows dead men tell no tales.

A LETTER FROM HELEN

Dear Reader,

I want to say a huge thank you for choosing to read *Silent Angel*. If you did enjoy it, and want to keep up to date with all my latest releases, just sign up at the following link. Your email address will never be shared and you can unsubscribe at any time.

www.bookouture.com/helen-phifer

I hope you loved *Silent Angel* and if you did I would be very grateful if you could write a review. I'd love to hear what you think, and it makes such a difference helping new readers to discover one of my books for the first time.

Thank you so much for choosing to read my stories, it means the world to me and I appreciate it. The Morgan Brookes series is one that's close to my heart. I know what it's like to work in a small police team, thankfully it was a lot less dramatic at Barrow station than it is at Rydal Falls most of the time. I suppose it did have its moments. I've worked days, long scene guards, done extensive house-to-house enquiries to help solve terrible crimes and worked with some amazing police officers, detectives, PCSOs, crime scene investigators, front desk staff, custody officers and all round lovely, hard-working people.

I love hearing from my readers – you can get in touch on my Facebook page, through Twitter, Goodreads or my website.

Thanks,

Helen xxxx

www.helenphifer.com

 facebook.com/Helenphifer1
twitter.com/helenphifer1

ACKNOWLEDGEMENTS

It goes without saying that I owe the biggest thank you to my gorgeous editor, Emily Gowers. I am so grateful, thankful and blessed that I get to work with you. Thank you, Emily, from the bottom of my heart for your help in bringing Morgan Brookes to life and for being so lovely.

Another huge thank you goes out to team Bookouture, honestly, I am so honoured to work with such a brilliant publisher. Who also throw the best parties and just all-round amazing people. It takes a whole team to turn a Word document into the eBook, paperback and audiobook that gets released and I don't think there is a finer team.

Where would I be without the fabulous publicity team? A huge thank you to Noelle Holten for always having my back on publication day; she is an absolute legend. As are the wonderful Kim Nash, Sarah Hardy and Jess Readett.

If I could thank each of my readers individually, I would. You are just so brilliant, supportive, amazing and have no idea how much you fill my heart with love. Readers are what writing is about and for me I thank my lucky stars every day that I have the best readers in the world. Your comments, shares, likes, reviews, laughter and support are what makes all of the hair pulling and sometimes tears all worth it. I feel honoured that you choose to read my stories and thank you from the bottom of my heart for being on this journey with me.

Thank you to the gorgeous Jess Yeo for all the help with the social media side of things; you're brilliant and make my life so much better.

A massive thank you to the Audio Factory Crew for bringing these stories to life, especially Alison Campbell who is brilliant.

Thanks to the fabulous Bookouture Authors who are the best, most supportive, Prosecco sipping, bunch of writers. Not to mention party animals, there ain't no party like a Bookouture Party – hahahaha. I'm just recovering now Emma Robinson, Sue Watson, Casey Kelleher, Emma Tallon, Susie Lynes, Victoria Jenkins, Lizzie Page.

Thank you to the gorgeous blogger, Kirsty Whitlock, and the rest of the fabulous blogging community for being so brilliant.

A huge thank you to my superstar final reader Paul O'Neill for always reading the stories I send him at short notice and superfast. I couldn't do it without your assistance, Paul.

Finally, it wouldn't be the same if I didn't thank my family for keeping me sane or maybe insane, I'm not sure, but I love you all so much and hope that one day you might actually read these stories.

Honestly, I don't hold it against you at all, at least we all love *Stranger Things*!

Helen xx

.

Made in the USA
Monee, IL
21 November 2022

18261640R00173